REVOLUTION - BOOK EIGHTEEN OF BEYOND THESE WALLS

A POST-APOCALYPTIC SURVIVAL THRILLER

MICHAEL ROBERTSON

EDITED AND COVER BY ...

To contact Michael, please email:
subscribers@michaelrobertson.co.uk

Edited by:

Pauline Nolet - http://www.paulinenolet.com

Cover design by The Cover Collection - http://www.thecovercollection.com/

COPYRIGHT

Revolution: Book eighteen of Beyond These Walls

Michael Robertson
© Michael Robertson 2024

Revolution: Book eighteen of Beyond These Walls is a work of fiction. The characters, incidents, situations, and all dialogue are entirely a product of the author's imagination, or are used fictitiously and are not in any way representative of real people, places, or things.

Any resemblance to persons living or dead is entirely coincidental.

All rights reserved.

No part of this publication may be reproduced, stored in a retrieval system, or transmitted in any form or by any means electronic, mechanical, photocopying, recording, or otherwise, without the prior written permission of the author except in the case of brief quotations embodied in critical articles and reviews.

READER GROUP

Would you like a FREE exclusive standalone novel set in my Beyond These Walls universe?

Fury: Book one in Tales from Beyond These Walls is available to everyone who joins my spam-free reader group at www.michaelrobertson.co.uk

You can unsubscribe at any time.

CHAPTER 1

The half-moon hung in a cloudless sky. Nature's spotlight, it guided William, Matilda crawling behind, close enough to grab his heels at the first sign of trouble. They used the long grass for cover and drew closer to the tower blocks. The soft, damp ground and dewy meadow had turned his sleeves and trousers sodden, but they'd not gotten this close before. They were just twenty feet away from shelter beneath the elevated plaza, the food tube another thirty. It hung from the blocks like an unravelled colon, waiting to be slit open to grant them access to the enemy's base. Stage one in a plan that had so many variables. To consider them made his head spin. But they were getting closer. And whatever happened, they'd committed to attacking these blocks in ten days' time.

The Icarus towers had sent a beacon to the other blocks, opening lines of communication with many other ex-vampires. They all agreed. They were all ready for this war. Each camp had their own target. In ten days' time, they'd attack their respective blocks in what could be the most important day in the revolution.

Artan and Nick were somewhere over to their left, Karl with a K and Knives to their right. If Karl didn't make it back, would anyone miss him? Diseased loitered in the gloom beneath the plaza. The night and the long grass had kept William and his friends from their bloody gaze for now. But sooner or later, they'd have to risk exposing themselves.

It had taken them five nights to get this close to the enemy. Until now, they'd observed them from a distance. But they still had more questions than answers. How many were in the blocks? What weapons did they have? Did they know they were coming? What would happen in ten days' time when they attacked?

Panting with the effort of his crawl, William paused for a break, his damp elbows and knees stinging with the cold. He caught the binoculars hanging from his neck and peered through them. "Shit! Duck!"

Matilda dropped behind him as a spotlight cut across the meadow like a scythe. It skimmed over the long grass, sweeping across the landscape.

As the light moved towards Artan and Nick, Matilda crawled up beside him. "Did you know about that?"

"You think I would have kept it a secret if I did?"

"There's no need to be a dick."

"Sorry. It's just, I'm getting so impatient. It's taken us five nights to get this close. And before that, two weeks of waiting for them to all decide what they wanted to do. We've got ten days left, and we're no better off now than we were a fortnight ago."

The massive spotlight swept the landscape. They were just twenty feet away from getting beneath the plaza. Twenty feet from hundreds of idle diseased. But they could cope with them. They were part of the plan. After all, they'd survived this long in a land filled with the horrible cretins, and despite the vile beasts still turning his stomach every time he came into contact with them, they were at least predictable. If they got beneath the plaza, they'd avoid them and cut open the food tube. Stage one in a long and complex plan. Small gains. Until they'd turned on that fucking light.

The powerful beam dissected the darkness like a laser. Hopefully, those operating it would find nothing more than idle diseased. Hopefully, the others had seen it in time to hide like William and Matilda had. "I thought we'd done it this time." William remained fixed on the plaza, the wind blowing so hard the swaying grass obscured his view more often than not. "There's just two of them on the spotlight."

"Surely there would be more if they knew we were here?"

"You'd think, wouldn't you?" William tutted. "But why now? With us this close."

"Bad luck."

"That's the only luck we have."

"We're still alive."

"You're right. Sorry, I'm just frustrated."

Matilda took his hand. "We'll get through this. We've come this far."

"Yeah." He nodded to himself. It wasn't like they had a choice. "So, what do you reckon?"

"Huh?"

A nearby diseased wailed as they wandered through the darkness. They cried out as if searching for their humanity, like they were calling to a missing dog. Screaming, they slashed at the air. They swiped at imagined enemies. "Should we wait it out? They'll get bored at some point."

"Are you mad?"

"Surely it's crazier to leave now we're so close. It's taken us five nights to get this near."

"What about the others?"

William shrugged. "Who knows what they've decided?"

"What if they run?"

Karl with a K probably already had. "It's quite a way to run." They'd crawled for about one hundred and fifty feet, the tank over the brow of the hill behind them.

"You know what I mean. Retreat. What if they choose to retreat?"

"What if they don't and we end up leaving them on their own?" They were so close, looking up at the plaza made William dizzy. "Pinky and Perky up there have to switch the light off eventually." The cool night air nipped at him, his body temperature dropping from the inaction. But he'd take discomfort over death any day. And it was nowhere near cold enough to get hypothermia. They'd had nights in Edin that were ten times colder than this.

"Okay," Matilda said.

"We wait here?"

"While we're safe, it seems like the best plan."

William jumped at another diseased wail. Would he ever get used to them? It came from somewhere much closer than the others. Closer and quieter. A lamenting sob rather than a screech. The swaying grass rustled. The shambling figure stumbled into view. Ten feet to their left. The moonlight revealed its gaunt features. Sharp angles. A vampire before they turned. Malnourished before the disease sucked their skin to their bones. Their life had been drained by something far more sinister than a virus.

Matilda dragged her gun around, covering her laser target with her free hand. William copied her, his eyes burning from where he refused to blink. They carried knives, but any scuffle with the diseased this close to the plaza would blow their cover.

The spotlight swung back over their heads and locked on the diseased.

The beast halted. It emitted a stuttering rasp from its half-open mouth. Something deep in its throat flapped like a blown exhaust. Its long greasy hair hung like a dead weight. Slashes down its left cheek revealed its yellowed teeth and white jaw. It wailed and swiped at the air like it could fight the light.

"When do we run?"

William blinked to relieve his stinging eyes.

Matilda raised her eyebrows and kept her voice lower than the swish of the perpetually swaying meadow. "We stand a chance if we go soon."

Something rustled over to their left. Nick and Artan were leaving. Getting out of there while those in the plaza were distracted. But they didn't need their help. William could go on his own. They were so close.

The diseased stumbled towards them. William raised his gun, but kept the laser covered.

Crack!

The back of the diseased's head erupted, driven back by a bullet to its face. It fell into the grass, hitting the ground before the gunshot's echo died. One silhouette in the plaza lowered their gun while their mate found another diseased with their spotlight.

"We need to go, William."

"But we're so close!"

"It doesn't matter how close we get if we die."

"No." He snorted a humourless laugh. "You're right." The guards shone their spotlight over to their left. William turned his back on the tower blocks. On the food tube and the diseased horde waiting for something to chase. They were so close. He led the way back up the hill. "I'll scan ahead; you check behind. Either of us sees any reason to stop, we let the other one know."

Matilda tapped his ankles. "Sure thing."

An inch at a time, William retraced the path they'd taken to get there. On their bellies like snakes, he led the way, crawling back through the long grass. He used his head to nudge a tunnel through the thick stalks. They were a hundred and fifty feet away from the tank. An uphill climb ahead of them. It had taken a lot of effort to get that close, and for what? To give up like cowards.

CHAPTER 2

Knock-knock!
Eleanor tensed in her bed. She rolled onto her other side and fixed on the door. If she said nothing, would they go away? Her eyes and the skin surrounding them burned from her constant crying. Her nose buzzed, wiped red raw from repeated rubbing.

Knock-knock!

She cleared her throat. "Hello?"

Whoosh!

Rayne slipped in. She whacked the door's button twice before it had fully opened. On her third hit, it closed behind her. "Hey, kid."

"Hi." The weight in Eleanor's chest lifted ever so slightly. Rayne gestured towards the end of her bed. She shrugged.

The mattress sagged beneath Rayne's weight. She rested her hand on Eleanor's shoulder. "How are you doing?"

Hijacked by another searing wave of grief, Eleanor turned into her sodden pillow while Rayne stroked her arm, running her fingers over her healing tattoos. "Every time …" Eleanor caught her stuttered breath. "Every time I think I've run out of tears, more come. I don't know what to do with myself."

"I felt that way after Aggie died." Rayne stared at the wall and teared up. "When I was on my own, I cried and cried. I still do. It's not been long since your dad crashed. And with everything calming down for now, I can imagine it's hard to think of anything else. I'd be more worried if you weren't crying."

"How do you stop it?"

"I don't try."

"You don't worry what people think?"

Rayne's eyes shimmered. "We're crying for a reason. If someone doesn't understand that, that's on them. Also, where are you going to put it?"

"Put what?"

"All this sadness. It has to go somewhere lest it consume you. I like to remind myself I was lucky."

"Lucky?"

"To have had someone like her in my life. To have had a relationship that's worth this many tears. Not everyone has people like Aggie and your parents, you know?"

She nodded, her soft pillowcase like sandpaper against her sore skin.

"I'm not trying to be your dad."

"I know."

"But I love you." She stroked her arm again. "Know that."

"I love you too, Rayne."

"Also, not that it matters, and I'm not saying you should stop, because I think it's healthy to let it out, but I find I cry less when I'm around people. They keep me distracted. For better or worse."

"I suppose being at the head of a murder investigation would do that, eh?"

Rayne laughed. "Yeah. That wasn't ideal."

"Thank you, Rayne. Other than Mum and Dad, I'm not used to people being kind to me. People only do it when they want something. And it would seem, when that happens, I always find out too late."

"I don't want to discount the suffering you've had to endure, but for what it's worth, your timing was perfect with Lines and Mads. Because of you, we had irrefutable evidence to use against them."

"They deserved everything they got, didn't they?"

"Of course."

"Thank you for caring."

Rayne smiled and stroked Eleanor's hair away from her face. Her mum used to do the same to her at bedtime. It was the only thing that would get her to sleep. And even now, as she cried tears over which she had no control, her eyelids grew heavy. Her hammering heart stilled.

Rayne spoke in a whisper. "I'll leave you to it for now. But I'll keep checking on you if that's okay? And I'm here for you whenever you want to leave this room. Whenever you're ready."

Smiling for the first time in days, Eleanor nodded. "Thank you for not giving up on me."

"I'll *never* give up on you." Rayne kissed the side of her head. Just above her temple. Just like her mum used to. "I promise."

CHAPTER 3

Crawling through the grass and mud had left William soaked from head to toe. Even before the spotlight had turned on, he'd gotten about as damp as he could get. Yet, weighted with the burden of a cowardly retreat, and having found no new information, he somehow grew wetter. His clothes fought his movements like they were questioning his choice, and the cold moisture wormed into his being, making even his spirit sodden.

The spotlight swept overhead, and he froze, Matilda halting behind him. It fixed on a diseased thirty feet to their right. The *crack* of a fired gun whipped through the night. The diseased fell into the long grass.

William set off again, sweat running into his tired eyes from the effort of the crawl. It set his already stinging orbs ablaze. He blinked repeatedly, but it did little to ease the burn.

The sweeping spotlight fixed on a once-woman in a black cocktail dress. It might have fitted her when she put it on, but it now hung from her wiry frame like an old sheet. William waited, and Matilda tapped his heel. She was doing fine. She'd follow his lead. The illuminated woman stood just ten feet away, up the hill and to their left. She swayed with the surrounding meadow, a slave to the wind. Despite being exposed to the elements for what must have been days, half of her bouffant hair remained intact. The other half hung lank and greasy. It clung to her wounded face, glued in place by weeping pus.

Crack!

William flinched as the woman threw her arms away from her body and fell backwards. The spotlight moved on.

Slithering up the hill on his belly, the soft mud gave way beneath William's elbows and knees. A coward's retreat. And one they'd have to own when they faced the expectant crowd in their block and explained to them they were no more informed than when they'd left. Again. At this rate, they'd be going to war in ten days' time, armed with little more than hope and aggression. Not quite the master plan they'd expected to devise.

The spotlight halted their retreat again. It shone on a short round man with a black beard, which glistened with blood. Matilda pulled up next to William, her tanned skin damp with sweat.

Crack!

The man fell, and the spotlight shifted to the woman behind him.

"I feel like a failure. There's so much we need to discover about these blocks, but we're still none the wiser."

Matilda frowned, rested her hand on his back, and leaned closer. "We know they have a spotlight. I'd rather find that out now than when we're attacking the place."

"You're right."

"And we have to accept we won't find out all we need to know."

"No. But something would be nice."

"We might not even get that, William. But what we know is we have to attack in ten days' time."

"You say it like it's a good thing."

"We have a deadline. I think that'll be the push we need. We'll attack armed with what information we have. We can improvise. It's what we've been doing since we left Edin. It's worked so far."

"For some of us."

Matilda's eyes pinched, and she dropped her head.

Crack!

The next diseased fell into the grass.

"It's the world we live in, William. You want information about this place so we can act, but imagine if we knew what lay ahead of us before we went on national service. We wouldn't have ever left. We work with what we've got, and we improvise when needed. And look, we're having to retreat, but at least the thing we're running away from is also aiding our escape. They're clearing a path."

Crack!

Another diseased down, the spotlight swept away from them over to their left.

"Come on." Matilda rubbed his back again. "Let's keep moving."

They negotiated the corrugated tin roofs and brick walls from the vampire camp's fallen shelters. They'd crawled about halfway up the hill before they paused again; the spotlight fixed on a diseased directly ahead about ten feet away. Matilda came to William's side and held his hand.

Crack!

The diseased fell like the others. William nodded in the fallen creature's direction. "We know they have a spotlight, and we know they're a good shot."

"See." Matilda smiled at him. "That's progress."

They remained static, the spotlight still shining ahead of

them despite the way being clear. They were about seventy-five feet from the brow of the hill. Seventy-five feet to freedom. Seventy-five feet until they had to spend more time with Karl with a K. What a prick. And who invited him, anyway? William squeezed Matilda's hand tighter.

She lifted her head a little higher and weaved from side to side like it would improve her view through the meadow. "Why haven't they moved the spotlight?"

Crack!

A beast screamed. They'd missed. "Maybe not such a good shot." A child stumbled into view. About five or six years old, she wore the tight-fitting tailored clothes of a block brat. She bit at the air. Snarled. Threw slashes with her hands at invisible enemies. Block brat or not, it still sent a pang through William's heart. Such a waste. Such devastation. She stumbled with her progress. Tripped across the debris-strewn ground.

Crack!

They missed again.

The block brat was now eight feet away.

Six.

Crack!

The angry little thing fizzed and hissed. Dazzled by the beam, she threw more swipes and slashes, like she could battle the glare.

Crack!

"Shit!" William squirmed where he lay. "She's too small and too far away."

"And she's heading straight for us."

The grass swished around them as more diseased closed in, drawn to the spotlight's beam.

Crack!

They missed again.

The child stumbled to just a couple of feet away. She had

a glistening ring of teeth marks on her cheek. So red, they damn near glowed with infection.

Crack!

Each bullet flew so close it whistled through the air.

William dragged his gun around, covered the laser, and aimed up at the small thing. The shooters in the plaza couldn't hit the child from this distance. But if he shot her, he'd blow his and Matilda's cover. They'd have to run. But maybe they were also too far away to hit. And what else could they do? He'd shoot the little cretin, and they'd run for their lives. Improvise. But could he make that choice for them both? And what if Matilda didn't make it? And even if they both survived, could they afford to show the blocks they were being watched? Turn their paranoia dial up to eleven and put them on high alert? How would they be able to gather information then? How would they be able to attack a community who was expecting war?

Crack!

The diseased girl was now two feet away at the most. Seconds away from uncovering the snakes in the grass. And even if she didn't. Even if the light blinded her, if she stayed on her current path, she'd walk straight into them. And what of the diseased drawn to the beam?

Matilda pushed the end of William's gun down. In her other hand, she clung to half a brick.

"What are you …"

She pressed a finger to her lips.

The kid stumbled close.

Crack!

Matilda grabbed her around the ankles and yanked.

The kid fell backwards like she'd been shot.

Pulling her close, Matilda leaned on the diseased girl and wedged the brick in her mouth. It forced the kid's jaw wide and ripped open the cuts on her cheeks. The girl twisted and snarled, bucked and kicked. Bloody snot shot from her nose. But for all her effort, Matilda weighed too much to budge.

William drew his knife while Matilda pushed off against the brick, lifting herself clear of the diseased. The girl's jaw snapped further open with a popping *crack*. William stabbed her in the temple with the penetrating *pop* of a breaking skull.

He wiped his blade on the damp grass. "It's never easy when they're kids."

Matilda rolled away from the tiny corpse. As the spotlight moved on, her cheeks bulged with her hard exhale. "That was close!" She pulled a tight-lipped and humourless smile. A smile he'd seen from her too many times before. They were in this together. Just like they'd been since primary school. They were in it together, and they'd endure. Like they always had. Like they always will. With her beside him, he could do anything. The strongest woman he'd ever met. She'd overcome enough struggles for ten lifetimes, but she still had the fight in her to face more. To go into battle and be willing to improvise if that's what it took.

Kissing her, William pulled back and fixed on her large brown eyes. "I love you."

"I know."

"Hey."

She kissed him back. "I love you too."

CHAPTER 4

Crack!

William ducked again. They were twenty feet from the brow of the hill. They were almost close enough to get up and run. Were they only concerned about being shot, they were definitely close enough to get up and run. The spotlight shone over to their right, fixed on a solitary diseased that those in the plaza failed again and again to hit.

Crack!

But they couldn't afford to be seen. Running, when it put just William's life in danger, was his choice to make. But if he lost patience and made a break for it now, he'd be putting the lives of hundreds at risk.

Crack!

The vampire huts' remains provided far fewer obstacles than before. They'd crawled beyond the camp's footprint. The scraps of tin, bricks, and wood now in their path must have been dragged during the chaos of the collapse. William's eyes still burned. Fatigue. Sweat. Scanning the darkness. But he maintained his focus. If he cut himself on a rusty piece of metal, it could be game over. The infection could knock him out for weeks. Or worse.

Crack!

More diseased charged over the hill. They converged on the illuminated beast those in the plaza were yet to hit.

Crack!

The single target doubled, trebled, and now ten or more stood in the glare in a tight cluster. The guards still missed.

Crack!

A bullet whistled through the air and into the night.

Fifteen feet from the brow of the hill. Sodden. Cold. Exhausted. But with Matilda beside him, William would crawl through broken glass if that was the safest way to get them out of there. Whatever it took, they'd do it together. It had been that way since they were kids. Thick as thieves, his mum would say. Peas in a pod.

Crack!

Another diseased called out. Closer to William and Matilda than the others. The canted form shambled into view and got closer still. It teetered on the edge of its balance like it could fall at any moment.

Matilda found another brick, but William placed his hand over the back of hers. Her fingers were as cold as his. Did they also tingle on their way to turning numb? His touch settled the fire in her eyes. She let him press her hand down. She dropped the brick.

Crack!

The fully grown man wouldn't go as quietly as the girl. And with so many diseased nearby, they had to keep the noise down. William held his breath while he lifted a sheet a corrugated tin. Matilda slid beneath it, and he rolled in next to her. They were so close their foreheads touched.

William spoke beneath his breath. "Not only might it make too much noise and call over the others, but if we take that diseased down like we did the little girl, those on the spotlight will know something's up. They're yet to hit *anything* from this distance."

Crack!

Her lips tight, Matilda's nostrils flared from breathing through her nose. She nodded.

They'd angled the roof towards the diseased. It hid them from sight, but also blocked their view of the beast. Over the swishing grass and *crack* of gunfire, they tracked the creature's clumsy gait and rattling respiration. An idling engine that'd never get going.

Stalks snapped, and tin popped beneath its steps. The ground squelched, and it cried out in response to every shot from the elevated plaza. Who needed to see when they had so many cues? But all the cues told them the same thing. The beast was drawing closer, and they were directly in its path.

Crack!

Small wrinkles ran away from Matilda's tightly scrunched lips and nose. She snapped board stiff as a spider ran over the side of her face, skirted around her eye, and vanished into the shadows. Her breaths grew heavier.

Slow and steady, William reached up and laid his hand against the side of her face. Her breaths settled. Her wide eyes relaxed. But all the while, the diseased closed in. Maybe the brick would have been better.

Crack!

A series of small rusty holes let the spotlight's shine in through the tin roof. They'd moved their attention to the diseased man. Closer than the mob, maybe they stood a better chance of success. Although, from what William had seen of their aim so far ...

Crack!

A bullet whistled through the air.

The diseased wailed and stamped. His petulance sent a vibration through the damp ground.

Crack!

The diseased fell and landed across the corrugated sheet, which whacked William on the back of the head. The tin roof buckled beneath its weight and wrapped around them.

William caught Matilda's hand again. Prevented her from throwing the sheet aside. Her deep brown eyes flitted from one of his to the other. Had he lost his mind?

The diseased corpse sloughed off the roof. They'd finally hit something.

The spotlight returned to the cluster on the brow of the hill.

William's dry throat made his voice croak. "Maybe they gave the gun to someone who knows how to use it?"

Matilda laughed.

"You okay?"

That smile. That same smile. Always there. Through it all. Since they were kids. "Yeah."

Lifting the corrugated tin sheet, William rolled away and held it for Matilda to slide out too. A few more minutes and they'd be over the hill. They might not have much information, but they'd not blown their cover either. They still had ten days. Surely they'd get something in that time. And even if they didn't, they had each other. They'd get through this. They always had, and they always will. Ever since they were kids.

CHAPTER 5

They were just a couple of feet from the brow of the hill when William stopped and took Matilda's hand. Mud squelched between their interlocking fingers.

"Are you—"

She kissed him. They might not be any more prepared to attack the blocks in ten days' time, but they were home free. And they'd remained hidden the entire time. They could fight another day. And as long as they had one another, they'd overcome anything. The spotlight remained fixed on the mob of diseased a hundred feet away. *Crack!* They finally hit one of the crowd, its head snapping back, a cloud of mist rising in the air as it fell back into the long grass.

They kissed again. It never got old. It never would. He'd dreamed of kissing her for years. Kissing her and of spending a life together. The specifics of that life had never seemed to matter. If he'd tried a little harder, could he have manifested something better than their current shit-show of an existence? He laughed.

"Something funny?"

"No." He sighed. His mum and dad. Hugh. Cyrus. Max. Aggie. Flash. A list almost too long to remember. A list that still had space for more names. He pointed at the brow of the hill and held up three fingers.

Matilda nodded.

He dropped one. Then the next. Final finger down, they jumped up and sprinted over the hill.

The diseased hit William so hard, they both stumbled. He inhaled a lungful of vinegar rot. He fell back and reached for the creature on its way towards Matilda. He caught its fancy shirt. Ruffled, turquoise, silken. It slipped through his fingers. The beast broke away.

He would have called to Matilda, would blow their cover to protect her ten times out of ten, but she saw it coming. She cracked the beast clean on the chin with her gun's butt. It stumbled, but its momentum carried it forwards, straight towards her.

Karl caught it. He grabbed silk where William couldn't. He dragged it back, throwing the beast aside. He had the strength in one arm to end its attack. Broader than William, taller than William, and when he got enough food in him, he would be stockier than William.

Karl stamped on the creature's head. Silenced it with a crunch that made William's stomach twinge. Karl wore a sneer almost as ghastly as that of his victim. Smug bastard.

Panting and gasping, William's shoulders slumped as Karl smiled at Matilda, and she smiled back. Cocksure, the tall man had a swagger that would get him in trouble one of these days. He offered his hand to help her stand. When she took it, William's stomach twinged again.

The others were already in the tank. Nick silently clapped and jumped out. Even his whisper carried through the night. "Am I glad someone invited you, Karl."

He'd invited himself. Karl beamed at Matilda. Drank her in. William clenched his jaw, biting back his reply.

Matilda smiled. And why shouldn't she be grateful? He'd saved her life. William needed to recognise what he'd just done for her. What kind of arsehole got resentful at a time like this? She dipped her head. "Thank you."

As if expecting the same gratitude from William, Karl turned his way, but William avoided his eye. He followed Matilda towards the tank.

"We're so glad you're okay," Nick said.

William tutted. "We wouldn't have been in that situation had you not all run away like cowards. We should have held our ground in the meadow."

"You saw the spotlight and the diseased it drew in, right?"

"We were so close."

After a glance at Artan in the tank, Nick turned back to William and leaned his head to one side. His tone was always soft. "Are you being serious?"

"You think this is a fucking joke, Nick?"

"Clearly not. But they were shooting diseased."

"You're repeating yourself."

"Pulling more and more towards them."

"I know."

"And *us*. We were just twenty feet from the plaza—"

"That's my point, Nick."

His hand on his hip, his eyes wide, Nick stepped aside to let Knives exit the tank. She glared at William, but Nick continued, his voice still low, "And that's *my* point. They clearly have an awful shot, but we were so close that even those clowns on the spotlight would have hit us had we blown our cover. We *had* to get out of there."

"You *chose* to get out of there."

"If a diseased found us …"

"*If* a diseased found us."

"So next time, you want us to take that risk? Artan and I should endanger our lives to make sure we stick to the plan? Knives and Karl?"

Karl with a K could do whatever he wanted. And so be it if it got him killed. "I wanted us to cut open to the food tube. To actually do something for once rather than just watch the blocks. We were so close. In ten days, we have to lead an army against these blocks. What use are these trips if we make no progress?"

"What use are they if we die because of poor decisions?"

"And why didn't someone stop that diseased earlier?" William flung his arm towards the dead creature, the grass flattened by its fall. "The thing attacked us from nowhere while you were all hiding in the tank."

"Karl wasn't hiding in the tank."

William sneered.

"I'd say it was a good job we'd retreated. It meant we were here to help."

William's cheeks burned. His top lip twitched.

Crack!

A bullet whistled overhead, the hill's sharp decline hiding them from the blocks and the blocks from them.

"Next time"—Karl stepped closer to William—"I'll try to wait even closer to the brow of the hill. I'm sorry you got a fright."

"Next time you run away, you mean? Maybe when we attack the shining city, when it all gets too much for you, you can leave and fight the diseased in the meadow? Find somewhere safe and pretend you're doing something useful?" He gave Karl a thumbs up. "I'm sure glad you came along."

"Now come on, Will—"

Matilda cut Knives short with a hand on her arm. Not now.

William held the air in front of him in a pinch. He had a gap of about an inch between his thumb and index finger. "We were *this* close to making progress tonight."

Artan joined the others outside the tank. "And that close to losing our lives and blowing our cover. We can come back, William."

"Fuck you, Artan!"

Although something flared in Artan's glare, it died again from a gentle shake of Nick's head.

Passing them all, William entered the tank and dropped into the driver's seat, the padding letting out a puff of air beneath his weight. The half-moon lit the meadow ahead, showing them their way out. Downhill back towards their blocks.

The others entered one by one.

Whoosh!

Someone closed the tank's door, and Matilda dropped in beside him.

Releasing the parking brake, William let the tank roll. The ground squelched beneath them, the long grass yielding, some of the thicker stalks snapping with cackling cracks.

William pulled them onto the road, their squelching progress turning into a hum of their tyres against the concrete. He started the engine and stamped on the accelerator. The tank shot forwards, throwing him back in his seat.

The others had sat down on the benches in the back. Matilda, like William, stared out the windscreen. She kept her voice low, the tyres' vibration keeping their conversation private. "Want to talk about it?"

"No." He'd been a dick. Had felt threatened by Karl with a K. They all knew it, so what would talking about it achieve? The sooner they returned to the blocks, the better.

She momentarily laid her hand over the back of his on

the steering wheel. Her attention burned into the side of his face, but he remained focused ahead.

Matilda recoiled. She folded her arms and pulled her legs up beneath her.

CHAPTER 6

Gasping as she woke, Eleanor sat up in bed. She shuffled away from the figure looming over her. Her back hit the wall, and her heart kicked like it might burst. She panted as she rode the adrenaline dump. It took her several seconds to catch her breath. "Rayne?"

The kind woman smiled. She tucked her hair behind her ear. She waited while Eleanor settled.

A few days had passed since Rayne had told Eleanor she loved her, and Eleanor had said it back. And she meant it. She loved Rayne. She'd been kind to her. Wanted nothing more than for her to find peace. Understood it would come at the end of a long journey, but she seemed prepared to walk beside her every step of the way. Or intended to, anyway. Plans had a way of failing in a place like this. Even before the diseased had come south.

In the time since they'd shared that moment, Eleanor had remained in her small single room. She'd only gotten out of bed to wash and use the toilet. The days and nights hinted at their presence through her small bathroom window, but the frosted glass diluted the outside world to the point where it barely registered. Sometimes dark. Sometimes light. It rained once or twice, the heavy drops against the pane fighting for her attention. Rayne visited often and asked nothing of her other than how she felt. And to remind her that if she ever wanted to talk … And sometimes she did. Other times, the tears got in the way. But, of all the times she'd visited, she'd never woken her from sleep. "Is everything okay? Has something happened?"

Rayne stepped aside, Matthew poking his head through the open door behind her.

"What's he doing here?"

"Believe me"—Rayne sat on the edge of the bed and laid her hand over the tattoos on Eleanor's arm—"I would have thrown him from a walkway had you asked it of me."

The boy's face reddened, and he stared at the floor.

Eleanor shook her head. "I'm okay with him being here. I didn't mean it like that."

Her hand still over Eleanor's tattoos, Rayne tutted and scowled at the boy. "I did."

"Sorry, Matthew." Eleanor flatted her hair with her hands and rubbed her burning eyes. She'd cried so much over the past few days, every time she looked in the mirror, someone she didn't recognise stared back at her. Her eyes were so swollen, she looked like she'd been kicked in the face. She'd yet to check today, but the sting remained consistent, so why wouldn't her appearance? "I'm not in much of a state to receive guests."

"And I'm sorry to intrude." Matthew pressed his hands together, palm to palm. "But we have something to show you."

"We?"

Rayne shrugged. "It's taking a while for me and the boy to see eye to eye on most things, but on this we agree. We think you should come with us."

"Where?" Eleanor pointed at the door. "You want me to go out there?" She pointed at her face. "Looking like this?"

"You look fine." Matthew smiled, although his left eye twitched.

"Even if I did."

"You do."

"Don't forget, I still wear the face of their oppressor."

Rayne offered Eleanor her hand. "And their liberator. I'm sure people will stare when they see you, but I'm also sure they don't share your low opinion of yourself. Besides, we're only passing through the blocks."

"You want to take me out in the meadows?"

"Just get up, will ya?" Rayne hooked a thumb towards the door. "It's easier if we show you."

"No."

"No?"

"N …" Eleanor sat up a little straighter. She filled her lungs. She lifted her chin. Rayne had spoken about having something to focus on. A purpose. For her, it had been a murder investigation. Maybe they were trying to offer Eleanor the same. And what else would she do? Stay in bed forever, lamenting the passing of her father like her tears might somehow bring him back? "Okay."

"Okay?" Rayne smiled.

"Yeah. But I'm coming back if I don't like it. Now let me get changed."

∼

THEY PASSED a few residents on their way to the plaza. A few looked like they might approach them until they met Rayne's sneer. Were Eleanor's heart not beating in her throat and her stomach turning somersaults, she might have found it funny.

They passed through a basement similar to the one taken

over by the coup. Although this one didn't have a small stage on which to elevate their self-appointed king. Matthew led them towards the open door and the plaza beyond, while Rayne picked up a discarded rifle and handed it to her.

"Am I likely to need it?"

The edges of Rayne's mouth turned down. "I'd feel more comfortable if you had a weapon."

Eleanor pulled the strap over her head. The cold gun rested against her stomach. She stepped out onto the plaza and stumbled back. She raised her hand, but it did little to dilute the sun's glare. An overcast day, but it still burned her eyes.

The diseased's collective moan came up at them from the meadow. So many tones and tempos it almost sounded like a conversation. A discussion about their next plan of attack. Until Eleanor focused, the white-noise chatter nonsensical. Tormented, disturbed, and ready to ignite into a unified cry of rage the second they got even a sniff of an uninfected. The chill wind hit her with its cleansing force. Blew out the stuffiness accumulated from days inside. Although, it gave with one hand and thrust upon her a curdled vinegar rot with the other.

Since Eleanor's last visit to the plaza, they'd set it up to make it easier for people to leave. The tanks were now parked on the other side of the gap in the exit ramp. They'd anchored the ladders to their side of the plaza using hinged joints, which bridged the space and rested on the back of the tanks' roofs. "What happens when you drive off in a tank?"

Rayne shrugged. "The ladder falls down onto the ramp."

"That's what I thought. And the diseased can't get across?"

"They can barely walk in a straight line, let alone cross a fifteen-foot gap on a ladder."

"But what if they—"

Rayne pointed across the plaza. Two guards stood waiting with guns.

"Ah!"

Matthew stepped aside to let Rayne cross the ladders first. The ramp had quite a sharp decline, but because the ladder rested on the tank's roof, the elevation reduced the slope. Rayne crossed it on all fours, her hands and feet on the ladder rungs like a monkey, her rifle swinging down from its strap.

Matthew followed, but Eleanor froze. She'd done harder things than this. But she'd done harder things than get out of bed in the morning. That didn't diminish the scale of the task with her current mindset.

A glance down the ramp behind her at the diseased in the meadow, Rayne gripped her gun with one hand and waved Eleanor on with the other. Matthew slipped inside the tank through the turret hole.

Eleanor leaned forwards and gripped the cold and rough ladder rungs with both hands. The diseased had gone from grumblings of discontent to a more focused fury. They gathered about fifty feet below, many of them staring straight up, their eye sockets filled with dry blood. Many reached out like they expected her to fall. She pulled back and shook her head.

"Come on, Eleanor." Rayne waved her over before aiming her gun down the ramp at the approaching diseased.

Back on the ladder, Eleanor jumped when Rayne fired her gun. Her stomach lurched, but she had to keep going. The longer she left it, the more diseased Rayne would have to shoot. Her legs and arms shook, but she focused on the next rung. One step at a time.

Rayne fired again. The diseased responded with roars and wails. One step at a time. Hands. Feet. Hands. Feet. A rung at a time.

Rayne gripped the back of Eleanor's shirt when she reached the other side and dragged her the rest of the way. She guided her to the hole in the tank's roof. Eleanor slipped in and landed flat-footed. Matthew turned from the driver's seat with a grin. "Well done!"

She threw a weak smile at him as he drove away. "What about Rayne?"

Gunfire above, Rayne shot the diseased in their path as they left the ramp and pulled onto the concrete road. The diseased grew smaller in the rear window, and Rayne dropped into the tank with them. She hugged Eleanor. "Well done, sweetheart."

∼

She'd travelled this route many times in her mind over the past few days. So before they'd even reached the wrecked trailer, Eleanor's heart beat treble time. It still lay on its side, the back hanging open from where she'd released the latch on the roof. From where she'd sentenced the coup to their death. Diseased gathered around the wreck. Where else would they go? Maybe some of them had once belonged to the coup. They were too far away to tell, and she didn't need to know. She fought to keep the warble from her voice. "Why have you brought me here?"

Rayne pulled a weak smile, and Matthew picked up the pace as they hurtled towards the crash site. Towards what Eleanor had caused.

As much as she tried, Eleanor couldn't still her rising panic. Why here? What were they hoping to achieve? Did they want to shock her out of her state? Like this would help. "Uh, I don't …"

They shot past the trailer, watched by the gathered diseased. Eleanor's tight chest slowly unwound as they put it behind them. She laid a palm over her heart as it settled. "I genuinely thought you were taking me back there." She laughed. "Mental, right?"

Rayne dropped her attention to the floor, and Matthew cleared his throat. He shuffled in his seat.

Eleanor shook her head. "Oh no! You're not?"

∼

Whoosh!

Daylight filled the tank, and Matthew stepped out onto the road first. He scanned the meadow. As Rayne jumped out after him, he remained close to the open door. "I've been coming here for the past few nights."

Eleanor backed away until she hit the tank's far wall. "But why here?" She dragged in a wet sniff. "Why would you bring me here?"

"Closure."

"What the fuck, Matthew?"

The boy reached into the tank, encouraging her to step forward.

She folded her arms and stuffed her hands beneath her armpits.

Matthew remained in the open doorway.

Rayne divided her attention between them and their environment. She clung to her gun. "Matthew's spent a few nights on this. He only told me he's been coming out on his own this morning. And while I rarely agree with him, on this I think he has a point."

"But..."

"Just have a look."

Eleanor took Matthew's hand and stepped from the tank. The wind stronger out here than up in the plaza. She followed Mads' son towards the deep roadside pit. The vampire trap that had killed her dad. Diseased gathered in the meadow, but the long grass hid them from sight. Eleanor's heart galloped, and she shook her head. But she kept stepping forwards, edging towards her dad's grave as if on autopilot.

But just before she reached the pit's edge, she let go of Matthew's hand. Her surroundings blurred through her tears. The strong wind cut into her trembling form. She folded her arms again and shook her head. She fought for breath. Her ears rang with the echo of her scream from when she'd first lost him. Why had they brought her here?

Matthew waited, and Rayne kept lookout for the diseased.

Reluctance ran through her veins like molasses, but Eleanor stepped forwards despite herself. Joined Matthew at the pit's edge. Her world still blurred, her shoulders bobbed with her grief. She rubbed her eyes and peered in.

The echo finally made it out. She wailed like she had the first time. It came from deep inside, her body a conduit through which to release the braying, soulful cry. She fell to her knees on the muddy ground, the tank about eight feet below. Matthew had covered the turret hole with a thin yellow sheet. It shone bright against the tank's charred chassis. He'd laid flowers on and around the bright fabric. She flinched when he lightly held her elbow.

"Now, we can leave him here, but I've looked inside, and he's not been burned."

"But what else will we do with him?"

"We—"

Eleanor yelped and spun around, Rayne now directly behind her. She followed Rayne's glances. Her grief had called the diseased closer. They were running out of time.

"We could give him a send-off like we did for Aggie. Take him somewhere and have a ceremony. Matthew will get him out if that's what you want?" Another diseased cry took Rayne's attention. She raised her gun to her shoulder and peered down the barrel. "Matthew thought, and I agree with him, that it might be a good way for you to say goodbye. And I hate to rush you, but …"

"I understand. Matthew, do you have time to get him out?"

"I do. Will you go back to the tank and wait?"

Eleanor stepped away from the pit. "Yes." She clung to Matthew's hands. "Thank you." Rayne pulled them apart as Matthew nodded and jumped down to the burned tank with a *thud!*

CHAPTER 7

"Are we there yet?"

Gracie rolled her eyes and shook her head. She threw her hand in front of her at the wide wall in the distance. "You can see the farm as well as I can, Bear."

"Well, at least you're answering me."

Now they'd slowed, the tank's steering became much heavier. Grunting with the effort, Gracie navigated the spikes punched up through the farm's approach road, diseased closing in on both sides. "I'm a little busy, in case you haven't noticed?"

"You can't multitask?"

Olga turned to Bear in the back. "I'm sure, given the right motivation, she could knock you out and drive at the same time."

"I just want to know what we're going into."

After turning close to a spike on their left, the diseased corpse it had skewered watching them past through its dried bloody eye, Gracie tapped the accelerator, sending Bear and Kira stumbling back. The road had opened up, and more diseased were closing in from both sides. Spikes halted the progress of some, but many more got through. "Life's hard to predict at the best of times. Besides, you've asked us a list of questions about what's ahead, but Olga and I have raised just one Icarus tower. This one could be entirely different."

"The last one had these spikes on the approach?"

The next skewered diseased had some life left in it. It threw a lazy swipe at the passing tank, its hand hitting the windscreen with a dull *thud.* "Yes, it did."

"See, that's something that would have been useful to tell me."

"Why? You're not driving." Olga sneered. "We've told you enough. Now shut the fuck up and let Gracie drive."

Gracie, Olga, and Kira had chosen to come to the farm. Had accepted this mission. But Bear had come against his will. And had anyone else had his skill set, they might be here instead. A mechanic, if anyone from the towers could get the abandoned farm vehicles started, it was him. Not that he'd volunteered that information himself. It took for one of the other community members to out him. On the drive over, they'd given him information about their last trip. Had even told him about the flood. But the more they told him, the more he asked. His concerns only grew greater. Tell him too much more and the only way they'd get him down the stairs to the Icarus tower's base would be to launch him.

Gracie navigated the final few spikes between them and the farm's gate. They'd already strapped a ladder to the tank's roof. It protruded from it like a jousting pole. It wobbled with their progress, every lump and bump in the road exaggerated along its length. "You ready, Olga?"

The fierce woman straightened in her seat and held up her hacking device for Gracie to see.

Nodding, Gracie leaned forwards like it would give her a better view. But they were too close to the farm's gates to see all the diseased converging on their spot. The *thunk* of activated spikes continued calling out over the shrieks and wails.

Gracie slowed to a crawl, squinting in the weak sunlight as she slotted the ladder's end into the grooves by the gate's control panel. "Okay, Olga. In three ... two ..."

Olga slipped from her seat, opened the tank's side door with a *whoosh,* and climbed out onto the roof. She crossed the ladder like a squirrel along a tree branch. Kira leaned into the cockpit next to Gracie to watch her through the front window.

Bear on the door, Kira beside her, Gracie divided her attention between Olga on the ladder and the diseased closing in from their left. They were as likely to go for the open tank as they were Olga. "How's it looking on your side, Bear?"

"They're still a little way away. She has time."

Moving like she'd done this a thousand times before, Olga reached the gates, hacked the lock, clung to the ladder, and gave Gracie a thumbs up.

The gates opened as Gracie reversed, pulling Olga and the ladder clear. She went forwards again, driving them into the quarantine zone through the front gates. Before she'd stopped, Olga had dismounted and run back, securing the first gates, locking them in and the diseased out.

By the time Gracie had parked the tank, grabbed weapons for them all, and got out with the other two, Olga had opened the gates in the farm's inner wall.

They'd parted with a deep roll like distant thunder and revealed a layout similar to the previous farm. The Icarus tower's top field directly ahead, framed by a gap that dropped for what looked like miles from this high up. Both Kira and Bear gasped to peer into it, Kira throwing out her arms like she might lose her balance.

Give them too long to think and they might change their

minds. "Right, come on." Gracie descended the steel stairs, her steps calling into the darkness below. They passed the first of the shelves filled with soil desperate for sunlight. So far, so familiar.

Kira followed directly behind and smiled every time Gracie turned around. Despite her vertigo, her big brown eyes shone, and her curly hair bounced with her steps. She positively buzzed with optimism. If only a bit of it would rub off on Bear.

Their steps called into the gloom as they passed the final Icarus tower field. The pair of massive struts plunged down into the darkness. Gracie scrunched her nose at the musty damp. The place stank like a crypt.

Jumping off the final stair, Gracie spun around as Kira, Bear, and Olga stepped off after her. She spread her arms wide. "So, here we are."

Kira beamed, Bear's mouth hung open, and Olga blew out hard, her cheeks bulging. Here they go again.

Of course, there was no sign of the buggies they'd used in the last tunnel. If there were any, they were probably at the other end by the control room. Instead, they had poor visibility coming from the weak sun above and the dim bulbs lighting their path ahead. Dwarfed by the monstrous Icarus tower struts, they all remained still, staring into the gloom of the off-kilter tunnel. "So, this is it. We have to walk down this tunnel until we find the control room for the Icarus tower, activate it, and come back."

Kira nodded and grinned, her ringlets bouncing along with her chirpy tones. "Sounds straightforward enough."

Bear scoffed. "No."

"No?"

A sharp shake of his head sent Bear's long blond plait snapping like a whip. "No."

"No?" Olga this time. She leaned towards him.

"That's what I said."

"But what do you mean?"

"I don't like it."

Olga's tut went off like a cracking whip. "You're not supposed to *like* it, Bear. Fucking hell, precious, what were you expecting? A nice little getaway? A sunny spot somewhere where we can catch some rays and wait this out while the others risk their lives at war?"

Bear's long plait flicked like a tail with the next shake of his head. "I don't want to be here."

"As opposed to the rest of us?" Olga rolled her eyes at Gracie.

"You've no idea, Olga."

The short woman rocked forwards, but halted at Gracie's raised hand. "Stop! This is our part in this war. It's not pretty."

"I didn't choose it. I was sent."

Olga grabbed Bear's shoulder and dragged him around so he faced her. "Would you rather we sent you to war?"

Bear's lips tightened.

After a few seconds, Olga shook her head. "I didn't think so. None of us want to be here. This place is awful."

"But why didn't you tell me what it was like down here?"

Gracie tutted. "We did."

"You didn't explain this, Gracie."

Olga stood with her hands on her hips as she looked up at him. "Because we need your skills. Would you have come had we sold it as a journey into the abyss? A trip to hell?"

Bear's lips tightened again. What little light they had down there caught the brown in his eyes. "Well … no. I just would have preferred it if you'd been more open about what lay ahead."

"Would you have moaned less?"

"Probably not."

Gracie threw up her arms. "So shut up, then, yeah?"

"Wha—"

"If you have nothing positive to say, Bear, then shut up. None of us would have chosen this, and none of us are looking forward to it." She glared at Kira until her smile fell. "So stop killing the mood."

Folding her arms, Olga snorted a humourless laugh. "My point exactly."

"You can shut up too."

Olga laid her hand on her chest. "What have I done?"

"You're antagonising him. He has every right to feel apprehensive."

"Didn't you just tell him to shut up?"

"Just leave him alone, yeah?"

Gracie gripped her gun with both hands and strode into the musty gloom. She aimed her laser target ahead of her like it would somehow reveal this tomb's secrets. Like it might explain the off-kilter tunnel where the walls and floor were at odds with one another. Or maybe help them understand why the air smelled like a crypt. And why the carvings surrounding them depicted a species that was not entirely human. Kira took it all in her buoyant stride while Bear wore a face like a scolded child. But as long as he continued sulking until they needed him, it had to be better than the incessant line of questioning. They were finally here. Now they had to make sure their mission was a success.

CHAPTER 8

After closing her eyes, Eleanor filled her lungs and leaned into the fire's warmth. It dried her tears and pulled her skin taut. The areas made red raw by her grief were now tingling like they might heal. The flames not only sucked the moisture from her exposed skin, but they drew a small amount of her sadness with it. Smoothed its sharp edges. Returned to her an element of control. Her soul would forever be torn, but standing on that large rock in the meadow, the fresh wind teasing the flames dancing on her dad's swaddled corpse, and with her friends beside her—Rayne rubbing her back the entire time—she found inside her a small amount of courage with which to face the world.

Diseased gathered around them. They'd rushed over, but crashing into an immoveable rock had shown them the futility of their fight. Even with their squalls and shrieks, with their furious focus locked on the mourners, they soon calmed down. They now stood as if they too were acknowledging a passing. The loss of themselves. Eleanor would never be the same again, but at least she still had her humanity.

In the days leading up to that moment, Matthew had not only gotten her dad's body ready to be removed by wrapping it in a sheet, but he'd also found the perfect rock in the perfect spot. Somewhere to park the tank beside so they could step across out of the diseased's reach. He'd built a fire in case they'd needed it. A bed of wood on which they laid her fabric-wrapped father, soaking him and the logs in fuel before they'd lit the match.

The fierce flames had initially taken her breath away, but the rock Matthew had selected gave them enough space to step back to a safe distance. At first, she'd wailed. Louder and harder than a hundred diseased. But as the flames abated, so did her despair.

"Even as I grew older …" Eleanor cleared her throat and started again. "When I wanted time by myself and didn't need to be tucked in at night, Dad would often knock on my bedroom door before I went to bed." She smiled, drawing some of the fire's warmth into her. "I'd often ignore him. Or I'd tell him to go away. But he never stopped coming. Every evening. No matter how rude I'd been to him the night before." Her smile broadened. Both Rayne and Matthew were beaming with her. "But on the times when I opened my door, he'd light up as if seeing me had made his day. As if we'd been apart for months, when I'd sat and had dinner with him just a few hours previously. He said he slept better when he tucked me in. That I was doing him a favour by letting him say good night. He'd pull my covers right up to my neck, like when I was little. He'd stroke my hair. He'd lean over me and kiss my head." Her hand shook as she pointed to her forehead. "Right there. And he'd say, *good night, peanut.* Every night. And no matter how cool I thought I'd become, I couldn't help but smile. And you know what, I think I slept better on those nights too." She pressed three fingers to her lips—her index, middle, and ring finger—and kissed the tips before turning them towards the flames.

She gulped, and her tears returned in full. But they were normal. She should be sad. Holding onto her grief had been the thing making her lose control. "And I'd always reply." She whispered those words for the last time. "Good night, coconut."

∼

Wham!

They sent another diseased flying, Matthew barrelling along the road back towards their tower blocks. They'd been out for hours, and the day had grown long. Eleanor sat beside him, riding shotgun, while Rayne leaned forwards from the back.

The setting sun shone in through the windscreen, and their destination loomed large. Eight tall tower blocks interconnected by elevated walkways. Matthew scowled against the low sun's glare. "So, I've heard a lot about the shining city, but it's always been from a vampire's perspective. I appreciate I need to take some of it with a pinch of salt, but what do you know about the place, Eleanor?"

"In general or specifically?"

"Let's start with in general."

Resting her feet on the dash, Eleanor leaned back in her seat. "It depends who you talk to. For many, it's paradise. It's like heaven on earth. But I'm more inclined to believe my mum and dad's version. They fought fiercely to keep me away. Whenever they talked about it, they did so with conspiratorial whispers and the paranoia of being overheard. They said it's run by an oppressive regime who aggressively discourage opinions. They get compliance through coercion. Be it blackmail, the threat of being ostracised, or worse."

Rayne leaned closer. "Worse?"

"I've heard they torture those who don't toe the line." She

took Rayne's hand. "And it's worse for women. Of course, like I said, on the surface it's paradise. But everyone knows about its dark underbelly. The punishment for non-compliance has to be public enough to be a threat, but private enough to be ignored. They hide their torture dens down side streets. Keep their slaves trapped in basements."

The tank twitched when Matthew turned her way. "It's that bad?"

"Apparently. It's a place run by old men who can barely stand without putting out their hips. In any other life, they'd be powerless and pathetic little cretins. But in the shining city, they're self-appointed kings."

Wham!

The next diseased cartwheeled away.

Wham!

Matthew hit another as he steered onto the block's entrance ramp. He maintained his speed, slamming into the pair waiting for them, sending them over the side to clear the way.

"Matthew!" Rayne reached forwards, but she couldn't brake for him. He overshot the ramp, the tank's front two wheels dropping into the gap, the underside of the tank's chassis hitting the concrete with a *crunch!*

"Shit! I'm sorry. I wanted to clear the way."

The tank's front dropped, and the back lifted, flipping Eleanor's stomach. It angled them towards a hundred or more diseased forty feet below.

Eleanor slipped from her seat and twisted past Rayne.

"What are you doing?"

She climbed out through the hole in the tank's roof. "Follow me."

Her gun raised, Eleanor ran to the tank's rear as it lifted. She laid her red laser target on a diseased's face and pulled her trigger, blowing the back of its head out behind it like a soggy flare. It fell and tripped two more.

Joining her, Rayne shot the diseased. "Are you sure you're okay?"

"I'm better than I've been in days. Thank you." Eleanor bent her knees as the tank dropped. Rayne copied her, their combined weight driving the tank's rear two wheels closer to the ramp.

The wheels spun from where Matthew threw the vehicle into reverse. They screeched against the ramp, but the tank lifted before they got any grip.

As the back lifted, Eleanor shot three more diseased. On the way down, she and Rayne bent their knees again. Matthew kept the wheels spinning in reverse.

The tank lurched backwards, dragging the front tyres off the ledge and throwing Eleanor and Rayne onto their backs. Matthew brought them to a screeching halt.

"Cover me, Rayne."

Although Rayne tried to grab her, Eleanor rolled clear of her reach and slipped off the side of the tank into a small gap between them and the one they'd parked beside. She fired down the ramp at the onrushing diseased. There were so many, every shot hit.

Letting her gun fall to its strap, Eleanor sprinted for the small space in front of the tank. She whacked the driver's side window on her way past so Matthew knew where she was. She lifted the hinged ladder and held it above her head. Rayne, back on her feet on the tank's roof, fired on the diseased while Matthew edged slowly forward.

The diseased on the ground drowned out the wails of those sprinting up the ramp.

Matthew had already proven if he moved too fast, he'd knock her into the baying crowd below. But if he took too much longer ... "Hurry up!"

Eleanor dropped the end of the hinged ladder onto the tank's roof just as five diseased broke clear on her side. She leaped, Rayne's scream a match for the diseased's collective fury.

She caught a rough ladder rung, the jolt of her weight snapping up to her shoulders as the five leaped after her. One whacked the back of her boot, but the rest of them fell. Flailing and swiping, they turned somersaults and landed on their kin like fleshy bombs. Eleanor's cheeks bulged as she breathed out and swung over the mob, her legs hanging down.

Sweating and weak, but she'd done this before. The best at monkey bars when they were little kids. She still had it. Taking her time, cheered on by the diseased, she swung from one rung to the next, each taking her closer to the plaza until she finally jumped clear and landed on the other side on solid ground.

Eleanor waited for Rayne to climb across and hugged her. "Thank you." Matthew joined them, and she hugged him, too. "Something's changed, and that's thanks to you both. I will forever be sad, but I feel a little more able to cope. To act when it's needed." She smiled. "After I've had a rest, that is. I dunno about you two, but I'm knackered." She waved as she walked away from them. "I'm going back to my room to rest."

∽

AS ANOTHER BROADCAST ENDED, Eleanor sat on her bed and sighed. Alone in her room, but better than before. Now she'd given her dad the ceremony he deserved, things were ever so slightly easier. Who knew when Rayne would come to check on her next. And how she'd react when she found her room empty. Would she forgive her? Surely she'd understand.

Eleanor had a role to play. Hopefully the note would make sense to her. She read it one last time.

Dear Rayne,

Please don't be mad. What a way to start a note! Sorry, but this is something I have to do to help both the community and myself. This is my murder investigation. Please don't be mad.

She laid it flat on her bed and opened her bedroom door. She stepped out into the quiet hallway and made for the stairwell. Rayne was going to be livid.

CHAPTER 9

"Stop!" Gracie thrust out her arms to either side, holding her three friends back as her call ran away from them down the tunnel. She'd not spoken since telling Olga and Bear to sort themselves out. She didn't blame either of them. Bear had every right to be nervous, and Olga every right to find his moaning annoying. But that didn't mean she wanted to hear the pair of them go at one another like squabbling children. The tunnel was at least twenty feet wide, so had the others wanted to pass, they'd have no problem skirting around her, but they took her warning and waited.

Olga leaned around Gracie's right arm and looked ahead. "Why are we stopping?"

"There."

Olga followed to where Gracie pointed. "Ah!"

"What?" Kira's curly hair bounced with her scanning. "What are we looking at?"

A raised mound sat in their path about five hundred feet away. "See that?"

Leaning past her like the extra few inches would improve

his view, Bear's long plait fell forwards into Gracie's back. He scowled. "What is it?"

"A sun."

"On the floor?"

Gracie tutted. "A *representation* of a sun."

"I didn't think it was the *actual* sun. And my question still stands. Why's it on the floor?"

"I told you about the flood?"

Bear looked up at the ceiling like it might come crashing down on them. He gulped and nodded.

"There was a sun like this on the ceiling of the previous tunnel. When we pressed it, the water drained away."

"So we should expect water?"

Olga flashed him a maniacal grin. "We should expect the unexpected."

Kira turned on the spot. Of them all, she'd been the most fascinated by the wall carvings. The alien inscriptions that depicted a species with forms unlike anything on Earth. Once again, she scanned them like she believed her attention would somehow make them make sense.

Although Kira acted like she had something to say, she kept it to herself, so Gracie said, "I agree with Olga. Expect the unexpected."

"Get down." Kira dropped into a crouch.

Olga and Gracie copied her, but Bear remained standing. He looked ready to run and knocked back Olga's hand when she tried to pull him down with them.

"Why don't you listen, Bear?"

"So I can't question anything now?"

Olga rolled her eyes. "You can, but that doesn't mean you should question *everything*."

"Be a good little vampire and accept what I'm told?"

"This is about trust, not compliance."

"Whatever you name the stick, you're still beating me

with it."

The pair's nonsense turned into white noise while Kira grabbed Gracie's arm and gestured at their surroundings. Long horizontal slots ran through the carvings on either side of them. They started at their current position and ran all the way to the mound on the floor and beyond. They were at the same height on both sides. A mirror image of one another. They started at three feet from the ground and climbed all the way to the wonky ceiling. There were seven pairs of slots in total.

Olga squared up to Bear. Her chest against his. "She knows what she's talking about. And she has more experience than you. Ignore what she's saying at your peril."

"Is that a threat?"

"Of course it is, you fucking moron. You'll die down here if you don't remove your head from your arse. Besides, you don't hear Kira complaining."

"She *volunteered* to come."

"Look, I wish we didn't need you, but we do. Is that what you want to hear? Please come with us, Bear. Oh, we need you so much in case we have to get the farm machinery working. You're *so* important to us. Although, I suppose I get it. I can't imagine there are many points in your life where you've been useful to anyone. Now that day's finally come, it must be hard to believe."

"But what good is me fixing farm machinery down here?"

"You're right. We should have left you in the quarantine zone above. Had I been running this mission, that's where you'd be right now. Diseased got in there in the last farm. We should have left you to see them off."

Gracie clicked her fingers at the pair. She pointed at the floor. She'd ducked before, but she now lay flat on her front beside Kira, her rifle resting against the base of her back.

Olga copied her, but Bear shook his head, gripped his

rifle, and passed the three of them, heading deeper into the tunnel. "Fine, we've come here to get to the end of the tunnel, so that's where I'll go. I don't care if I get wet."

Olga leaped up, sprinted after him, and tackled him around the waist. She knocked him over, landing on top of him as they both hit the ground hard.

Whoosh!

A steel sheet burst from the highest slot on their left, about three feet lower than the tunnel's ceiling. A sheathed blade filled with holes a few inches in diameter. A horizontal guillotine. It slammed into the gap in the other wall with a *crack* and rang like a struck bell.

Throwing Olga off him, Bear pressed down against the ground as if to stand. "I still don't see why we need to lie on our bellies like snakes."

Crack!

The next sheet shot overhead. Another three feet lower. Filled with holes like the one above. They filtered the tunnel's already weak light.

Bear dropped, lying flatter than the rest of them.

Crack!

Yet another, the tunnel getting increasingly cramped.

Crack!

Crack!

Kira remained flat, but she gestured at the wall on their right with a flick of her hand. "We should be okay if we remain on our bellies. That's the lowest of the slots."

Crack!

"Just two slots left." Kira ducked despite the penultimate slot being about six feet above them.

Thunk!

Thunk!

The final sheet slammed into place, joining the chorus of ringing steel, which somehow grew louder with every passing second. The sound swelled through Gracie's skull, her cranium thrumming like the vibrating steel. She rolled onto her back and flinched from the sand raining into her eyes. "You three need to retreat."

Olga hunched, the sand raining on the top of her head. "What?"

Bear shuffled backwards and stood clear of the horizontal blades. A layer of sand already coated the floor.

Although she frowned at Gracie, silently questioning her judgement, Kira took Gracie's rifle when she handed it to her, and pulled back, leaving a snake's trail in the sand.

Gracie shooed Olga away. "Go with the others."

"No."

"No?"

"You're not coming, are you?"

"Stop fucking about and just go with the others, Olga. This doesn't need both of us."

"Don't be a hero, Gracie."

"I'm being a leader. I don't want to risk your life on a hunch. I need to press that sun, and you're wasting precious seconds."

"You are." Olga pulled her rifle from over her head and slid it back towards Bear. He stopped it with his foot and wore it with his own.

"Fucking hell, Olga."

Olga shoved Gracie's feet, shunting her towards the sun.

The sand not yet deep enough to cushion her progress, Gracie clenched her teeth through the sharp sting in her elbows as she dragged herself forwards. Sand rained down on her. It got in her hair. Beneath her collar. Stuck to her sweating skin. Stung her eyes.

The sun was about three hundred feet away and completely covered in sand. "We're running out of time, Olga. I won't slow down for you."

"Fuck off, Gracie."

The sand fell heavier than before and with a white-noise hiss. It now sat a few inches deep, which at least made it easier on Gracie's elbows. But it also slowed her crawl. She'd expected to swim based on the previous farm, but not like this.

Two hundred feet from the raised sun. The grains fell faster with every passing second, and the levels rose quicker, lifting Gracie closer to the blade directly above her. Olga couldn't keep up. She should have gone with the others.

One hundred feet away, and Gracie had adopted an improvised breaststroke to help her progress. The mound had all but vanished. Her back scraped against the blade, and her chin cut a groove through the rough sand.

Gracie closed her eyes, the sand kicking up in her face. With every breath, she inhaled more grains. Her throat itched with her need to cough. She reached an air pocket, lifted her face to a hole above her in the steel sheet, and stole a breath. "Olga?" The tight sand blocked her view and absorbed her call. Even if Olga had called back, she wouldn't hear it.

Digging back the way she'd come, Gracie found another air hole and tried again. "Olga? Shit."

The sun was about fifty feet away. Who knew where Olga was? And how would it help to get back to her now? "Shit! I told you not to come, Olga. Shit!"

But what if the sun didn't work? What if she had a chance to save her friend and get them both out of there, but instead she followed a hunch that led to naught? She dragged the sand away from another hole in the steel and gasped on the air. She tried again, but too much sand came through. She had to make a choice, and now. Any further inaction and they'd both suffocate.

CHAPTER 10

A full day had passed since William last saw his friends. Since he'd turned on them all because Karl with a K had made him look weak. Although, his reaction to it all had proven the arrogant prick right. Matilda could do better, and so could his friends.

Butterflies danced in his stomach as he and Matilda crossed the elevated walkway towards the ballroom with the shattered mirrored floor. His friends waited inside. Matilda had asked them to meet him there prior to their meeting with the top table. No doubt they were ready to tell him he'd been a total dick. Like he didn't know. But it didn't matter how much he hated Karl, he shouldn't have taken it out on them. He'd tried to explain to Matilda, but she didn't want excuses. She'd made him accountable for his actions, accepted his apology, and then forgave him. She had the strength to be compassionate and the solidity in herself to tell him he was wrong. It served as yet another reminder of just how much he loved her.

Matilda slowed to let him enter the room first. His bed, now he had to go lie in it. And afterwards, at some point, they'd have to tell the top table just how little progress they'd made with their scouting missions. Nick, Artan, and Knives waited for him. No Karl with a K. Fuck Karl with a K. And no Gracie or Olga either. The first sign they'd get from them would be another raised Icarus tower. If they were successful. Hopefully they were doing all right. Eleanor and Rayne were also absent. They'd needed time alone. "Look, about the other night ..."

Artan batted the comment away. "Don't mention it."

"I ... uh ..."

Knives' blade glinted as she tossed it in the air. She remained fixed on William the entire time, caught it, and smiled. "Honestly, it's fine. You were a dick. You've apologised. Now let's move on."

And Nick had forgiven him before they'd returned to the blocks. Even waited for him at the top of the food tube when they'd climbed back in to see if he wanted to talk about it. He didn't. They still returned to the blocks via the food tube instead of driving the tanks up the ramp and using the ladders to cross the gap. They had limited room on the ramps, so why take the space now they were used to the other way? Also, they needed the practice. It was how they'd enter the enemy's block, and with no rope ladder in their food tube, they needed to stay fit for the climb.

Tossing her blade, Knives caught it again. "So we're going out again soon?"

William nodded. "Yeah. In an hour or so. We should have gone out last night, especially as I have to tell the top table tonight just how little we've discovered."

"No." Knives shook her head.

"No?"

"We were right to stay in last night. We all needed a rest. Needed to take some time. Who knows how many more chances we'll get to look after ourselves before this war ends."

"You're right."

"And seeing as we have some time to kill while we wait for the top table …"

"Huh?" William said.

She winked at him. "How about I give you a haircut? You look a mess."

He ran his hand along the side of his head. It had been a while since he'd had a trim. His tightly curled hair gave him a tatty halo that'd only get bigger. "You'd do that?"

"If you'll trust me with a knife that close to your neck?" She made a cutting motion as if slicing his throat.

"Even when you're delivering it with a direct threat, I feel more relaxed with your blade close to my face than ever before. Thank you."

"Welcome." She led them into the control room at the end of the corridor. The top table's meeting place, but it sat empty for now. She dragged a chair away from the table, the legs screeching across the steel floor. William sat down.

Knives' blade glinted in his peripheral vision. He might have been more comfortable with her, but the sharp edge so close to his face still made him tense.

Knives squeezed his right shoulder. "Relax." She cut some of his hair away, a single swipe removing a black clump that fell into his lap.

The screech of Artan's chair against the steel floor pulled his shoulders tight again.

Matilda's brother sat down with a sigh. "I'm tired."

Nick sat beside him and laid an arm around his shoulders. "Me too. But the end's in sight."

Hanging his head, Artan nodded. "It's always dark before the dawn, eh?"

"Something like that."

Artan looked at the others. "What do you all have planned for when this is over?" He took Nick's hand and smiled. "We're going to find somewhere quiet. Maybe return to the north. We want a small house with a vegetable garden and—"

"Massive fucking walls!" Nick said.

William laughed along with the others.

Nick beamed. "We want to slow down and grow old together."

"Sounds lovely." Matilda winked at William. "But you'll have to be close enough so you can help with babysitting duties."

William's heart kicked, and Artan sat up straighter. "Something you're not telling us, sis?"

"No. But you're not the only ones who've talked about a future."

After taking off another chunk of hair, Knives patted William's shoulder.

Whoosh!

The control room door opened.

Hawk entered, streaked with dirt from where he'd been out hunting. He carried a plate of cooked deer, the smell of barbecued meat making William's mouth water.

Hawk moved around the room, giving each of them a slice.

"Another successful day, then?" William took a chunk and chewed on the juicy steak. "The hunters are getting better?"

"They were always all right." Hawk put the plate on the table. "It was the diseased that were the problem. They needed a few days to see they're not so unpredictable. Since then, we've been doing great. Our little hunting party has become formidable."

Knives ran her blade along the side of William's head, and more clumps of hair fell into his lap. He swept them to the floor. "And you?"

"And me, what?" Hawk said.

"How are you?"

"Okay."

"But?"

"If I'm honest, William, I can't wait for this to end."

William gestured towards Artan. "We were just saying the same thing."

"I just hope it doesn't take much longer for us to conquer these blocks and the shining city. I can't wait to live a life without worrying about what's coming next. About who else we might lose."

Hawk's comment plunged the room into silence save for the scrape of Knives' blade against William's stubble. William caught Matilda's eye and pulled a tight smile. They'd been luckier than most. They still had each other. But so many had gone. And poor Hawk. Reaching out, he held his friend's hand. Rough with hard graft and covered in dirt, he squeezed. "Thanks for the meat. And we're here for you, man."

His eyes glazed. His scarred throat bobbed. Hawk nodded. "No problem." He hooked his thumb over his shoulder at the door. "I'm tired. I'm going to head back to my room to get some rest."

"Thanks again, Hawk." William spoke with his mouth full. "You're doing an amazing job. You should be proud."

"I'll be beside you when we go to war."

"We have no doubt."

Although Hawk left the room with the *whoosh* of automation, his grief remained in the air. Matilda's eyes filled, and a single tear ran down her cheek. Because William had his back to Knives, he couldn't see her face. But she'd stopped cutting his hair. He reached back and laid a hand against the side of her leg. She coughed to clear her throat and continued cutting.

Whoosh!

Queen Bee entered. Behind her, Katrina, Whale, Star, Tom, and Karl with a K. Fucking Karl. Couldn't he take a night off? He sat beside Matilda and smiled at her. Prick!

Resting her hands on the table after she'd sat down, Queen Bee interlocked her fingers. "So, how are we getting on?"

"You've probably heard most of it?" William gestured towards Karl.

Queen Bee shrugged. "From your perspective?"

"We got closer to the blocks than we ever have. But they turned on a spotlight and started taking potshots at the diseased. Were they doing it for fun or on a hunch?"

"You think they knew you were there?"

"If they did, they didn't try to shoot us, so I'd guess not. But they seem paranoid. And how will they react when Gracie activates another Icarus tower? Their light and shooting called more diseased over the hill, and if we hadn't retreated, eventually a diseased would have found us. So we had to leave despite being close to getting to the food tube to slice it open."

Although she kept her tone even, Queen Bee winced. "And you found out nothing new?"

"Nothing. All that's changed between our last debrief and now is we now have seven days before we have to take those blocks rather than nine. Seven days before I lead a several-hundred-strong army, blind, into hostile tower blocks in the vain hope we're a match for them. The ramp's blocked with tanks and guarded with Gatling guns. They have a spotlight, so they'll see us coming in the night if we make too much noise. And so far, we've not even got close enough to cut open the food tube to give us a way in. We could do with more time."

"We set a date and time to attack," Queen Bee said.

"I know."

"And we can't change that."

"I know. And we can trust they'll attack when we do?"

"As much as we can trust anything in this world."

"So we have to lead an army into war, against an unknown enemy, into an unknown battlefield, at a set day and time to co-ordinate with an attack from people we've never met in the hope they will live up to their end of the bargain?"

Queen Bee's signature smirk returned. "Pretty much, yeah. Hopefully, over the next few days, we'll find out something more about their blocks that'll help."

"I hope so too."

"But those coming with you to attack the blocks understand what they're up against. They know you're doing your best. We've been delivering them honest updates with our broadcasts. They understand the situation."

"And they're still willing to go to war with us?"

"They are."

"So what exactly have you found out from talking to the other blocks? How many communities are we attacking in total?"

"Sixteen."

"*Sixteen?*"

"It's a lot, huh? Which is why we have to all act at the same time. We'll only have the element of surprise once. Attacking sixteen blocks in one hit will better set us up for phase two."

"How many more blocks in phase two?"

"They reckon fewer than sixteen. So we might lose the element of surprise, but we'll gather and attack in force. We'll pick them off one at a time. No single community will be a match for us."

Knives stepped back, and William ran his hand over his head. She'd cut it to the scalp. "And then the shining city."

"And then the shining city."

"I mean, it's an end. It might not be in sight, but it's an end."

"Focus on the now, William. A day at a time. A step at a time. We have seven more nights to find out what we can about the blocks we're attacking. A lot could happen between now and then to make it easier."

Whoosh!

"Eleanor?" William sat up straighter.

The girl stumbled in wearing a dark blue cocktail dress with puffy shoulders. It had long sleeves slashed with cuts, and dirt caked the cuffs. She had disheveled hair and mud-streaked cheeks. Katrina gasped the loudest. No matter how tatty, Eleanor had just interrupted their meeting dressed in the uniform of their oppressors.

Matilda ran over to her and took her hand. "What's happened?"

Her chest rising with her deep inhale, Eleanor turned to the rest of the room. "I wanted to come here while you're all together. I have an idea that might help us win this war ..."

CHAPTER 11

Keeping her eyes closed, Gracie clawed the sand from her path and pulled herself towards the sun like a mole. It made no sense to go the other way. Even if she reached Olga, what then? They suffocate together? And unlike Olga, the sun would stay put. Even blind, she could make a good guess at its location. But what if she made it, and what if it did nothing? But if she went the other way, she'd die, and Olga would die too. The sun had worked last time. Hopefully it'd work again.

The sand, although dense and growing denser with every passing second, remained loose enough to shift. For now. She pumped her legs until her toes touched the ground. She pushed off with her feet and dug with her hands, dragging it behind her. She used her head to nudge her way through, shuffling forwards a few inches at a time.

The fine grains filled her ears, deadening the gritty swish of her progress. It stung her eyes and slipped beneath her clothes, making her skin itch.

She broke into another air bubble. The pocket ran several feet long and amplified her desperate gasp, turning it into a donkey's bray. Skittering across the space, she caught her breath and dived into the other side.

The sun had to be about twenty feet away. At the most. She pressed her lips tight and moved like a machine. Clawing at the loose sand, she pushed forwards with her toes against the ground, propelling herself into her freshly cleared path.

The tightly packed sand slowed her progress. Stole the last of her breath. She should have gone back to Olga. How could she find the sun in this?

Slowed to a near halt, Gracie cupped her hand in front of her mouth and breathed. Her itching throat dared her to cough. To spend valuable oxygen and choke on more grains. She gagged. She dropped her head. The rising levels covered her face. She fell limp. What was the fucking point? Who was she to think she could get out of this?

You're Gracie. You don't give up. Ever.

She raised her head against the sand's oppressive weight.

That's it.

Her brother's face. Smiling. He'd never displayed such warmth towards her. The Aus he showed his mates. Their dad. The Aus people liked. The Aus no one could ever believe had been so nasty to her. She must be imagining it.

You need to keep going. He waved her on. *You're almost there.*

A trick. It had to be. One cruel twist of the knife from beyond the grave. She'd killed him. He'd come back to have the last say. To lead her to her death. She dropped her head again.

Gracie!

She jolted.

You're one of the bravest people I know. You won't go out like this. Trust. Move forwards with intention. Everything will work out.

It had to be a trick. Why should she trust him? What had he ever done for her?

Move, Gracie. Now.

Her head spun. Stars danced in her closed eyes. Her lungs ached. Her pulse throbbed in her ears. A tinnitus whine drilled into her brain. Was her brother contacting her from beyond the grave? Was the sun close? Had Olga made it back to safety? How could she know any of those things? Just one fact existed in that moment. The only certainty she needed. If she stayed put, she'd die.

Gracie worked her arms free and plunged her fingers into the sand ahead. She dragged it back and pulled herself on.

Using her head like a drill, she twisted and turned, cutting into the shifting wall while she fought to bring her arms back around. She kicked herself on, pushing into the tightly packed grains.

Covered in scratches. Her face. Her neck. The folds in her body. Crook of her arm. Armpits. But she pushed on. A thousand tiny scrapes. She pushed on.

She brought her arm around in front of her again. Wormed her fingers into the tight sand. She dragged it back again. One step at a time. Keep moving. Her fingertips scraped something. An embossing on the floor.

Thunk! The entire tunnel shook.

Gracie cupped her hand in front of her mouth again. She lowered with the draining sand.

Thunk!

The sheets above her withdrew.

Thunk!

Thunk!

Thunk!

Gracie sat up before she stood on wobbly legs. She wiped herself down. Kira and Bear were several hundred feet away. Kira was crying. Bear stood with his eyes wide and his mouth forming a slack O.

Most of the sand had drained through the ground,

although she couldn't see where or how. Just a light coating remained.

Gracie tried to speak, but her itching throat hijacked her words. She coughed and heaved. She leaned over and spat stringy and gritty saliva. She tried again with a rasp, "Olga?"

Kira cried even harder and shrugged. Her entire face twisted out of shape. She turned her palms to the ceiling. "I don't know where she's gone."

CHAPTER 12

Taking the rifle from Kira, Gracie slipped the strap over her head and exhaled hard. Olga's rifle, it hung as a dead weight around her neck. Why didn't she just listen to her and stay back? She took the second one and clung on, her fingers turning white from how tightly she gripped the cold steel.

Kira cried harder than ever, her brown eyes swollen and red with grief. She wiped her running nose with the back of her sleeve. Gracie gripped the girl's shoulder like she had her rifle. She waited for her to look up. Her voice echoed through the tunnel, the force of her words the only way to shove aside her hurt. "We don't have time to grieve. Not now."

Kira nodded, but her tears still flowed. Gracie turned to lead them on, and Bear followed. It was what Olga would want. They had a job to do. But Kira turned the other way, returning to the spot where they'd last seen Olga. She dragged trails with her feet over the sand-dusted ground as she scanned the floor.

After a glance at Bear, who shrugged back, Gracie threw

up her arms. When they fell back down, her hands slapped against her thighs. "What are you looking for, Kira?"

She jumped at Gracie's raised voice, but continued searching.

"I think we'd see her if she were still here. She's not a lost ring, you know?"

Kira flinched again, but continued her search.

"Kira! We have to keep moving."

But Kira walked over to the wall on her right and scanned the strange carvings. Some shapes were more familiar than others. She traced the images with her fingers. A sun. What looked like a donkey with strange proportions. A horse. Some flying creature. A flying man? Icarus? The signs were there, but he kept on towards the sun. He should have turned back. Waited with the others.

"Ki—"

"How can she just vanish?" Kira shook her head. "I don't get it."

Bear remained close. His eyes were wide and his lips tight. Firmly closed like he fought to keep his opinions to himself. For once.

"We would have been fine if she'd listened to me. I told her to let me go on my own." Gracie's grief shredded her words. "I saw what had to be done and could have done it. I *did* it. If she'd have only listened."

If anything, Kira grew ever more interested in the nonsensical depictions cut into the wall.

"We need to keep moving." Gracie scratched her head, sand spilling from her tight plait. "Unless either of you have a better suggestion?" Or unless Aus wanted to return with a little more guidance … "I mean, what else can we do? Stand around and hope she materialises out of thin air? Wait for some divine intervention, all while praying we don't get chopped to pieces by another steel sheet?"

Bear looked at the walls on either side and shuffled down the tunnel in the direction they were heading.

Clunk!

A ceiling panel opened.

Thud!

A corpse hit the hard floor.

Kira screamed, and Bear ran the rest of the way, past the end of the final groove, should the sheets shoot from the wall again.

"What the …?" The ceiling had returned to the same wonky sandstone expanse of moments before. Like it had had nothing to do with the evicted corpse.

The tall male body had landed face first. Gracie hooked her toe beneath his shoulder and grunted with the effort it took to flip him over onto his back. She clapped her hand to her mouth and heaved. A dense nest of maggots writhed in his empty eye sockets and mouth. His sandy tomb had sucked the very essence from him, his skin wrinkled and dry.

Kira came to Gracie's side and stared up at the ceiling. "Where did it come from?"

Frowning through her tears, Gracie shook her head, grabbed Kira's arm, and pulled her along with her. "Come on."

"Huh?"

"We're going, Kira." She pointed in the direction they were heading. "We have an Icarus tower to raise."

"But what about Olga? What if she's up there?"

"What about her? And what if she is?"

"We might be able to get her out."

Gracie stamped her foot as she said it. "How? Do you have any idea?" She pointed at Bear. "He clearly doesn't."

Kira stepped back a pace.

"You're looking at me like I'm a monster."

"You're behaving like a monster, Gracie."

"What choice do we have? Shall we just stand around and wait for months until this tunnel decides to shit her from the ceiling? Or until we drown in another wave of sand?" Her voice broke, and her eyes burned. "She's *gone*, Kira. And if we're smart, we'll get the fuck out of this place while we still can. We came here to do a job. Let's make sure we at least manage that."

Gracie clung to her rifle as she strode past Bear.

∼

OTHER THAN THE scuff of their steps and the occasional gasp from a grieving Kira, they walked in silence. Gracie maintained her pace, her legs aching, her tears flowing. She kept her head down.

"When you said flood."

Gracie scowled at Bear.

"Was it as bad as what just happened with the sand?"

"Probably worse."

"Worse?"

"It flooded everywhere. We were all submerged, and we had no idea how to get out. Finding the sun was blind luck. At least we went into that last trap informed. Informed enough for you and Kira to stand back. Informed enough to see Olga was making a stupid choice."

Bear rubbed his gaunt face. "Had I known it was so bad down here, I wouldn't have come."

The bend opened up ahead of them, revealing the control room and the tunnel's end. "Don't pretend you had a choice in the matter. We needed you then, and we need you now. I still stand by that, but Olga was right, your moaning is tedious. And right now, more than at any other point on this little excursion, I'm *really* not in the mood to hear it."

"I'm just not sure I'm cut out for this."

Gracie spun his way. "And the rest of us are totally at ease with being buried alive by fucking sand?"

"I'm frightened is all."

"We're all frightened. Frightened, dejected, depressed. But we have the awareness to keep it to ourselves. To not be so selfish as to turn this moment into a conversation about us."

"But I jus—"

"I swear"—Gracie pointed at him—"if you don't shut up, I'm going to leave your corpse down here with Olga's."

Kira sobbed again like Gracie's realism stung. Did she really think Olga had somehow survived? With Bear, she had a selfish little prick who thought the world was his therapist. In Kira, a child who refused to accept the hard reality right before her eyes. Gracie led them on again. The sooner they got into that control room and out, the better.

Olga's hacking device had gone with her, but when Gracie pressed the door's button, it slid open with a *whoosh!* She entered, and Kira followed, her mouth hanging open as she took in the circular room. The plain ceiling. The bland steel walls. A single computer console sat in the room's centre.

Gracie woke the machine by tapping a key and input the code. *Icarus.*

Like in the previous control room, the walls shook with a *thunk!* The floor trembled.

Kira thrust her arms out for balance. "What's happening?"

"We've activated the Icarus tower. We've done our bit. Now let's see if we can get out of this place alive."

CHAPTER 13

It seemed obvious to William that Eleanor had dishevelled her hair on purpose. But as the shy girl approached the top table, she dragged it down as if trying to improve her appearance. Her hand shook as she dragged out one of the many spare top table seats and sat down. She leaned forward, rested her elbows on her knees, and drew a deep breath while taking them all in. William moved as if to speak, but halted when she sat up straight and steepled her fingers. "Dressed like this—"

"Let's talk about that!" Katrina raised her eyebrows and looked around the room. She fixed on William, but he turned away like everyone else had. What did she expect? While he got it, if they interrupted Eleanor after every three words, the reason for her visit might take a while to transpire. It had already turned dark outside, and with them missing their nightly trip to the blocks last night, they couldn't afford to risk losing another day with no further information to help their attack.

"Dressed like this, scuffed up for effect, I reckon I can

walk straight into those blocks you've been surveilling, and they'll accept me as one of them."

Katrina visibly shuddered, and Matilda shot her a scowl.

A flare of retaliation glowed and died in Katrina's glare.

"I'll give them a sob story. I mean, I have one. We all do, right? Lost my mum and dad. Lost my home. Now I've lost my way. And if they don't let me in, the vampires will get me." She delivered the last line to Katrina as if daring her to bite. William smiled. She might be a self-conscious teenager, but the kid had spirit.

"I can say I've been in the wild for ages. Avoiding the diseased while looking for a friendly block."

His arms resting along the steel tabletop, William turned his palms to the ceiling. "And then what?"

"Well, if I've found my way in ..."

She left it hanging, but William frowned along with everyone else around the table.

Her cheeks flushed, and she dragged her fingers through her hair, tugging on a troublesome knot. "Getting in will be the hard part. Achieve that, and the rest should run smoothly."

Knives scoffed. "I wouldn't bank on it."

"When I'm in, I'll find out as much as I can. When I either have enough information for us to take down these blocks, or our time runs out, I'll leave and bring you what I have. Tell me if I'm crossing a line, but from what I've deduced from the broadcasts"—she nodded in Queen Bee's direction—"I'm guessing whatever I get will be better than what you've managed so far?"

Another person might have gotten William's back up with the same accusation, but if anyone had earned the right to a voice ... Hell, they might have been better sending her on the scouting missions. "And Rayne?"

"What about her?"

"She's on board with this idea?"

"Yep."

Nick glanced at the closed door. "Then where is she?"

"I said she's on board, not that she likes it. She didn't want to come."

Matilda dragged her seat a few inches away from Karl with a K. "When do you want to do it?"

"You're going out tonight?"

William said, "We are, but we have plans."

"To lie like snakes in the grass and hope you get close enough to cut open the food tube?"

"You really have been telling the blocks everything?"

Queen Bee shrugged. "We have a lot of trust to rebuild."

"But what if tonight's the night we open up the food tube?"

"There's no evidence to suggest it will be. And even if it is, I'd still be willing to bet getting me into the blocks will be more advantageous. And there's always tomorrow night for you to get to the food tube."

"Or not."

William flipped Katrina the bird.

Whoosh!

A slim man poked his head into the room. In his mid-twenties, he had cropped fair hair. His pale skin reddened to be the focus of their collective attention. His voice wavered. "Icarus." He cleared his throat. "Another Icarus tower is going up."

Karl with a K led the exodus, following the man at a jog.

William stayed close to Matilda, crossing the shattered mirrored dance floor and out onto the elevated walkway.

The first tower stood strong and resolute, while a deep rumble rolled through the air like distant thunder. Matilda grabbed William's shoulders and turned him to the right.

The Icarus tower lifted into the sky. A prehistoric beast

awakening from a timeless slumber into an alien world. Stopping with a thunderous *clack,* the giant phallus' tip stood almost as high as their elevated walkway. The tower released the fields. They fell to the sides with a louder and final *clack!*

"Wow!" Matilda clung to the walkway's railing like she needed its support.

Karl flashed her a cocky half-smile. "I know, right? It's the second time we've witnessed it from the blocks. Amazing, huh?"

Slipping in between Karl and Matilda, William shoved him aside. "Just imagine what it must have been like doing the hard work."

Karl's smile faltered.

Matilda said, "But at least it suggests Gracie and Olga might be okay."

Artan and Nick nodded along.

Matilda chewed on the side of her nail. "But what does it mean for the blocks?"

The strong wind and her muffled words had drawn William closer. "You think this might make them more paranoid?"

"You don't?"

William stumbled from where Eleanor shoved him a little too hard. "I'd say it's the perfect night to forget about trying to get close to the blocks, and to get me inside instead."

Two standing Icarus towers. A clear indicator Gracie and Olga's mission had been successful, but to what degree? Were they all still alive? Could they replicate what they'd done? Holding his bottom lip in a pinch, William passed Eleanor on his way back to the mirrored ballroom. "Let's talk about it."

∽

Back at the top table first, Matilda beside him, William held his love's hand and waited for everyone to enter and close the door behind them. Karl with a K sat next to Knives, slightly recoiled like he'd drawn the short straw. Like he wanted to be out of swiping range. Not that she'd shown him any more animosity than she showed anyone else.

William said, "Eleanor, can you give us a moment?"

"Leave the grown-ups to talk?"

"If you like."

"Fuck you, William."

"Whoa!"

"You'd all be dead had I not infiltrated the cult and passed on information to Queen Bee. While you were all pissing about at the farm"—she gestured at Karl with a K—"and you were watching towers rise like a tourist, *I* was in *real* danger. So don't treat me like a child. I'm staying here."

"And Rayne?"

"I've told you what Rayne thinks."

"I just wonder if we should have her he—"

"I'll say to you what I said to her, *William*. I'm going to those blocks whether you like it or not. I'm in a unique position to help. I have something no one else around this table has, and that's a bastard heritage. It's burdened me my entire life, so help me use it to my advantage. I'm going with or without your support, but it would be a hell of a lot easier if you helped."

"And what if it goes wrong?"

"There are no guarantees in this life."

"Ain't that the truth." Artan lowered his head.

"But when I get in, I can convince them my story's real. It'll help us win this war, stop this stupid fighting, and hopefully prevent a lot of lives from being lost. Are you telling me you don't dream of a life with Matilda where you don't have to worry about being killed every day? Also, because of the tower, they'll be on high alert. It would be mad for you to slither close to the blocks tonight."

"Slither?"

"I can use the Icarus towers to say how scared I am out in the meadows by myself. So scared it was worth the risk of me approaching a strange block." She clapped her hands to the sides of her face with a *crack!* Her voice rose in pitch, and her eyes watered. "Help me. What are these strange structures? Are we all doomed? Please, I'm so scared."

The room had hung on Eleanor's every word. And now she'd paused, Nick smiled. "So, you think we should support her in leaving?"

"I am here, you know?"

"Only because you wouldn't go," William said.

Artan this time. "How about we take a vote? If enough of us think this is a good idea, we'll help her. Agreed?"

William nodded along with the others. With how unsuccessful they'd been so far, how could they ignore what Eleanor offered?

"Fine." Artan raised his hand. "Who wants to help Eleanor infiltrate the tower blocks?"

CHAPTER 14

There were many similarities between this tunnel and the one they'd been in previously. Having activated the Icarus tower, Gracie led them from the control room to find the two recesses on either side of the exit had opened up like before. But unlike the previous tunnel, the space on the left sat empty. They only had one buggy in the right recess. They only needed one. As long as it worked.

Kira followed Gracie out, and Bear exited last. He clapped his hand to the top of his head and looked up.

Gracie copied him, wincing as sand speckled her face. Tiny pinpricks. A light dusting. For now. She ran to the buggy and jumped into the driver's seat. The flimsy cart swayed with its soft suspension. She pressed the start button beside the steering wheel. "Damn it."

Kira slipped into the passenger seat, and Bear jumped into the back. Gracie pressed the button again. "Shit!" The sand came down harder. She pulled her shoulders into her neck, the grains sliding down her collar and tickling her bare back. She jabbed the start button again.

"The definition of insanity."

"What are you talking about?"

Bear pointed at Gracie's hand. "Repeating the same action and expecting different results."

"Is there anything useful going on in that vacuous skull of yours?"

"Steady on."

"We're about to be buried in sand. Again." She jabbed the power button harder, like the force of her press would somehow inspire the vehicle into life. "How are you at running?"

The flimsy cart creaked when Bear vaulted from the back and walked past her. Sand already covered the road like a heavy snowstorm. He dropped in front of the cart's square nose, shoved his fingers into the grille, and popped the bonnet open.

Before Gracie could exit the cart, he leaned around the vehicle's front. "Try it now."

"But how can you have—"

"Just try it."

She pressed the button. The cart shook like someone had walked over its grave, and the electric motor hummed with life.

Bear removed his top and scaled the cart's side. It had a roll bar as high as the front windscreen frame. He tied his shirt between the bar and the frame so it formed a canopy over Gracie and Kira.

"Thank you."

"Welcome." Sand covered Bear's naked torso. A light dusting on his lithe form. He swiped it from his shoulders before pointing down the tunnel. "Now drive."

The cart's small wheels spun on the sandy path before finding traction. The small vehicle packed a surprising punch, forcing Gracie to go easy on the accelerator.

The missing windscreen made Gracie wince from the

expected sandblasting in through the front, but Bear had angled his shirt so it shielded them from the worst of it. She blinked, her eyes still sore from being buried earlier, but at least it wouldn't get any worse.

The sand fell so hard it filled the air like mist. It hadn't yet covered the corpse that had fallen from the ceiling. It might have hidden the maggots from view, but they still writhed in Gracie's mind's eye. She shuddered like they crawled beneath her skin. She gave the corpse a wide berth.

"You need to stop."

"What?" Gracie turned to Kira, the cart swerving with her sharp movement. She levelled out, slowly coaxing it back on track. Another twitch like that could end them all.

Kira grabbed her arm, and they swerved again. "You need to go back."

"You need to not grab me while I'm driving."

Although she pulled her hand away, Kira fixed on Gracie and leaned close. "Take us back. Now!"

"In case you haven't noticed, Kira, it's raining sand. This buggy will be useless if it gets too deep. You think we'll be able to swim all the way back to the entrance?"

"I think I know where Olga is."

Gracie eased off a little. "Don't do that to me."

"Stop the cart."

She shook her head. Tears blurred her already cloudy view. "No." The lump in her throat turned her words shrill. "*Think* isn't enough. You're hoping, and we don't have time for that. Hope doesn't belong down here. We can't risk our lives on a hunch. I'm as desperate as you to want her to be okay, but it's too late. The only thing we can do is make sure we don't die down here too."

"I *know* where Olga is."

"Don't say that." Gracie gripped the wheel harder.

"I do. Now stop."

"What if you're wrong?"

Kira grabbed the cart's handbrake and yanked hard. The cart's back wheels locked, throwing them into a spin.

Gracie clung to the steering wheel while Kira and Bear flew from the cart.

Landing hard, Kira jumped to her feet and sprinted back to the corpse in the road. The sand came down harder than ever.

"We have to go back for her." Bear climbed into the cart. "We can't leave her here."

Clenching her jaw, Gracie sneered. "This had best be fucking good!" She stamped on the accelerator, and the wheels spun. The back of the cart kicked out. She chased after Kira, who slowed as she drew close to the corpse. She ran to the left side of the road and dropped to her knees in the sand.

Gracie skidded to a halt. "Kira! What are you doing?"

Kira pressed into an indented handprint low down on the wall. A small door popped open. Only about two feet square, the panel revealed a tight tunnel. A head of black hair.

The corpse moved. Gracie jumped as it reached out of its small hole.

Kira took their hands and dragged them out.

"Olga!" Gracie slid from her seat. She helped her small friend stand. She swiped the sand from her hair and face and hugged her.

Olga gargled like someone being choked. "Easy on the squeeze. Are you trying to kill me or what?"

Having got out with Gracie, Bear leaned down and peered into the small tunnel. "It's like it's been designed to house a body. Maybe she would have been the next one to rain from the ceiling when someone else triggered the trap."

"The coward's survived, then?"

"The *coward* got the cart working, Olga. Without him, we wouldn't have gotten here in time to free you."

"So you want me to thank him now?"

"I know you better than that."

"And what are you talking about, anyway? Bodies raining from the ceiling?"

Letting go of Olga, Gracie gestured towards the dead man, the sand over his eyes and mouth undulating from the furious activity beneath.

"Why's it not a skeleton?"

"Huh?"

Olga spat sand from her mouth. "These tunnels seem old. Like no one's been down here in years. But if that's the case, how is that body still covered in skin and flesh?"

Cowed by the sandy assault, Gracie swiped it off her like it would make a difference. She lifted Olga's gun over her head and smiled. "I don't know, and right now I don't care. But why did you follow me when I asked you not to?"

Olga smirked. "You know I know better."

Gracie pointed at the open tunnel. "That's better?"

"Than listening to a bossy old bitch like you?"

"Dick!" Gracie shook her head. "Come on, before we're all buried alive."

"Again." Olga grabbed one of Kira's hands. "And thank you."

Kira bowed. "I knew you were still alive."

CHAPTER 15

Pulling her shoulders back and holding her head high, Eleanor crested the hill's brow, the silver moon shining down on her like a spotlight. Butterflies danced in her stomach, and she trembled from a mixture of the chilly wind and adrenaline. But she had a unique heritage among the vampires, and she owed it to them to use that to their advantage. She'd never acted like those who ran her community, never treated anyone as lesser because of who they were, but she'd been a part of the system. She'd benefited from their engineered status. She'd lived a privileged life compared to those they oppressed, and if she could use her affiliation with that awful regime for good, then of course she should help.

The meadow swayed around her. The scattering of diseased dotted along the hill moved with the surrounding grass as if they were also enslaved to the elements. A horde of silhouettes gathered beneath the plaza. Hidden in shadow, they moaned like they wanted out. Out of the darkness. Out of their miserable existence. Everything acted as it should, so despite her rampaging heart and leaden legs, Eleanor pushed on, down the hill, the meadow's moisture turning her ragged dress damp. Dressed like a scruffy version of them, surely they had to allow this ghost of a Christmas yet to come into their community. If they couldn't save her, then what hope did they have?

William had offered to accompany her. Keep an eye out for diseased and have her back if things turned bad. But if they were being watched, a chaperone would destroy any chance she had of being admitted to the blocks. And what if they saw him, let her in, and only then revealed they were wise to her façade? She had to do this alone.

She'd torn slits into her dress' long sleeves. The wind's icy fingers wormed through the gaps and lifted gooseflesh on her arms. She'd made sure the rips didn't reveal her tattoos. If there were ever a mark she didn't belong … She didn't belong anywhere. Not a vampire, and she'd rejected the community that raised her.

Mud weighted her cuffs and her dress' hem. The puffy fabric around her shoulders danced in the wind. She stumbled across the uneven ground. She wore flats, but even then, her heels sank into the soft earth.

Naked without a gun, but she carried one of Knives' blades in her right hand. Maybe for the best. With hundreds of diseased beneath the plaza, firing a gun might kill one or two, but it would provide little protection for someone on their own against a hunting pack.

The fronts of Eleanor's thighs burned from where she walked with a low crouch. Hidden from sight. From the diseased, and from anyone watching from the blocks. The elevated walkways were too far away, even if she walked upright, but someone might see her from the plaza.

Something rustled on her right. Just feet away.

She dropped even lower. She gripped her knife tighter.

The phlegmy and rattling snort of a diseased. Truffling. Lost. Aimless. Unsettled. Desperate to latch onto something.

Anything. Meaning. Prey. If she ran, they'd give chase. If she waited, she could be waiting all night.

Walking on tiptoes, Eleanor edged closer. She scrunched up her nose, but it did little to dilute the thing's stench. Just feet separated them. The long grass kept them hidden from one another. She filled her lungs, inhaling their foetid reek. Her already shaking legs damn near spasmed. Adrenaline and cramps combined. She couldn't hold it any longer. She jumped forwards and led with her stabbing hand.

The diseased squealed like a stuck pig. Its open mouth and fresh wound loosed a rancid stench. She withdrew her blade and slammed it beneath the beast's chin. She drove it with such force, it burst through the top of its skull with an eruption of blood and bone. She pulled her knife out as the thing fell away from her, flattening the surrounding grass.

Panting, and with her stomach in knots, she waited, the hairs on the back of her neck and arms standing on end as if they were tuning into her surroundings. Searching for a disturbance that told her she'd been discovered. She gave it a few seconds before moving on.

Eleanor halted about halfway down the hill. She'd passed five or six diseased, but none of them were close enough to matter. The long grass hid her from sight, or sense, or whatever they used to register prey.

The diseased mob beneath the plaza stood about two hundred strong. Two hundred furiously oblivious silhouettes. They were far enough away. She'd get to the broken entrance ramp unnoticed. They'd parked three tanks on the incline to prevent unwelcome vehicular approach. They'd provide her good cover from the diseased. Get her close enough to plead her case.

She changed course, descending the hill diagonally towards the road. With about twenty diseased between her and the ramp, she stood a chance of reaching the blocks unnoticed.

Eleanor paused at the meadow's edge. She leaned from the grass, drawing a mental route down the road and up the entrance ramp to the elevated plaza about thirty feet away. The looming blocks cast inky shadows. The massive towers stood resolute. They made a mockery of her plan. What a stupid girl to think she'd get inside. But what could she do now? Turn back after she'd promised so much?

She trembled like the evening had suddenly turned colder. Like her skin had thinned. But the only thinning came from her will. The chill of a certain death filled her bones.

Unlike the blocks she'd just left, this lot had parked their tanks horizontally across the ramp. Positioned them to block access rather than enable an exit. They'd parked two close to the gap, nose to tail. They overhung the ramp on both sides. The third parked across the pair a little farther down. It left space to pass it on either side. It sat more as an afterthought than serving any real purpose.

The silver moon shone on the road, ready to reveal her to keen eyes. Hopefully the diseased's bleeding orbs were as dull as their personalities.

Clinging to her knife like it might help, Eleanor burst into action. Head down, arms pumping, she sprinted for the entrance ramp.

A diseased screeched on her left. But it had its back to her. It shoved its mate, who wailed and shoved it back. They fought like spiteful toddlers, wrestling one another to the ground and vanishing from sight in the long grass.

Eleanor ducked like it would make a difference. Like the moon wouldn't shine as bright if she dropped lower. She gave a small group of diseased a wide berth and came around in an arc that brought her back to the entrance ramp.

Her feet scuffed against the concrete. The soles of her flat shoes. She'd considered heels to complete the look. It might have made her appear more authentic, but she'd have broken an ankle by now. Another diseased down to her right yelled.

Reaching the first of the three tanks, Eleanor crouched beside it and paused, fighting for breath.

A series of confused snarls and snorts, but nothing close to the focused ferocity of a diseased dialled into their prey. Leaning against the tank, she let her breathing settle before slipping around the side and heading for the pair just before the gap.

So focused on the diseased behind, she'd not checked ahead. The solitary beast between the pair of tanks wailed and charged.

Kicking out on instinct, she drove it back and jumped at the pair of tanks. She stepped up onto one of their large wheels and clambered onto the roof. Four more diseased joined their friends on the ramp below.

Snorting a laugh, Eleanor bit on her bottom lip and thrust her middle finger at the grotesque beasts. "Fuck you!" She turned around, and her strength left her. "Oh, shit!"

Both the Gatling guns on either side of the ramp were pointing straight at her. A cluster of several guards operated each one.

Her knife clattered against the tank's roof from where she dropped it. Eleanor raised her hands in the air.

CHAPTER 16

The diseased threw their cold hands against the side of the tank. They whacked it like they believed they had enough force to upset Eleanor's balance. They managed little more than a lazy percussion of weak slaps. Three guards operated the Gatling gun at her on her left and four on her right. She'd held her arms up so long, her fingers tingled with the loss of blood flow. "If you're going to shoot me, will you just get it over with?"

The guards on her right lowered their massive gun. A man with blond hair more voluminous than her puffy sleeves, a double chin, and ruddy cheeks stepped away from the others. He wore a black suit that hung loose on his narrow shoulders and stretched to bursting around his middle. He motioned for the other Gatling gun to relax. What threat did this girl pose? His nasal whine made her want to deafen herself. Pompous. Arrogant. Entitled. "Who are you?"

"My name's Eleanor. Nice to meet you."

The man shrugged.

"You asked who I am."

"We could still shoot you, you know?"

"And I appreciate you haven't yet." A diseased screamed louder than the others. She jumped and spun around. It still had some colour in its cheeks, and its eyes bled freely. It attacked the tank with the vigour of one freshly turned.

The man threw a pudgy hand towards the road. "We saw you coming when you broke from the meadow."

Eleanor gestured back the way she'd come. "My blocks have fallen. Everyone's gone. My dad, my mum, my fr—"

"Fucking hell, love." The man snorted with a half-laugh. "I didn't ask for your life story."

She laughed with him. Prick. "Of course. Ever so sorry. We've all had it rough. Please let me in. I have nowhere to go, and so many of these blocks are run by fucking vampires now."

The man's smirk twisted into a grotesque grimace. Those not from the blocks might read it differently, but Eleanor knew the type. He'd spent his entire life looking down on people. His condescending display was as close to mirth as he could manage. He swiped his blond hair back from his forehead. It returned to the same ridiculous and wispy halo. "You've got spirit, I'll give you that."

"That's a good thing?"

"It's a fine line. But right now, you're on the right side of it." He gestured behind himself, calling two more guards from the elevated plaza's shadows.

The woman wore a cocktail dress and the man a suit. It fitted him much better than his foppish leader. Between them, they carried a steel ramp. About three feet wide and twenty feet long, they stood it upright before lowering it across the gap until it rested on the tank's side. It gave Eleanor a bridge should she trust them enough to cross it.

The diseased behind Eleanor had grown to at least fifteen strong. More joined all the time. They'd only halt when they had no more space on the ramp. Many stood and stared up at her with the vacant glaze of incomprehension. They were here for her, but they were already out of ideas.

Eleanor pressed down on the ramp with her toe. It seemed solid enough. It should hold her weight. She stepped out over the gap, and her stomach lurched. She'd crossed the ladders in the other blocks, and while the drop was similar, it had been easier when she'd had rungs to cling onto. They'd helped her brace against the windy assault from the open meadow. One step at a time, she focused on the grimacing man on the other side.

Jumping the last few feet, she blew out hard and smiled. Any humour the jowly man might have shared with her from a distance vanished. He grabbed her arm so hard she gasped, and he led her towards the blocks. "Whether you stay here or not, funny girl, is not my decision. We run a democracy, and anyone who wants to join us has to appeal to the majority. You've got spirit, so they might like you." He leaned close, his halitosis reek a match for the diseased's stench. "But spirit can either endear or repel. They might as readily decide to launch you from a walkway." He finally flashed her a well-practiced smile. Were it not for her time in her blocks around people like him, she might have taken it for genuine. "Now come on, Eleanor. Time to tell your sob story to the masses."

∽

ELEANOR STOOD on the theatre's stage before a packed room. There were close to two hundred people in attendance. Men, women, and children. At least twenty teenagers stood in a gaggle nearby, their faces slack like they'd been infected.

Clearing her throat, Eleanor shifted her weight from one foot to the other. She cleared her throat again. It rang out in the packed room. Every face fixed on her. Very few smiled. "Th-thank you for letting me in." She wrung her trembling hands. "I've been walking for ages. I've avoided the diseased this far, but I'm sure I wouldn't have lasted much longer. Thank you for the lifeline."

"Don't get ahead of yourself." The man who'd let her in stood in the middle of the crowd and fixed her with his cold, dead eyes.

"I've been hiding in the long grass. I've been sleeping on rocks so they couldn't get me at night. I'm tired, cold, and hungry."

Many eyes had glazed over, and a couple of people yawned at her timid performance. "I've been—"

"Get on with it!"

A man's voice. It came from somewhere over to her right. Several people snorted, and the teenagers giggled amongst themselves.

For the past several days, she'd done nothing but cry. A constant stream of grief. Rayne and Matthew had shown her she could let it out in public. People would understand. And even if they didn't, why should she act small? She gripped her hands together. She swallowed the lump in her throat. She looked up at the ceiling, the bright glare stinging her tired eyes.

"Uh …" One teenager laughed louder. "What's she doing?"

Eleanor cried freely.

He laughed again. "Bit weird."

Holding up a shaking hand, she pinched an inch of air. "This is how close I was to saving my mum's life when we fled. I reached for her hand and missed. She fell. A second later …" She drew a deep breath and set her backed-up tears free. They ran rivers down her cheeks, and her mouth buckled out of shape. "A second later, diseased bit into her head." She fixed on the boy who'd laughed at her. "I saw my mum's blood spray away from the thing's mouth."

The boy stared at the floor.

Her voice broke. "Then we ran into *fucking* vampires. They cut my dad down and tried to take my head too. But I dodged them and ran. As they were storming our blocks, I left. Snuck away. Used the meadow's long grass for cover."

Many of the crowd had lost their cynicism. Several people, mainly the older women, cried with her. "I didn't know what to do. I've always had my mum and dad around." She cried harder, fact and fiction blending together in a teary mess. "I didn't realise just how lucky I was."

Eleanor pointed behind her. "I stayed out there, catching rabbits and deer, and drinking rainwater. I didn't know which blocks were safe and which weren't. One block where I used to live has collapsed. And what are those massive towers in the farm about? Did you all see the second one go up?"

The sea of vacant faces suggested many hadn't.

"It only went up this evening. But it made me realise I've been lucky to last this long alone. I can't do it forever. I need a community." She pressed her hands together, palm to palm. "I need your help." She wiped her eyes and ran her sleeve across her running nose. "This is my last roll of the dice. If you don't take me in, I don't think I'll survive. I'll do my bit. Pull my weight." She cried again. "But I can't do this alone. Please help me."

The man with the ridiculous hair and ill-fitting suit laughed while he ascended the stairs at the side of the stage. "Ladies and gentlemen, I give you Eleanor." He nudged her while she rubbed her eyes, and she accidentally poked herself.

She drew a breath in through her nose. He'd get his. But not here. Not now.

"So, I told this little scavenger that we're a democracy. We go with the majority. I'm asking for a show of hands from those who think we should let her stay?"

At least two-thirds of the room raised their hands. Men, women, and children. But not a single teenager. And not the man beside her.

"Wonderful." The man flashed Eleanor his practiced smile. "Welcome to the community. I'm Noris, by the way." He gestured at the boy who'd laughed at Eleanor's open display of grief. "Stan."

He flicked his head up in response.

"Be a good boy and lead Eleanor to one of the guest rooms, will you?"

Stan's peers laughed and shoved him forwards. His face glowed red, and he shook his head while he waited for her beside the stage. When she got close, he walked away without looking back.

She'd completed stage one in a complex and ever-shifting plan. She'd gotten in. Now she needed to keep her head down and find out as much about these arseholes as she could. By the time she left, she'd know every one of their dirty little secrets.

CHAPTER 17

The cart shook as Bear and then Kira climbed in over the open back. Gracie sat in the passenger seat because Olga insisted she drive. She'd clearly felt powerless inside her sandy coffin and needed to regain some agency. Gracie reached back and fist-bumped Kira. "Here's to the woman of the moment." Her laugh ran away from her down the strange tunnel. The carvings. The wonky floor. The canted walls. The sand raining down like a fine mist, the layer on the floor growing increasingly thicker as if to remind them to get moving. "Who knew someone could make sense of this madness?"

"Not all of it." Kira scratched her head and then shook it, her black curls fanning out. "If every symbol has a meaning, I'll need years to decipher them."

"And we certainly don't have years." Bear bounced where he sat, the entire cart shaking. He ducked like he might avoid the sand. Shirtless, it covered his skin like dust, and despite having it in every crevice, just the sight of his exposed body made Gracie's skin itch. He patted Olga's shoulder. "We need to get moving."

Clinging to the wheel like she might tear it clean off, Olga tutted. "Of course *you* want to get moving."

"What's tha—" Bear slipped from his seat, thrown off by Olga's sharp stamp on the accelerator.

Olga scowled at the road ahead. "You've been wanting to leave the second we got down here."

"In case you haven't noticed, *Olga*"—Bear climbed back into his seat, hung onto the cart's side, and screwed up his face when he looked at the ceiling—"there's a shitload of sand raining down on us that doesn't look like stopping anytime soon. I'd say the fear of being buried alive is a fair motivator, wouldn't you?"

"You were shitting your pants even before the sand started falling."

"Maybe, but we'd also be much closer to the stairs out of here had we not stopped to drag you from your coffin. Or have you forgotten that already?"

"At least I was willing to get involved."

"Too willing."

The buggy twitched when Olga turned towards Gracie.

Gracie shrugged. "I'm just saying. If you'd listened to me in the first place, then you would have already been with us."

"Well, screw me for trying to help."

"Screw you for ignoring my request. Had I gone back for you, I would have died. And Bear's right, we have had to slow down for you."

The muscles along the sides of Olga's jaw bulged from her tight clench. She pushed harder on the accelerator.

The grains of sand stung, and Gracie turned sideways to avoid the worst of it.

Olga pointed behind her at Bear, the cart twitching again. "You're sticking up for this shirtless wonder?"

"I'm agreeing with him."

"With the coward who had to be forced to come here for

the greater good? Who clearly only gives a shit about himself. Who has done nothing but moan the entire time."

"We're all frightened, Olga. He's entitled to that."

"At least I take action."

"Stop wearing taking action as a virtue. The wrong action is more damaging than none. When you get on one, your anger blinds you. You need to gain some perspective."

"I'm not a child!" Olga sped up, the cart slipping even as they tried to drive in a straight line.

Gracie shielded her face with her hands. The grains stung her cheeks and filled her mouth. "And you're wondering why he's shirtless?"

Shrugging, Olga shook her head. "To make him even more physically repulsive?"

Gracie pointed up. The canopy flapped with their increased velocity.

"Big deal. He took off his shirt. That's hardly a contribution."

Kira leaned between them and shouted over the humming engine, "And he got this cart working. Without this, we would have been up to our necks in sand by the time we reached your hidey-hole. You'd have been buried alive."

Olga's eyes shifted out of focus, and the cart drifted with the road's lean. She flinched at Gracie's touch. "You're okay now. You're safe."

"I was okay before." Olga righted their course.

Gracie snorted.

"What?"

"Come on, Olga. You were lucky you didn't die down there. Lucky Kira worked out where you were, and lucky Bear had the skills required for us to reach you quickly enough." Gracie shielded her eyes, but refused to blink. Olga drove as if possessed. The cart's small wheels dragged and spun. Every few seconds, the vehicle snapped and twisted.

The small sand moguls that had formed on the ground tossed them around like a boat in a storm. "You're sure you're okay to drive?"

"You want me to ask your permission for that too?"

"You're driving too fast. You need to calm down."

As fixed ahead as Gracie, Olga gripped the wheel harder. "We need to get out of here while we still can. I'd say that's a reason to rush."

The cart's right side lifted off a small dune. Gracie's stomach flipped, and she clung to the door beside her. "We can take it slower and still get out of here in time. You're safe now."

"Don't patronise me, Gracie."

The sand fell harder. The cart slipped again. The sand moguls grew increasingly treacherous. The tunnel leaned to the right. The tyres slipped and chewed into the deeper surface.

Thunk!

They hit a larger dune. The contact slammed through the small cart. Bear yelped as the front wheels lifted. They whined from where they spun in mid-air before slamming down again and biting into the sand. The buggy snaked and rocked. Lifted and groaned. But Olga maintained their furious pace.

"See!" Olga pointed ahead at the stairs. She loosed a laugh as maniacal as her wide-eyed gaze.

Thunk!

They hit another hard lump of compacted sand. One side of the cart lifted, raising Gracie above Olga.

Gracie clung to the door, but it did little against the cart's momentum. She screamed as it lifted higher. They went past their tipping point and flipped into a clattering barrel roll.

The cart screeched and groaned as it flipped. The steel chassis yielded from multiple impacts. Gracie lost her grip and flew from her seat like a stone from a slingshot. She landed shoulder-first on the soft sand and came to a near instant halt, the dune consuming her momentum.

Pushing through her aches, Gracie stood up and swayed. Olga stood about ten feet away, her hair disheveled. Her face hung slack as she stared at the upturned cart with Kira's leg trapped beneath it. The sand fell harder than before, as if determined to bury their stricken friend.

"The fucking snake!" Olga cupped her mouth with both hands. She called after Bear, who ran away from them, heading for the stairs leading out of there, "How dare you run, you coward! See!" She turned on Gracie and pointed after him again, like she couldn't see the man abandoning them. Like she needed the reminder she'd backed him to come good. Like nothing mattered more than Olga being right.

CHAPTER 18

The rope ladder swayed with their climb. Probably no more than usual, but with Karl with a K directly behind him, William carried the intention to kick him loose balled in his right leg. Could he blame the ladder? One day, the temptation to set Karl free with a swift boot would prove too compelling.

As they were leaving the tank, he'd slipped in between William and Matilda. Yet another attempt to get close to her. To show her he could protect her better than William. Could save her from the diseased. Could fight better than William. Could climb better than William. Could he fall better than William, or would the tank break his weak body just like it would break William's? And if the fall didn't kill him, would he get infected from the diseased's attack like William, or was he so fucking wonderful he was impervious to infection?

William climbed into the food tube, the thick plastic funnel stained red on the inside. It ran at a forty-five-degree angle, granting them access to the lowest residential floor. An abandoned room. And while he carried hostility towards Karl in his heart, at least they were returning to a friendly block, and they no longer needed to hide their secret access point. They now had four hundred plus people so aligned with their cause, they were about to follow them into battle.

Doing what he always did, William braced against the tube with his hands and feet. He held himself like a spider in a drainpipe. Slow and steady, he shuffled towards the room. His heart fluttered. Sure, he could slip and fall, but worse than that, he could climb into a hostile room like when they'd returned to find the coup waiting for them.

Poking his head from the tube, William balked at the figure in the shadows. Until she stepped forward. "Rayne." He laughed. "Is it good to see you. The last time—"

She charged, her features twisted. She punched him in the face. His head snapped back, white light flashed through his vision, and he lost his balance, teetering on the edge before falling backwards. He screamed like a little girl.

Although William's stomach continued falling, he halted after a few feet. He'd slammed into a grunting Karl. Strong. Resilient. Dependable. Alpha. He remained pinned in place at the top of the ladder and spoke through gritted teeth. "I can't hold you for much longer, William."

And maybe he should have let them both fall. Plummet to his death. Take his shame and his nemesis in one hit. But William braced against the tube again, a few feet from Rayne's mangled hatred. His nose bled, and his limbs shook from the blow. His voice echoed in the tube. "What the fuck, Rayne?"

"You sound surprised. What have you done with Eleanor?"

"What you agreed to."

"You think I would have agreed to that?"

"Uh, I hate to interrupt."

"Then don't, Karl."

"But how about we have this conversation inside?"

William's reply died on his tongue. "Rayne?"

Although she paused for a few seconds and her jaw clenched, Rayne stepped back.

Just before he emerged into the room, William waited for Rayne to retreat a few more paces. Far enough away so if she charged again, he had a fighting chance of getting clear of the tube. He vaulted into the room and jumped to his feet. His gun hung from the strap across his front. He had no intention of using it, and Rayne didn't seem to care if he did. His bullets were no match for her fury.

She stepped farther away from William. Like she couldn't trust herself to be close. Like he repulsed her.

Karl stepped out next. Then Matilda, Artan, Nick, and Knives.

All the while, Rayne glared at William.

"It's not my fault, you know?"

"*Really,* William? Who delivered her to the blocks? That's if she made it?"

"She made it."

"So it's not your fault, but you executed this shit-for-brains plan. It's not your fault, but you sent her to her death?"

Knives said, "We all did, Rayne."

Her hands on her hips, Rayne looked Knives up and down. "When did you two become such good friends?"

William stepped in front of Knives. He could fight his own battles. "Eleanor said you knew."

"You've already said that."

"And we took a vote whether we'd help her. But she seemed set on leaving, with or without us. Surely you'd rather we made sure we got her there safely?"

"So you want me to thank you now?"

"No."

"Turn around."

"What?"

Rayne pointed at the tube. "We're going back."

"Rayne." Knives grabbed her shoulder, but Rayne threw up her arm, knocking her grip away.

"William's right."

"*Don't*, Knives. I'd expect it from him, but not from you."

"She convinced us you knew. That was clearly a mistake."

"You think?"

"But you know what this life does to people. It's hard to think straight. And William's right, whether we helped or not, Eleanor was adamant on going."

Tears filled Rayne's eyes, and she turned away. The strength left her voice. "We need to turn around now."

Nick took Rayne's hands. "Going back won't help anyone. She's already inside the blocks. Returning will only blow her cover."

Rayne's shoulders sagged.

"She said she'll go out on the walkway every night, starting from tomorrow. So we can check up on her. Make sure she's okay."

Rayne looked up at Nick. "But what if she's not?"

"She's a tough kid. I think she will be."

"Is that all you have?"

"I'm afraid it is."

Lifting his binoculars over his head, William handed them to Rayne. "You can come with us tomorrow night while we try to sneak closer to the blocks."

"You're not doing that anymore."

William glanced at Matilda and then Knives. They both frowned, but neither backed him up. "What do you mean?"

"Now Eleanor's in those blocks, there's no way I'm having you lot clomping about outside and risking being seen. You've done fuck all so far, so what makes you think you'll suddenly start being useful now?"

William pointed at her. "Now hang on. Yo—"

"Keep pointing that finger at me and I'll snap it clean off. You've risked Eleanor's life because you were too shit at your job to find out anything about those blocks. Those are the facts. If you keep going back for the next six or seven nights, you'll screw up at some point. It's a wonder you haven't already. You can't have it both ways. You've put Eleanor at risk. Now you need to back your shit plan and step away to let the girl work."

"We need to at least slice the food tube open. What if she doesn't make it?"

Rayne's rigidity returned. Her face reddened, and she trembled. "You'd best hope she does, William. For your sake."

CHAPTER 19

While Olga cursed and stamped, kicked sand and spat, Gracie ran to Kira. She had every right to be annoyed with Bear. And Gracie had gotten him wrong, but that didn't matter right now. The cart lay upside down, half of it buried with Kira beneath it. She dropped to her knees and dragged handfuls of sand behind her, tunnelling like a dog. "Are you hurt?"

Kira blew out, her cheeks puffing. Her eyes were wider than usual. Big brown orbs, their familiar softness sharpened by fear. The ever-hopeful had lost hope.

"We'll get you out of here."

"Come on, Gracie. Not even I can see a way out of this."

"What part of you hurts?" For every handful of sand Gracie dragged behind her, two handfuls fell into the crater she'd made.

"My leg."

She panted with the effort, sand raining down on her. "Broken?"

Olga finally dropped in beside her and helped.

Kira groaned. "I can't tell." She screamed when Olga tugged the cart. "But if it's not, it will be soon."

"We need to lift it." Gracie dragged more sand away. With Olga's help, they were making progress. Albeit slowly. "If we can get underneath the frame, hopefully we can get it off her."

Olga went turbo; possessed and dripping sweat, she attacked the sand, throwing out massive clouds behind her.

"There it is!" Gracie pointed. She drove her fingers into the sand and felt her way along the cart's edge. She yelled with the effort of trying to lift the heavy vehicle.

The cart shifted, and Kira screamed.

With Olga grabbing beside her, she tried again, the pair of them lifting the cart by an inch or two.

"It's too heavy." Olga threw an arm towards the stairs and the fleeing Bear. Her shout damn near shook the tunnel's walls. "He could have helped us!"

"Focus on what we *can* do." Gracie shook with the weight of the cart. With Olga's help, she lifted it by a few more inches.

This time, Kira held onto her scream, and her puce face turned incandescent.

The falling sand burned Gracie's eyes and stuck to her skin. "It's too much, and with every passing second, it's only getting heavier."

"Fuck this." Olga let go of the buggy.

Catching the extra weight sent fire ripping through Gracie's already burning shoulders. Kira, coated in a layer of sand, winced and cried. If Gracie let go of the buggy now, it'd crush her. "What are you doing, Olga?"

Olga's feet sank into the sand as she walked away and picked up her gun. She snapped it into her shoulder, closed one eye, and peered down the barrel. Bear had gotten so far away he'd become a silhouette in the gloom. The red laser target cut through the shadows and danced on his back.

"Olga!"

"Why's it not him beneath that cart?" Olga turned back and lingered on Kira's twisted face. "He should be the one who's drowning, not her."

"Killing him helps no one."

"Maybe not." She fixed on Bear again. "But at least he'll get his."

The sand piled up around Kira. Around her neck and beneath her chin. Slowly drowning her. Gracie kept a hold of the cart, but for how much longer?

Olga twisted her feet into the sand as if to stabilise her aim.

What if Bear had a reason? He'd not been afraid to show his fear, but he wasn't a snake. Maybe Olga had misjudged him. And even if she hadn't, how would killing him help? Gracie's gut had told her to trust him. That hadn't changed. Bear paused by the stairs. Hopefully enough sand had fallen to cushion the impact of lowering the cart. "I'm sorry, Kira." Gracie let go of the vehicle's weight. It sank into the sand, and Kira yelled.

But before she reached Olga, her short friend had already lowered her rifle. She dropped her head. "He's not worth it." She passed Gracie and dug some more. "Whatever happens, Kira, we're getting you out of here."

"That's kind, Olga, but I fear you trying to help me will be the end of us all."

"Wait!" Gracie pointed at Bear. He'd gripped one of the steel uprights on the stair's railings. He rocked back and forth, tearing it free. A steel pole about eight feet long, he waved it above his head while running back to them. "Dig, Olga."

Falling in beside her friend, Gracie dragged the sand

away. She redug the hole that had filled over again. Exposed the cart's frame again.

Bear sweated and panted. He passed Gracie and Olga and plunged the pole into the sand at an angle. He hit the hard ground with a *clang*. He got beneath it with both hands. He stood with his legs shoulder-width apart and yelled with the effort of his lift. The vehicle rocked up and away from Kira.

Gracie and Olga grabbed the frame again. They lifted the cart higher, and Kira dragged herself clear.

"Okay, let's drop it again on three." Bear winked at Kira. "One, two, three."

Bear jumped aside, the cart's weight slapping the pole against the sand.

Gracie ran to Kira and stood on one side of her while Olga stood on the other. They supported her weight, helping her towards the stairs and the lift out of there.

Gracie led Kira into the lift while Bear held the door open. She guided her against the railing running around the inside and stepped back. "You okay?"

The ever-hopeful Kira smiled and winced. "I'm alive. Thank you. And I don't think anything's broken."

After rubbing the top of Kira's arm, Gracie untied her plait. She ran her fingers through her loose hair and shook the sand away.

Olga laughed. "Maybe when you're done, you can tie Bear a new one too?"

The gaunt man grinned. "I didn't want to ask, but …"

Smacking the elevator button with her clenched fist, Olga sent them shooting up, and Kira screamed. Her shrill cry turned into tittering hysteria as they flew past the tower's levels towards the night's sky. They passed each field with a *thwip*.

Aching and exhausted, Gracie smiled at first, but soon laughed with Kira.

Olga winked at Bear. "You know, you might be a coward, but you're a useful coward."

Bear cocked an eyebrow. "Thanks. I think. And you might be an angry little troll—"

Gracie blocked Olga as she stepped forward.

"—but the strength it must have taken to lift that cart. Maybe your fury's your superpower. Maybe you don't need to be tamed."

"You make me sound like a wild animal."

Bear pressed his lips tight and raised his eyebrows.

The pair glared at one another until the lift broke the surface, the air both fresher and cooler. They shot up the side of the erected tower like they were going to go into orbit. Kira's next gleeful shriek shattered the standoff and made them all laugh.

CHAPTER 20

She'd spent just over a day in these blocks, but it already felt like a week. Time always dragged in the towers. It always had, and based on the past twenty-four hours, it always would. Eleanor had no friends in her old home, and she had none in this. But at least she had the distance of being a stranger. Most of the residents didn't know her well enough to be anything but polite. Even if their smiles didn't make it all the way to their narrowed eyes. And even when their conspiratorial whispers followed her down the hallways. As long as it held until they went to war, she could get behind this pretence.

Unlike most of the residents, the teenagers struggled to put on a façade. They were arseholes from the start. Openly hostile and cuttingly cruel. It would have been worse if they weren't. At least she knew where she stood. Unlike her time with Lines and his lot. She'd managed to keep her head down and blend into the crowd. Became invisible. Smiled politely and spoke only when addressed. To get the information she needed, she had to move through this place like a ghost.

Dressed in another puffy cocktail dress, the cerise

garment's baggy flourishes flapped in the breeze while the wind on the elevated walkway cut to her core. The dress' main body clung to her skinny form like film. Since she was little, it didn't matter what she ate, she never gained weight. Although, she'd eaten better in the past twenty-four hours than she had in a while, so the tight dress exposed her slight paunch as if displaying something for which she should be ashamed.

She'd chosen the highest walkway of the three, the clatter and chatter of a packed dining room behind her. The white noise of vacuous conversation punctuated by the clink and chink of cutlery and crockery. She'd often sought solace on the elevated walkways. No matter how hectic and claustrophobic her life became, she could always step outside and let the wind blow it all away. Also, she'd told William she'd be here every night for Rayne. Miss just one, and she'd be storming the blocks for her. Although, who knew how furious she'd be about the deceit. Maybe she'd storm the blocks anyway.

Four guards gathered around a spotlight in the plaza. Two directed the beam, shining it on diseased in the meadow, while another tried to shoot them. They missed more than they hit.

"They like to do that some nights."

Eleanor gasped and spun around.

The woman smiled. In her late forties, she had wrinkles before her time. But her sparkling eyes shoved aside any traditional signs of aging. She pointed at the guards. "They do it to improve their aim for when we move on."

"Uh ..."

"Belinda." She offered Eleanor her wrinkled hand. "My name's Belinda."

Eleanor shook it. She gripped hard enough to be assertive, but she'd not come here to break bones. She quickly tugged down her cerise sleeve, re-covering her tattoos. If Belinda noticed, she kept it to herself.

Clasping her hands in front of her, Belinda winced. "I'm sorry to hear what's happened to you."

"Thank you." The wind burned Eleanor's eyes, making them water, but revisiting her loss restarted her tears. But she shouldn't be ashamed of her grief. "Have you lost anyone?"

Belinda's eyes shimmered. "We all have, dear."

"Move on?"

"Huh?" Belinda snapped straight and dabbed the corners of her eyes.

"You said they were practicing their aim for when you moved on."

"To the shining city."

"That's where you're going?"

"It's where we're all going. No one's told you?"

"No one's said much to me yet. I think they're still working out if they can trust me."

"I'm sorry."

"It's okay. I'd probably find it harder if everyone wanted to be my friend."

"Like I am, you mean."

"I didn't mean it like that."

"It's okay."

"I'd just rather not be the centre of attention."

"I understand."

"So, you're planning on heading to the shining city? I suppose that was inevitable."

"You're not excited?"

"I dunno." Eleanor threw up her puffy shoulders. "Its reputation precedes it. I'm not sure what to believe about the place."

"Whatever it used to be, I'd say now it almost certainly represents security and a life of plenty."

"You've been?"

"No." Belinda lost focus. "But we have to hope for salvation, right? Come on …" She hooked her arm through Eleanor's. "You must be getting cold."

She'd been out long enough for Rayne to see her. Eleanor let Belinda lead her back into the packed dining room. As she passed through the doorway, she reached up and angled the camera so it faced the ceiling.

Belinda raised her voice over the din. "Why did you do that?"

"The cameras are all off, right?"

"Right."

Eleanor winked at her new friend. "So what does it matter if I move them? If someone turns them back on, I'd like to know I still have a vague chance at privacy. I always hated being watched in my old blocks."

Tapping her nose, Belinda winked back. "I like you, Eleanor."

"Thank you. I like you too."

She stroked Eleanor's back. "You take care of yourself, love."

But before Eleanor could thank her, Belinda left.

The funk of cooked meat turned the dining room's air humid. Its sickly sweetness slithered up Eleanor's nostrils and clung to her skin like sweat. Like she'd eaten too much and might hurl. It had nothing on Hawk's barbecued deer, which made her want to eat just one more piece, no matter how full. She held her breath as she weaved through the room. No one paid her any mind, which was just how she liked it. She made a beeline for the stairs.

"Oof!" The collision drove the air from Eleanor's lungs

and sent her stumbling back. She stepped up to the boy. "Watch where you're going."

Stan, who'd just emerged from the stairwell, glanced past her at the busy room. At Noris, who lowered his gaze when Eleanor turned his way. "I am. On top of that, I'm watching where *you're* going too."

"That's why you walked into me, was it?" The boy brought with him an earthy reek of sweat and dirt. Eleanor scrunched her nose, but it did little to dilute the tang. "What do you want?"

"I don't trust you."

"I don't care."

"I have a hunch about you, you see."

"Do you now?"

"And if I'm right, I'm going to take great pleasure in exposing you."

Thrusting her forearm into Stan's neck, Eleanor drove him back into the stairwell's door. As it closed behind them, blocking Noris' view, she pinned him against the wall, grabbed his crotch, and squeezed, forcing from him a febrile gasp. "I've had a hard fucking time, you little cretin. The last thing I need is some jumped-up fool thinking he can push me around. I don't know what you think you'll get out of this, but I promise you it won't end well."

Stan grunted and gasped. "That a threat?"

"It's a fucking promise, you mug." She stepped away from her urge to headbutt him.

"We made a mistake in letting you in." Stan wiped his watering eyes.

"You made a mistake thinking you could bully me." Before he could say anything else, Eleanor descended the stairs. Back towards her room on a floor of her own. Away from Stan and away from Noris in the dining room on the other side of the door.

CHAPTER 21

They'd put Eleanor on her own floor. They didn't have room anywhere else. And you can never be too careful, right? So which one was it? No room, or never being too careful? Not that it mattered. Given a choice, she'd have opted for solitude. Everyone else stayed on the blocks' top two floors. Close to the communal areas. They'd put her on the third one down. She would have gone lower had it not looked suspicious.

The camera above the hallway's exit remained pointed at the steel ceiling. Angled up like every camera she passed beneath. The cameras and ceilings were low enough for her to reach up, adjust them, and draw little attention. If the surveillance systems were active, they'd allowed her this privacy. If the surveillance systems were active, they were yet to undo what she'd done with every one she'd passed. Maybe they were telling the truth?

She could have chosen any room, and while the one at the far end of the hallway appealed, it would be the hardest to sneak from when she went out at night. She ducked into her room close to the stairwell and closed the door behind her.

Eleanor sat on her single bed, the mattress springs creaking beneath her weight. On her first night, she'd been a good girl and stayed put, but she'd come here to do a job. Later, when the block slept, she'd go out exploring.

~

Maybe she should give it another night, but they were running out of time. In less than a week, they'd be taking these blocks for their own. Phase one in their plan of attack. Take over half the blocks in the south, get control of the rest, and then take the shining city. Take it, or raze it to the ground. The place might be worth picking clean, but after that, surely they had to topple the symbol of the old regime? The city had a poisoned legacy that could never be cleansed.

Whoosh!

The door's servos announced her exit. Her shoulders lifted to her neck, and she held her breath as she waited in her doorway. The block remained silent. It either held its breath with her, so the guards could listen out for the whispers of subterfuge, or the residents were sleeping. Basking in the complacency of their old lives. The thing that would be their ultimate undoing.

Eleanor tiptoed towards the stairwell, the dirty blood-red carpet muting her footsteps. She paused at the end, lifting her left ear a little higher. An occasional drip of water. Wind played the open doors leading to the walkways several floors above. The snort and snore of the sleeping residents. Diseased moans rode the wind far below them.

She descended the stairs. Best to search the unoccupied areas first. She'd get braver with time, but she needed to know what went on in every block, so why not start here?

Eleanor bit her bottom lip with her descent as if the action would somehow mute the gentle *tock* of her boots against the steel stairs. She passed the floor below and then the next. She kept going down. A combination of the stairwell's chill and a heavy adrenaline dump raised the hairs on the back of her neck.

Every floor a carbon copy of the previous. The maddening uniformity added to the torture of a lifetime spent in these blocks. Each had a blood-red carpet that ran all the way to a window at the end. So dark outside, it had turned into a black mirror. She looked away from every one. Mirrors at night had a way of revealing things no one wanted to see.

"You're right, Dad, it is scary."

She spoke beneath her breath. Her lips moved, but her words were quieter than her steps. "But it'll be worth it. It'll save lives when we come back."

"I dunno. Maybe see what they have in the basement. What do you think?"

"I don't know either, but where else should I go? I'll check the other blocks, but not tonight."

"When? When I can move more freely. When it doesn't feel like I'm sneaking around a haunted building."

She'd passed four, maybe five floors. Hard to tell. And what did it matter? She continued down. She'd visit the basement first. What were they holding down there? "And the ground floor, I know. If they've designed these blocks like the others, this is where we'll find the food tube. If nothing else, I can make sure they have a clear exit for when the—"

Eleanor froze, halted by the muffled voices. They came from a room along the hallway directly in front of her. From behind the third door on the left. She could return to where she'd come from. Her lonely floor where no one would be any the wiser. But what if they came out soon? What if they followed her up? They'd surely hear her. And what were they doing in there?

She should go back to her room. She'd have time to get away. She could come back tomorrow night.

"You agree, Dad? You're right, information's no use to anyone if I'm dead. But what are they doing in there? And what else is going on in these blocks? And it's not like we have all the time in the world."

Eleanor continued down the stairs. Down a flight to the plateau between floors. She paused halfway and climbed back up. She could vanish in a heartbeat. And they were more likely to go up the block than down. Right?

Whoosh!

The third door on the left opened. Light spilled out and shone on the opposite wall. Broken by the silhouette of someone leaving. Multiple people leaving.

"Fuck!"

Eleanor ran to the plateau between floors and down the next few steps. Hidden from sight, she pressed her back to the cold steel wall. Her heart hammered, and she breathed in short pants.

Despite her dad's insistence she should go down lower, she waited. Three, possibly four people, they chatted amongst themselves. No one would hear them this deep in the block.

They climbed the stairs, and Eleanor released a deep sigh. "See, Dad."

Their conversation quietened not only because they got farther away from her, but also as they climbed closer to the occupied residential floors. Were they hiding something or simply trying not to disturb the others from having a good night's sleep?

"I agree, Dad. Best to give it a minute. I'll come back later." She descended the stairs.

~

Three floors down, the final residential floor in the block, Eleanor stood before the room at the end. She paused by the door's control button and once again held her breath. Once again, her hammering heart answered her call. With a wince, she opened the door.

Whoosh!

Like in her blocks, and the ones she'd just left, they'd put the food tube in this room. The gaseous hit of decomposing veg caught in the back of her throat. How could anyone shove rotten food, and the heavens only knew what else, down here and sleep at night? But these fuckers slept like they had not a care in the world. Like they didn't even understand the concept of a conscience. She'd been born into this existence, like many others. But she'd not chosen it. If this life ended with a day of reckoning, Eleanor's judgement would be based on the choices she made in life, not the misfortune of her birth.

~

Whoosh!

Eleanor smiled as she stood in the open doorway. Instead of visiting the basement, she'd returned to the room three floors up. The third door on the left. The one the men had exited on her way down. Like with every other room in these blocks, the door opened with the press of a button. Another sign of their privilege. Why lock doors? These people wouldn't know a threat if it bit them on the arse.

Even if she found out nothing else about his place, she'd be able to tell William and the others how they could arm themselves within a few minutes of entering these blocks. They'd have to travel light to climb up the food tube. Now they could travel light, get to the blocks' ammo store, and hit them hard and fast, armed to the teeth with their own weapons.

CHAPTER 22

They were back in the blocks, and the second Icarus tower they'd raised over a day and a half ago stood tall like the first. Gracie squeezed Olga's shoulder. "Maybe you should be gentler this time?"

"Gentler?" Olga fixed Gracie from beneath a heavy scowl. Hands twitching to be balled into fists, one side of her top lip flickered with a sneer. "What do you mean?"

Fighting to suppress her smile, Gracie let the strong wind on the elevated walkway fill the silence.

But Olga continued to stare.

Gracie sighed. "Well, we're about to tell Kira she's not coming with us when we raise the next tower. On account of her leg injury."

"She'll say she's fine. It's been a few days."

"But we know she's not."

"Okay, so she won't be happy to hear that. I get it. Are you worried I won't be gentle with her?"

"No, you like her."

"So again, your point?"

Gracie rolled her eyes. "My point is, we'll need to recruit

someone else. Whoever that is, how about you go easier on them? Bear was jarring, but when you write people off as quickly as you do, you fail to see their value."

"I saw Kira's value."

"But you nearly shot Bear. Even after he'd proven to be integral in keeping us alive."

"You can't have a go at me for every thought in my head. Shit, in my mind, I murder you at least three times a day."

"Aiming your gun at him is slightly more hostile than wishing him ill, wouldn't you say?"

The acoustics changed when they entered a kids' play area. The cavernous space amplified their footsteps and conversation. "But I decided he wasn't worth it."

"And I'll give you that."

"How gracious."

"All I'm asking is you give the new person more of a chance. They're bound to be frightened. I'm sure we were as bad when we raised that first tower. And you have it in you to be compassionate. It was you who saw what Joni had to offer."

Olga sighed.

"What's changed?"

"I'm tired, Gracie."

"Aren't we all?" Gracie led them into the stairwell going down to the residential floors. Down to tell Kira they were leaving without her. "But we're nearly there."

"Nearly where? Kira's?"

"No, we're nearly done with this bullshit. A couple more Icarus towers. A war against the shining city. After that, we're home free."

"I get the need to be positive, and I'm trying, but there's positive and there's deluded. We've nearly died while raising both towers. And if we survive two more, the shining city is an impenetrable walled fortress where they have only the heavens know what weaponry. And that's not to mention an army to rival every diseased in the wastelands."

"We don't know that. That could just be hearsay."

"Plan for the worst, hope for the best."

Gracie shrugged. "Either way, we have an end in sight."

"Even if the horizon's miles away."

Gracie rolled her eyes.

"I'll try to be friendlier. How's that?"

"A good start."

Olga turned at the next plateau and descended the next flight of stairs. She looked around. Like in many parts of these blocks, gunmetal grey steel surrounded them. "Do you think it's been worth it? All this. As awful as Edin was, if someone gave me a chance to return to that life, knowing what I know now … I'd find it hard to leave for a second time."

"It's too early to know for sure. I suppose only time will tell."

"Will you remain in these blocks when we're done?"

"Fuck no. After years in Dout, the last thing I want is to be encased in more steel. I want space. Fresh air. And more than I can get from just going out on a walkway once in a while. I want to leave my old life behind. Make this all worthwhile." She flinched as her brother's face flashed into her mind's eye. The kindest he'd ever been. But if she saw him again, would she trust him? Should she?

Another red-carpeted hallway. The window at the end let in the morning light.

"She won't be happy, will she?"

Gracie stopped at Kira's door and shook her head. She knocked.

"Come in."

Olga punched the button like it had crossed her.

Whoosh!

Her big brown eyes were alive. Eager and clearly pleased to see them. Kira sat up straighter in bed, her pained grimace cracking her cheerful façade.

While Olga went around to the other side of Kira's bed, Gracie sat on the edge closest to the door. She laid her bag beside her and pulled out a small pack of meat and placed a fresh bottle of water on her bedside table. "How are you doing?"

Her smile enough to light up any room, Kira swiped a hand through her hair, her ringlets bouncing. Even now, with a few days passed, Gracie expected sand to fall from her springy curls. "I'm good."

"Good?"

She unwrapped the meat and took a bite. "I'm getting tired of Queen Bee's updates. She makes quite the song and dance of telling us nothing's changed."

"Other than we're getting closer to going to war."

Kira smiled at Olga. "Right." She chewed more of her mouthful and took a sip of water. "But I'm on the mend."

"That's good." Gracie glanced at Olga. "Have you seen Bear?"

Olga's scowl returned.

After a glance from one of them to the other, Kira shrugged. "No. I've been in here since we got back. He's coming with us when we raise the next tower?"

Olga's focus burned into Gracie. Her cheeks grew hotter and no doubt glowed. She just needed to get it over with. Tell Kira. "Unless we find a replacement with his skill set."

"That'll be hard. For all his complaining, he really is quite capable."

"You can say that again." Gracie laughed. Too hard. Over-compensating much? "We'll put out a broadcast for him when we're ready to leave. He'll come if called."

Kira nodded. "I think Bear understands what needs to be

done. Despite what he wants, he won't shirk his responsibility."

"Do you know him from before?" Gracie turned away from Olga's searing attention. Shifted on the bed to make herself more comfortable.

"Not really." Kira scrunched up her nose. "I saw him around, but it was a big camp. While we were a community, we mostly kept to ourselves. Everyone was fighting to survive. If you were lucky enough to come across something worth having, like food or supplies, it made it easier to keep it to yourself when you weren't friends with your neighbours."

"Gracie knows about keeping things to herself."

Kira glanced at Olga and then back at Gracie. She tilted her head to one side, but Gracie batted the comment away.

"Also"—Kira lowered her head—"I was looking after my dad."

Gracie narrowed her eyes at Olga. She needed to back the fuck off. She was getting around to it. "Why were you looking after him?"

"He was poorly." Her big brown eyes glazed. "He had bad lungs. Some days, he could barely walk a few steps without falling into a debilitating coughing fit. He had to keep his activity to a minimum."

"So you were trying to keep the both of you alive?"

"And I would still be doing that had the diseased not arrived at our camp."

The diseased Gracie and Olga had played a part in releasing.

Gracie flinched again at Kira's next touch. "I don't blame you for them getting free. We've all seen the footage. But when the diseased came, we had a few minutes' warning at best. Dad begged me to leave him. Told me he was done. That he might have years in him still, but how valuable were those years in his state? He said they weren't worth his daughter's life."

The bed squeaked beneath Olga's weight as she sat on Kira's other side. "So you left him?"

"No, but I turned my back for a second when I heard the diseased. When I turned back around again, he'd run off. He moved like I'd not seen him move in years. And although he was heading towards the largest horde, I'd been so conditioned to think about his lungs, I was more worried he'd run out of breath than get infected."

The silence dared Gracie to finally tell her. Kick her while she was reliving one of her lowest moments. Tell her she'd slow them down too much. Like her dad had slowed down her.

"I would have taken him with me." Grief played with the edges of Kira's mouth. "Regardless of their physical state, we don't leave people behind, do we?"

"Uh ..."

Olga raised her eyebrows. Gracie had to tell her.

"Promise me ..." Kira took Gracie's right hand with both of hers. "You won't leave me here when you go to raise the next tower? I'm okay. Honestly."

Gracie pursed her lips.

Kira kicked her legs and grimaced through the pain. "See, they work fine."

"It looks like it."

"They're only bruised. I want to come out with you to the next tower."

Olga rested her hand on the back of Kira's. "What if we need to run?"

"You'll be chasing my tail."

"What if you need to fight?"

"I can point a gun and pull the trigger. Any fool can do that. Besides, I've been thinking about the symbols on the walls. I reckon I can decipher more of them. Were I not there last time, you'd still be in that coffin in the wall."

Olga shuddered.

"If you want, I'm ready to leave now." She looked from Gracie to Olga and back again. She pulled her covers aside.

Gracie put a restraining hand on her shoulder. "We're not going now."

"At least promise me one thing?"

"I can't if I don't know what it is."

"Even if you decide you're leaving without me, promise me you'll tell me when you're going?"

It would be much easier to just leave. To beg forgiveness when they returned.

"We promise," Olga said.

Why had she promised that? Gracie stood up from the bed. "We'll leave you to get some more rest."

Kira pointed at Olga. "You promised."

Maybe Gracie should make Olga come back on her own when they had to break it to her. They were going to leave soon, and whether Kira thought she had it in her to help or not, to take her with them in her current state would be madness.

CHAPTER 23

She'd found out about the ammo store being close to the food tube in the middle of the night, but while she could hide in the shadows, the night-time didn't give Eleanor the same freedom of movement as during the day.

The blocks woke and slept with the sun. So bright out on the walkways, she had to shield her eyes from its glare. But she strode with confidence from one room to the next. Explored the communal areas like she belonged. Which had been easy enough. She only had to believe her created narrative. Just another citizen seeking salvation.

Moving from one block to the next, diverting cameras as she went, Eleanor reached a sports hall in the block directly opposite hers. A sports hall as abandoned as all the others. No use for physical exercise. How uncouth to break a sweat. Although, every time she'd seen Noris, he perspired like a pig in a sauna.

Adjusting the camera above the doorway as she left the sports hall, shoving it at the ceiling like all the others, Eleanor slipped into the stairwell and descended.

Like in the block they'd put Eleanor in, they occupied the top two residential floors. Doors opened. People came and went. She acted like she belonged, but remained far enough away to not warrant further scrutiny. She continued down the stairs, leaving the chatter above.

"I know it's risky, Dad, but it has to be easier than sneaking through the blocks at night. This way, I'm invisible in plain sight. Also, it's not like we have time to spare. I might not find everything we need to know if I only move under the cover of darkness."

Like in Eleanor's block, each floor looked the same. A red carpet ran to the window at the end. The doors were all closed. Seemingly abandoned. Seemingly. But who knew what hid in each room? More ammo stores? Something else that might aid them when they took these blocks?

Eleanor's heart kicked when the stairs concluded at a door with a porthole window. A low-ceilinged basement like the one where Mads and his band of nutters met. Where she'd faced the vitriol from Lines and the other coup members. She pressed her face to the cold glass, her breath turning to steam against the round window. The gloomy basement sat empty. The daylight shone in through the small windows over by the exit. She shoved the door wide and strode in.

Unlike the carpeted hallways, the hard steel floor reported Eleanor's every step as she crossed towards the basement's hatch. She hooked out the large ring on top of the steel trapdoor. It lay flush with the floor, a small notch for her finger so she could lift it away and grip on.

"Three, two, one …" She tugged, but the hatch didn't budge. She widened her stance to make her base more solid and tried again. The hatch remained stuck. Locked in place. She had no key for the small hole beneath the handle. "Damn it!"

Dropping to her knees, Eleanor pressed her ear to the cold steel. The thick panel gave away little, although the slightest decomposition stench tickled her nostrils. Reminiscent of the food tube. This must be where they stored their rotting supplies. And if the smell could penetrate the thick steel, they clearly had a lot down there. More than they could ever need, so what else would they do but let it rot? The diseased had little use for red dye, rotten food, and only the heavens knew what else they put in the mulch they sent down the tower blocks' colon.

Without a key, she'd not get any farther. And the longer she spent down there, the greater the risk of being caught. A chef. A patrolling guard. Someone on a stroll. Whoever she bumped into, she'd have to give them an explanation she didn't have. Pressing off against the cold floor, she stood up and left. At least she had more information for the others. Even if this particular piece of knowledge was less than useless.

∼

ELEANOR HAD SPENT her life climbing and descending stairs. She moved at a jog and barely broke a sweat. She passed the empty hallways, the daylight shining in through the windows at the end. She closed in on the chatter above. The residential levels. She paused at the plateau before the first occupied floor. Conversations spilled from open doorways, but the residents remained in their rooms for now.

She jogged past the first residential floor and slowed to a walk. Now just another resident. She slipped back into the flow of people.

The sports hall as empty as before. Maybe she should devise a training plan for Noris. He might appreciate it. It might give him something to focus on other than her. A way to spend his clear frustration.

Steps followed her into the room. She spun around. A little too quickly. Stan watched her through dark little eyes beneath a furrowed brow. He hunched his shoulders and balled his fists. "Been somewhere?"

Eleanor tutted, turned her back on him, and continued walking. "Well, I'm not in my room, am I?"

"Where have you been?"

Exiting the sports hall onto the walkway, she breathed in the fresher air, the sun's warmth lying against her skin.

Stan ran to catch up with her.

She clenched her fists. She'd use his momentum against him and do him with one good punch. Send him into a railing and swipe his feet up as he stumbled. Another *accidental* death on the elevated walkways.

"I asked you a question."

"I heard."

"Well?"

"Well what?"

"Are you going to answer me? Where have you been? What have you been doing?"

"No."

"No?"

"I won't answer you." Eleanor turned her back on the boy and his puppet master. Maybe Noris thought he knew how to hide. Thought she wouldn't see him on the next walkway up. But he'd passed overhead like a storm cloud blocking the sun. She headed for the dining room in the next block. Stan followed, and Noris tracked her from above.

Through the dining room, she entered another stairwell and followed Noris' footsteps. Latched onto the snorting rasp of an overburdened respiratory system. She passed a ballroom on her way to the theatre on the top floor.

Someone performed onstage, but she lost the meaning of their words as she fixed on Noris. The waddling man had weaved through the crowd and skulked into the shadows backstage. He slipped in through the door leading to the second control room. No doubt the primary control room in this place. Much like the one Duncan had used against them.

~

THROUGH BALLROOMS, dining rooms, and the simulation room. Stan tracked Eleanor the entire way. He followed her down the stairs, back to her room. The residential floors were quieter than usual. Fewer people to hear the boy's slurs.
"We know you're up to something."
"*We?*"
"*I* know you're up to something."
"I'm sure you do, Stanley."
"Don't call me that."

Past the first residential floor and onto the second. Eleanor paused at the plateau before her level.

The boy joined her, but kept his distance. His eyes dropped to her opening and closing hand. If she grabbed him again, this time she might tear it off.

"Do you want to have it out now? If not, this is where your pursuit of me ends. I want to return to my room in safety. I'll do whatever it takes to make sure I can rest easy. Are you a problem that needs to be dealt with?"

He sneered, but jumped back when she stepped towards him. On her next advance, Stan turned tail and ran, his steps slapping against the stairs with his clumsy retreat.

Eleanor descended to her floor. But what had Stan and Norris deduced about her? And how much more time did she have in these blocks before she needed to make herself scarce? She'd come here to help those attacking the blocks, but if she blew her cover, she'd be handing the advantage to the enemy.

Back in her room, Eleanor sat on the bed with her head in her hands. "I know, Dad, they're a problem. And I'll deal with them. I just need to work out how. And when."

CHAPTER 24

William sat beside Rayne in the tank's passenger seat. The hard downpour covered the windscreen like a liquid blind, blurring their view of the road ahead. Blurring his view at least. Rayne had her foot to the floor and her jaw squared from her tight clench. She played chicken with the elements, and even the elements could see she'd rather die than yield.

Eleanor had entered the blocks a few days ago. Rayne and Matthew had gone every night since to make sure she appeared on the walkway. William accompanied them tonight.

Rayne had also put a stop to William's reconnaissance missions until Eleanor returned. So instead of going on more fruitless trips to glean information about the blocks and maybe slice open the food tube, William and his friends had joined the hunting party. At least when they went out with Hawk and his team, they returned with something useful.

But William being out with Rayne that evening left Karl with a K alone with Matilda. He shook his head like he could remove the indelible thought. He leaned closer to the windscreen like it might help. Too dark. Too wet. "Do you think … Maybe … you, uh, might want to slow down a bit?"

"Nope."

"Good chat."

But at least he'd get a chance to check on Eleanor for himself. She'd been on his mind for many of his waking moments. Had they made the right choice in helping her get into the blocks? Rayne didn't think so, but only time would tell. Could he forgive himself if she didn't make it? She was a tough kid. Smart too. She'd be fine.

"Gracie and Olga seem to be doing well with the farms. They're going out again soon to find another Icarus tower."

"Good for them." If Rayne had blinked, William missed it. The tyres hissed against the damp road.

"The hunting's going well."

"Is it?"

"You're eating meat every night?"

"Yep."

"And that doesn't tell you it's going well?"

"Don't be smart, William. It doesn't suit you."

Matthew continued minding his own business in the back. The only ever-present on these tank rides with Rayne. Maybe he could teach William a thing or two about how to handle her.

"We didn't need anyone coming with us, you know?" Rayne followed the right bend, the front of the tank lifting with the road's incline.

"We want to help."

"If you'd wanted to help, you wouldn't have delivered Eleanor to the blocks."

"She would have left on her own. By escorting her, we made sure she reached them safely."

"Well, aren't you a gentleman? And do you have a plan for getting her out?"

"I didn't have a plan for getting her in."

"Yet you still dropped her off."

"You talk about her like she doesn't know her own mind."

Rayne turned towards him, snapping the tank left with her twisting torso. "I talk about her like she's a *child*, William."

"Look, I'm sorry, okay? We didn't know how you felt about it." He folded his arms and turned to the window on his left. Pitch black outside from where the storm clouds blocked the moon, and the rain came down in sheets. In his mind's eye, he plotted the scores of canted silhouettes that were undoubtedly out there. "I'm not sure it would have made a difference, anyway."

"Some apology."

"It's the truth. Short of tying her up, it was all we could do to help."

"You could have tied her up."

"We don't do that, Rayne."

"Well, maybe you should." Rayne eased off the accelerator, the hiss from the tyres against the road turning into a gentle splash. The incline ate into their momentum as they rolled close to the hill's brow. The tower blocks loomed large. Just before they reached the hill's top, Rayne guided them into the boggy meadow, the long grass whipping against the tank's chassis.

"You think I'm not worried about her?"

"Someone who's worried about her wouldn't have put her in danger like you have."

"When will you fucking listen, Rayne? She. Was. Going. To. Go. With. Or. Without. Our. Help."

Braking harder than necessary, Rayne sent William

sliding forwards in his seat as she came to a halt. "Why did you come?"

"Someone had to."

"I don't need babysitting. And even if I did, why you?"

"I drew the short straw."

"Look, seeing as you believe this is necessary, how about you do us all a favour and shut your mouth until we're done? We wait for Eleanor in silence. When we see her, we go back to the blocks. After that, how about you stay the fuck out of my way for another few days?" She held up her fingers, showing him a gap between her thumb and forefinger of about half an inch. "Because I'm this close to breaking your legs and leaving you here for the diseased."

William turned to Matthew in the back. The boy's lips tightened, and he lifted his eyebrows. He undid his seatbelt and opened the tank's door with a *whoosh!*

William followed the boy outside, the rain throwing icy needles against the top of his freshly shaved head. His steps squelched in the boggy ground, and with the heavy clouds in the sky, their only guiding light came from the blocks over the brow of the hill. He and the boy lay on their fronts, their clothes instantly soaked. Diseased moaned all around, furious at the weather and its unrelenting assault.

After a few minutes, Rayne joined William and Matthew on the hill's brow. She lay beside Matthew and peered through her binoculars.

William leaned closer to the boy. Rayne had told him to keep silent, but she could fuck off. He kept his voice low. "Have you discovered anything about these blocks over the past few nights that might help?"

"No." Matthew gestured towards the towers. "We've seen plenty of people on the walkways. And the other night, they turned on the spotlight like when you were here. Their shooting practice called over a shitload of diseased. Thankfully, Eleanor came out soon after. Once we'd seen her, we got away before it became too crowded." He pointed at the blocks. "Is that her there, Rayne?"

Rayne snapped left and aimed her binoculars at the walkway. She visibly relaxed. She might have been taking it out on William, and that might be her right, but he shouldn't take it personally. She and Eleanor hadn't known one another long, but they were like mother and daughter. She'd cut through Rayne's hard outer shell. She'd become a part of her. And every evening, when she went out, she carried with her a fear the girl might not be there. A fear they'd wait all night and she wouldn't appear. That fear probably permeated her sleep and would surely have been at the front of her mind from the second she woke. It would slowly stew all day until her anxiety bubbled inside her like lava. No doubt all the possibilities for what could go wrong filled her mind. All the awful ways Eleanor could meet her end. This wasn't about William, and if it made her feel better to make it about him, then so be it. If it gave her even a small release, then he'd take her rage.

After Matthew looked through the binoculars, William held out his hand. "Do you mind?"

Rayne tutted when Matthew handed them to him. His hands tingled on their way to turning numb. The frigid downpour had soaked every inch of him. Like Rayne, he'd spent most of his waking moments thinking about Eleanor. Something inside him eased now he fixed on her on the walkway. She'd cleaned up since they'd seen her last. She looked like she belonged. Resting on the walkway's railing, the wind in her hair, she stared out across the meadow. Stared into the night. He handed the binoculars back to Rayne. "Thank you."

She took them with a grunt.

Were it Matilda up there, he'd be the same. He'd probably

never leave. His relief at seeing her probably didn't even scratch the surface of Rayne's, but it had been several days since Eleanor had gotten into the blocks, and she looked to be doing all right. Thriving even. She'd return to the blocks in time, and hopefully she'd bring with her the information they needed to win this war.

CHAPTER 25

The fourth morning in these blocks and Eleanor still ate her breakfast alone. There were other spaces at other tables, but she had neither the courage nor inclination to take them. It would be nice to have friends, but how could she connect to anyone here? In a few days' time she'd be one of the architects of their destruction.

Maybe the basement veg had grown staler over the past few days. Maybe the way they cooked their meat turned her off. Maybe the burden of guilt had swelled in her gut like a tumour, banishing her appetite. Whatever the reason, she swallowed a mouthful of overcooked potato and pushed her plate away.

Stan sat with a group of mates several tables away. He watched her from the other side of the room. As always, his vicious little eyes narrowed on her while he laughed and joked with those around him. They didn't seem to share his obsession. His obsession, or Noris'? The vile man hadn't yet found his way to the dining hall.

Every morning of her stay, Eleanor had awoken to a

buffet breakfast. They left food in hot trays for the residents to help themselves. This morning, she'd not only taken more food than she could eat, but she'd also taken a sharp knife from beside the meat joint and slipped it up her sleeve. Sharp and about five inches long, it hung heavy inside her top, but other than Stan, no one paid her any mind.

Even when she stared back, he watched her. Holding Stan's glare, Eleanor dragged her plate closer again, stabbed her fork into another chunk of meat, and chewed the fatty chunk. It tasted like pork. But if they had pigs, the heavens only knew where they kept them. She still had a lot of exploring to do.

Just the thought of swallowing tightened Eleanor's throat. Still fixed on Stan, she let the meat fall from her mouth to her plate. She left the half-chewed chunks on her lips, left the grease dribbling down her chin, and left the strands of meat in her teeth. She smiled at the boy, who finally turned away and focused on his own meal. She wiped her face with the back of her sleeve and pushed her plate of food away. Should he stare at her again, she'd be more than happy to perform an encore.

Stan flicked his head up at the door. Noris stood in the shadows. He beckoned the boy towards him. Eleanor dropped her attention to her plate before he looked her way. Better he didn't know she was onto him.

The second Stan left, Eleanor exited via a different door. She strode out onto the walkway leading to the VR room.

"Are you okay?"

The wrinkled woman from the other night. Beatrice … Beril … "Belinda." She smiled.

Belinda winced and frowned at her.

She'd never been good at faux sincerity. One of the many things that had worked against her in her old blocks.

"Hi, sweetie." Belinda ran her fingers from the corners of

her mouth, dragging them down and gripping her bottom lip in a pinch. "Uh ... are you okay? It's just ..." She pointed back at the dining room and pushed her tongue from her mouth, miming what Eleanor had just done to Stan.

"You saw that?"

Belinda pulled a face like she wished she hadn't.

"Sorry. Yeah, I'd eaten too much. Thought I was going to be sick." She fanned her own face. "I've come out here for some fresh air and a walk."

"Would you mind if I joined you?"

Despite herself, Eleanor nodded and walked on.

Belinda fell into step at her side. "I figured I could help you get excited about the shining city."

"Oh?"

"They have weapons. Weapons that are more than a match for the diseased."

"Do they now?"

"And the word is they'll force them back to the prison where they belong. And then back to the north. To return everything to how it should be. I don't like change, dear."

"It's hard to change when all the options available are a step down from where you were, eh?"

Belinda's eyes narrowed, sending yet more wrinkles from the corners of her eyes.

"I'm not taking the piss. We've had it good, right?"

Belinda shrugged.

"I had a mum and dad. A comfortable life. Prospects." Just before vanishing into the VR room, she threw an arm away from her to show the surrounding wastelands. "And now we have this."

Sighing, Belinda caught her arm and steered her towards the next walkway. Eleanor fought the instinct to snap free and take a different route.

"I think we need to remain hopeful for what's coming."

Belinda pressed the back of her spare hand to her forehead like a damsel about to faint. "Because if we look back ... well, it's rather bleak, isn't it?"

"Rather." Eleanor and Belinda stepped back out into the strong wind. The brow of the hill she'd crossed to first get into these blocks was down to their left. Even during the daylight, the steep decline hid anything that might be on the other side. Had Rayne and the others come here each night to see her? How had Rayne reacted upon hearing the news Eleanor had left? Who faced her wrath for that one? And would it even scratch the surface of the fury Eleanor would have to face when she returned?

Belinda pointed away from their blocks at a raised Icarus tower. "I heard the shining city erected them. They've built them as another part of their plan for the future. A way to make sure we'll all still eat well."

They entered an art studio. Eleanor tugged away from Belinda, but the woman clung on tighter. She had a forceful grip, and they were going exactly where she chose. She took them down the stairs, towards the residential floors.

At the second floor directly beneath the communal areas, Belinda smiled, leaned forward, and kissed Eleanor on both cheeks. It took all Eleanor had to not recoil from the woman's reek. She carried the same fatty stench as the meat they'd had for breakfast. Like she sweated grease.

Belinda smiled as she pointed up at the redirected camera. "I took a leaf from your book. Thank you for walking me home, dear."

It would have been nice to have been asked. Still, Eleanor forced another weak smile.

"Hopefully I'll see you soon. We can go for another walk, yeah?"

"That would be great. See you soon, Belinda."

Belinda left. Her fatty reek didn't. So thick it turned the air humid. Eleanor sniffed, waving and smiling at Belinda one final time before the woman entered her room.

If anything, the reek grew stronger. Like it hadn't come from Belinda at all. Like it came from somewhere deep in the building, funnelled up to them through the stairwell.

With no other residents around, Eleanor took to her toes and ran downstairs to the next plateau. A final glance back, the residential floor still quiet. She wouldn't get a better chance than this.

While the stench made knots of Eleanor's guts, its strong odour laid down a compelling trail. The deeper she went, the more her eyes watered from the pungent reek. It left a greasy film on her skin.

They'd smashed the window at the end of the hallway, but instead of it sucking out the stench, the breeze shoved it into Eleanor's face. The cooler air solidified the greasy film on her skin.

She jogged along the hallway to the end and whacked the door's button for the last room on the left. Steam billowed through the opening, the broken window finally doing its job by pulling much of it outside.

She lifted her shirt up over her mouth and slipped into the muggy room.

As hot as a sauna, the room hosted two vast copper vats. Like giant stew pots, each one stood over five feet tall. They were filled with gallons of boiling stock. They bubbled and popped, curdling the already rancid air.

Eleanor stood on tiptoes and peered inside.

Her stomach kicked when a head floated on the surface, face down.

She clapped a hand to her mouth. "They're eating humans?"

The head turned over and fixed her through empty eye sockets. A teeth-mark ring scored its pallid cheek.

Eleanor pulled away, rested her hands on her knees, and ejected her breakfast in thick chunks and braying waves. Her stomach acid burned her throat and clogged her nose. They were eating diseased meat. *She'd* eaten diseased meat.

CHAPTER 26

"Who'd have thought I'd grow tired of this?" Gracie gesticulated with her chunk of deer meat. She bit into it and tore away another strip. Juicy and cooked to perfection, her mouth watered as she chewed, but each gulp became harder to swallow. With her tongue, she stuffed her current mouthful into her cheek so she could finish her point. "I don't mean to sound ungrateful."

Olga winked at her, raising her voice over the white noise of collective conversation in the dining room. "Yet here we are."

"It's just..."

"Too much of a good thing?"

Gracie nodded. "Too much of the *same* thing. Also, it's hard to enjoy it when I feel so useless."

"Isn't that something you've managed your entire life?"

Gracie flipped Olga the bird. "I'm being serious. It's been days since we came back, and all I've done is sit around and stuff my face while everyone's getting ready for war."

"We've been looking for Bear."

"That's my point. There's not even five hundred people in these blocks. Hardly the manhunt of the century."

Olga's eyes narrowed. "He's a slippery fucker, isn't he? Besides, you shouldn't be too hard on yourself."

"Why not?"

"We'll be out again soon, putting up Icarus towers. That's no mean feat. I'm sure if half the people here got buried in sand like we did, they'd choose to go into battle instead of returning to that."

"Yeah." Gracie bounced where she sat. "Maybe I'll feel more useful when we're out again. Doing more than navel-gazing and waiting for Bear to show up. Or a suitable replacement."

"Maybe we need to go without him?"

"Without both him and Kira? Which, by the way, if we choose to leave her"—she pointed at Olga—"it's on you to break the news. You made the promise."

"Do you think there's any other way?"

"I dunno. But they've both proven themselves. When we truly needed them, they came good. To leave one behind is shit, but both of them? What if the next two prove a lot less reliable?"

"Or we go alone?"

Crash!

Rayne threw her breakfast tray on the table and sat beside Olga. She slammed her glass of water down, some of it spilling over the sides. She stared at her lap and breathed hard.

"Uh …" Gracie shrugged at Olga. When the backup didn't come, she reached across the table but stopped short of touching the irate woman. "Everything all right, Rayne?"

"No, it's not fucking *all right*." She pointed back the way she'd come, the people on the table next to them scowling at the accusation as if she'd aimed it at them. "That prick William."

But he'd not followed her in. Gracie appeased those nearby with a wave of her hand. "Has something happened to Eleanor?"

Rayne threw up her thin shoulders in a shrug. "No. I dunno. I don't think so. I dunno."

"Then what's the issue?"

"That he put her in this situation in the first place."

"Is that on him?"

The tips of Rayne's pale fingers turned even paler from where she gripped the tabletop.

"I understand your concern, but Eleanor tricked him. His only mistake was to trust what she told him. That might be naïve—"

"You reckon?"

"But he didn't do it to exploit her. He wouldn't. Are you still going to the blocks every night?"

"Of course. I was with William last night when we checked on her."

"Ah."

"What's that mean?"

"Nothing."

Rayne clung to her deer meat and bit off a chunk. She chewed with her mouth open, and her lips glistened with grease. She scowled at Gracie and Olga, daring either of them to say the wrong thing. When Gracie returned a tight smile, she rested her pointy elbows on the table and dropped her head again. "Sorry."

"It's a stressful time."

Rayne glanced around. The surrounding tables chatted amongst themselves. She kept her voice low. "Why are you still here?"

"Thanks."

"I don't mean it like that, but what's happening with the Icarus towers?"

"We went as a team of four for the last one. And that worked. But now one of them is incapacitated from nearly breaking her leg."

"And the other?"

Gracie turned her palms to the dining room's tall ceiling.

"I'm going to see Ash and Rowan this morning." Rayne swallowed her mouthful with an audible gulp. "Want to come?"

When Olga didn't object, Gracie smiled. "Sure. It'll be nice to see how they're getting on."

∼

Rayne led them through several blocks to the maternity ward. Gracie carried a plate of deer meat and Olga a bottle of water. Better to turn up with something, even if Ash and Rowan could have gotten it themselves.

Babies' cries filled the stairwell. Their shrill need for attention stabbed into Gracie's eardrums and pulled her shoulders tight. She frowned like it might fight off the intrusion, but the cacophony hit her with both barrels as she followed Rayne onto the ward. The ripe reek of soiled nappies nearly knocked her on her arse. She pressed the back of her hand to her nose. "Fucking hell, it smells worse than the diseased in here."

A line of white cots with white bedding ran down the room's right side. Each had an adult bed nearby. Many had women in them. Many had partners sitting beside them in hard plastic chairs. More didn't. Those who'd survived held their women's hands. They waited while their pregnant partners slept. Some held babies, some of them tiny and fast asleep, some of them incandescent with the strain of their wailing screams. The room was packed and active, but Gracie, Olga, and Rayne had walked into tens of private moments. Some women lay freshly vulnerable from childbirth. Washed out. Almost transparent with exhaustion. Too many of them lay without a partner at their side, the nurses too busy on the ward to give them the focused care they might have needed.

Olga walked on Gracie's left. Pale, she stared straight ahead like the cots didn't exist. Gracie caught her hand, but it did little to remove the haunted look from her eyes. The baby in the bathtub lived rent-free in her head.

Rayne waved. Ash lay in bed about twenty feet away. Rowan and Knives sat in the two chairs beside her.

Getting up, Knives hugged Rayne, then Gracie, then Olga. She left the room while twirling a blade. Always ready for a fight.

Ash glowed in their presence. Rowan gave up his seat. Gracie handed him the meat and took the spare chair beside Rayne. Olga placed the water bottle on Ash's bedside table and looked at the floor.

Even now, with the babies screaming so loud it made her ears ring and her head ache, Gracie spoke in hushed tones like she didn't want to wake them. "How are you both doing?"

Ash beamed. "Really well, thank you."

"You look good. And you? How are you doing, Rowan?"

Despite being one of life's perpetual pessimists, even Rowan smiled. "All right. It's just a waiting game now, isn't it?"

"Thank you for all you've done for us." Ash took Gracie's hands. "All of you." She looked at Olga and Rayne. "We don't take any of this for granted. I didn't appreciate just how important it was for me to feel safe right now. You and everyone else fighting for the cause have given that to Rowan and myself. Thank you."

"You're welcome." Gracie shrugged, and Olga finally looked up. She nodded along with her.

As Rayne and Ash fell into conversation, Olga tapped Gracie's shoulder. She pointed across the ward.

"Damn!"

Rayne said, "You okay?"

"The other person we were looking for."

"The one without the broken leg?"

"Bruised. But yeah." Gracie pointed across the ward. "That's him." She stood up, her chair screeching as it pushed out behind her. "Will you excuse us for a second?"

Ash smiled. "Sure."

Gracie jogged to catch up with Olga, who was laser-focused on their target. "Go easy on him."

"I'm hardly going to kick his arse, am I? Even if that's exactly what he deserves." She raised her voice as they drew close. "Well, well."

Bear sat on the chair beside a woman with an enormous bulge. She must have been close to full term. His face fell slack.

"Didn't think to tell us you were here, no?"

"You've been looking for me?"

Gracie tutted. "Cut the crap, Bear. We've—"

Olga cut her off by dropping into a crouch and beaming at a small boy who'd appeared from around the bed. He saluted her. About two years old, he had curly black hair like his mum, and his dad's brown eyes. He smiled, and Olga beamed back. "What's your name, little fella?"

His eyes widened, and he damn near shouted with his exuberance. "I'm Wilf."

"Hi, Wilf, I'm Olga." She saluted back.

The woman in the bed had kind green eyes and a healthy

glow. Her hair shone. Pregnancy, nature's glow-up. Gracie offered her hand. "Sorry, how rude of us. I'm—"

"Gracie?"

"Right. And she's—"

"Olga." The woman smiled.

"Sorry we came in a bit hard."

The woman waved the comment away. "We've been making the most of our time together before he goes out again."

"But he can't come out with us. Not when he has …" Gracie circled her hand over the woman and her small family. "This."

"He wants to. *I* want him to. And I still have at least a month of this pregnancy left. I'm Tammy."

"Gra—"

"Gracie, you've already said."

Olga now sat cross-legged on the floor, put her hands across her face, pretending to hide, and pulled them away. "Boo!"

Wilf's shrill giggle lit up the room. Gracie laughed with the rest of them as he ran around the bed and into his father's arms.

"I'm sorry, Bear, but we've not found anyone else who can fix the farm machinery."

"Like Tammy said, I'm ready whenever you want to leave." He flinched while hugging Wilf close.

"We were thinking of waiting a few more days."

Olga looked up at Gracie and grimaced. "We were?"

Gracie nodded. "Yeah. Kira's still healing, so we thought we'd wait until the night before they go to war to leave. Move in the cover of dark and before the chaos begins. By the time we're raising another Icarus tower, it will be the last thing on anyone's mind. To raise another one too soon might put the blocks we're attacking on high alert. We risk giving the game away."

"We do?"

"Yes, Olga, we do."

"Okay." Olga shrugged. "But Bear's not coming with us."

"What?"

Tammy took Bear's hand. "He's going. Aren't you?"

"Yeah, I mean it. I want to help. I want to make this world safer for our kids."

Gracie frowned at Wilf and then returned to Bear. "You're sure?"

"I am."

"All right. We'll confirm with Kira, but the plan is to leave in two nights' time. All good?"

Bear dipped a stoic nod, and Tammy smiled.

"See you soon." Gracie walked away.

But Olga stayed back and played another round of peek-a-boo with Wilf, who squealed with delight. She ran to catch up with Gracie. She now walked on her right. Like on the way in, she put herself as far from the cots as possible. Gracie rested her hand on her back. "I agree with you about offering Bear the chance to stay, but I think it's the right call to take him with us."

"Yeah. And you're right about giving them a few more days. I'm not overjoyed about the wait, but at least if we go as a foursome, we have a better chance of all coming back again."

CHAPTER 27

"I'm just pleased she's doing okay."

"But is she?" Matilda sat opposite William in the back of the tank. She clung onto the rail above her head. Knives took them on a bumpy ride, but it had nothing on the white-knuckle trip he'd taken with Rayne the previous evening.

"I mean ... She came out onto the walkway as promised. She *looked* all right. She showed no sign of needing help."

"Hopefully that means she doesn't."

William sighed. "Hopefully."

Artan, Nick, and Hawk rode in the back with them. Karl sat next to Knives up front. When William had suggested he remain back at the blocks, he was the only one who didn't see the funny side. Even Matilda laughed.

Evening settled in, and the little remaining light shone in through the front windscreen. Their tank still had a turret, making it much darker inside.

They were all together for the first time since dropping Eleanor at the blocks. Katrina had gone out with Rayne that evening.

"You've done a good job, Hawk."

Their scarred friend jumped, stirred from his own thoughts. "Huh?"

"A good job," William said. "Your hunting parties have kept us all well fed."

"We're doing our best."

Artan patted his stomach. "And we appreciate it. When the farms are fully operational, we'll be eating like kings and queens."

Karl with a K turned from the front and sneered. "We'll be eating like those greedy shits who used to run the blocks."

Knives maintained a consistent pace. They bounced and bobbed along the lumpy road, and the tyres hummed against the concrete.

"So …" Nick rested the back of his head against the tank's wall. "Three days? It's no time, is it? And what if Eleanor's not back by then?"

"She will be."

"But what if she's not, William?"

"Then we attack anyway, and we make busting her out our number one priority."

Leaning across the gangway, Nick rested his elbows on his knees. "And then more blocks after?"

"That's the plan. But I think we should focus on one battle at a time. It's overwhelming to plan too far ahead."

"To think about the shining city, you mean?"

William's heart sank.

"We don't even know what that place looks like."

"Which is why it's best not to think about it until we know more."

Karl's sombre tone cut through the conversation. "Imagine the most protected city you've ever seen. And instead of a brick wall, it's surrounded by thirty-foot-tall steel. It's so thick it'd withstand an earthquake, and they always keep the gates locked. You only get in and out of that place at their discretion."

Artan snorted. "Sounds lovely."

"It really isn't."

William rolled his eyes. "No shit?"

As if spurred on by William's sarcasm, Karl with a K said, "They keep children in basements. They bring them out whenever they want to …" He coughed to clear his throat, and Matilda's face sank. She'd heard about the city many times already, although with each retelling, she turned paler.

Hawk scratched his scars.

"They sacrifice vampires for fun," Karl said. "They make a show of it. They hang them in plazas. Sometimes they just string them up and leave them to starve to death while they have week-long banquets right in front of them. Some say they eat their corpses. I wouldn't put anything past them, but sometimes it's hard to separate fact from fiction."

Artan said, "And who's *they*?"

"Those in power." Karl shrugged. "Obviously."

"What I mean is, do we know much more about them?"

"Not really. They're politicians and their mates. Whoever's in favour that month. I've heard they're as ruthless with their own as they are with vampires. The power to evict people is both a carrot and a stick, which they liberally use in equal measure."

The others hung on Karl's words. And maybe it was all true, but Eleanor hadn't mentioned half of what he had, and she knew people who'd been inside. Of all the things, they could only be certain of one truth … the thirty-foot-tall walls. Whatever lay inside, they'd have to penetrate an impenetrable fort to discover it. "So how do we get in?"

Karl sat back in his seat. "Dunno."

Knives kept her eyes on the road, but leaned her head back. "Hang on."

Because of his trip with Rayne, William clung to his seat with both hands. The others were more relaxed as Knives brought them to a gentle halt.

Whoosh!

Karl opened the tank's door and jumped out. In William's mind's eye, the cocky prick got tackled to the ground and bitten by a diseased. He'd shoot it, of course he would, but who could blame him if he was too slow to react to save Karl's life?

The smarmy cretin waited just outside the door and took Matilda's hand to help her out into the damp meadow. He offered his help to William, but William jumped the few feet and landed with a squelch that sent a small splash of mud up the front of Karl's trousers.

"Hey, Tilly, what a hunt we had yesterday, eh? The way you took down that deer. Man, you're something special, you know that?"

Matilda acknowledged him with the slightest flick of her head. William tutted. When did that prick start calling her Tilly?

The hunting party was over thirty strong. Many of the same faces came out each night with a small rotation of older teenagers to teach them the ways. They each had a rifle. The lands were rich with wildlife. Especially with the diseased wandering the wastelands. They unsettled the animals, keeping them moving and distracted. Their distressed calls rode the breeze. The larger packs were too far away to be a problem. For now.

While they sorted themselves into groups, Hawk took up a central spot amongst them. He'd been sombre since Aggie's death, but out here he had a purpose. William smiled at his stocky friend. Their best hunter, their survival depended on him. He was more than up to the task. "Now remember, keep quiet and keep calm. They might be diseased, but we have the advantage. We have our wits. They only have rage. And if you're about to lose your head, think about Eleanor. If a fourteen-year-old girl can live with the enemy for days to gather intel, you can cope with a few pissed-off diseased. If you feel overwhelmed, find higher ground. A rock or one of the old vampire outposts. Wait there, and someone will come. At the very least, we can drive over to you in a tank later."

A rustling to William's left. He raised his gun and aimed into the long grass.

Hawk paused. They all watched the spot on which William fixed. When nothing came of it, he continued, "And getting your aim in now will be good practice for when we go to war in three days' time. If you can hit a deer, you can hit a Rupert in the tower blocks."

Pointing at the groups, one at a time, Hawk sent them in different directions. When he got to William, William pointed toward the rustling, and Hawk cocked his head to one side. Problem?

William shrugged.

Hawk nodded. Go wherever he felt the need.

Of course Karl with a K took over and headed where William had pointed. Matilda made to follow them, but William took her hand. "You go with Artan and Nick. I'll go this way."

"You sure?"

How else would he accidentally shoot Karl in the crossfire? And with only him and Karl heading that way, it would be the perfect opportunity. "Yeah. See you back at the tank." They kissed, and he followed Karl with a K through the long grass.

Using the prick's confidence to his advantage, William held back a few steps. Let him flush out the diseased.

A group of four had set off on a parallel path to William

and Karl. The long grass hid them from sight, but they made swishing progress. Three teenagers, all about sixteen, they had an adult with them. A more experienced hunter called Salomon. He'd agreed to be their mentor on this trip.

A swish in the grass to their left. Karl snapped his gun to his cheek and peered down the barrel.

Another swish.

A diseased would have attacked by now. William jogged to a nearby rock. It stood about six feet tall and ten feet wide. He scaled its cold and jagged side, using several ledges as steps to the top.

Karl joined him. The open meadow swayed in the wind. It hid whatever had made the rustling.

The small, inexperienced hunting party reached an old vampire outpost. A rickety wooden lookout tower that stood about ten feet tall. Higher ground. Somewhere to wait until the deer showed up. It rocked and creaked with their climb.

"There!" Karl pointed away from them. About halfway between them and the rookies. Something moved through the grass, but the meadow, combined with the fading light, kept it hidden from view. They tracked the movement with their rifles, but how could they shoot if they didn't know what they were shooting? The first person to fire started the countdown. They'd all have to attack before the diseased reached them. The rustling vanished behind another rock.

William jumped at the deep baseline rumble. "What the …" So loud the vibration ran through the rock beneath their feet. "What is it?"

Karl scanned the meadow. "Sounds like speakers. Around the vampire tower."

"What? Who would put them there? Surely that would only attract the di—"

The diseased screamed.

"Who would do th—"

A tank burst from behind the rock they'd tracked the rustling to. The vehicle jumped and hopped, cutting through the grass as it headed straight for the off-kilter tower.

"Fuck!" Karl stamped his foot. "We should have shot them."

The tank slammed into the structure's corner, shattering the wood. The teenagers cried out and clung on tighter, as if the very thing that would bring them down could protect them.

Karl's shots bounced off the tank as it raced past them towards the road.

Just one person in the driving seat. William made eye contact with him as he passed. They should have shot him when they had the chance.

Karl hit the aerial on the vehicle's back, knocking it off.

"He knows," William said.

"What?"

"That person, Karl. Driving the tank. He knows. Eleanor. Our plans to attack the blocks. At least I think he does."

"That's why I shot his aerial. It'll cut off his comms."

"You're sure that'll work?"

Karl shrugged. "I hope so."

"Hope?"

Karl shrugged again.

"And even if it works, it doesn't stop him from getting where he's going."

"What would you have me do, William?"

The diseased responded to the speakers. The teenagers clung to the swaying structure. Many of the hunters had gone the other way. Karl and William were the closest to Salomon and his rookies. But they were also closest to the fleeing tank. "I know there are four people who need our help, but if that tank gets back to the blocks, we're screwed. If he heard our plans …"

"And that's the question, isn't it? Did he hear them?"

"We have to assume he did."

"So then we have a choice. Do we give chase or save lives?"

William chewed on the inside of his mouth as the tank fled. "How many will be lost if we don't follow? If they find out our plans …" It hopped and bounced along the meadow. Cut through the long grass. Drew closer to the road and closer to the blocks Eleanor had infiltrated.

A boy, the highest up the tower, cried for his mum. His febrile warble came out like a lost lamb's bleat. The diseased closed in from all sides. The tower swayed. The tank got farther away. "What shall we do, Karl?"

For the first time, the cocksure prick had lost his swagger. Tears glazed his wide eyes. "I don't know."

CHAPTER 28

The screams dragged on William like an anchor as he and Karl ran from the rookies on the rickety tower. Their shrieks of despair, combined with the speakers' bass-note boom, called the diseased from far and wide. Hopefully, they'd still be there when they got back. Either way, they couldn't risk Eleanor's safety and put their attack on the blocks in danger for the sake of three teenagers and their mentor. No matter how shrill their cries.

Karl reached the tank first. He started driving as William jumped in through the open door. He pressed his foot flat to the floor. The armoured vehicle hopped and jumped, getting air several times as they chased the fleeing tank.

They left the meadow with a final leap that threw William against the tank's roof. He rubbed his bald head, his ears ringing from the contact. "Jeez." He swallowed back the rest of his retort. What did he expect Karl to do? Slow down?

The tank's six tyres hummed as they sped up, the road's flat surface like finding an extra gear. The rat in the tank ahead had a lead of about one hundred feet. But he had to pass their blocks on his way back to his own community.

William grabbed the mic.

"What are you doing?" Karl gripped the wheel harder.

"Calling in help."

"No."

"No?"

"Radio silence, William. Who knows who's listening?"

William tutted and slotted the mic back in its holder.

Karl pointed ahead. "The turret."

"You reckon?"

Like they'd heard them, the tank ahead's turret turned their way.

Karl grimaced. "I reckon."

"Shit! There's more than one of them in there." William slipped from his seat, stood on the turret step in the back of the tank, and peered out through the small slot window. It put a letterbox frame around their enemy.

"It makes sense. There were a lot of speakers around that lookout post."

Still clinging to the turret's control, William dropped a little lower and shouted over their clattering and humming momentum, "What?"

"There's at least two of them, like you said. It makes more sense how they got so many speakers in the field around the vampire lookout. That's not a job for one. That's why we have one driving and one on the turret."

"And that's useful information how?"

"Just saying."

Fwomp!

The end of the tank's turret flared. William's letterbox view framed the missile heading straight for them.

Karl snapped left at the last moment. William whacked his head on the inside of the turret. The explosion shook the ground behind them.

"Good driving, Karl."

"I know."

William rubbed the growing lump on the side of his head and aimed the turret at their enemy. "Hopefully, they'll shoot the second one while we're still far enough away to avoid it. And far enough away from the blocks to not attract their attention."

The enemy tank's turret dipped. The end hit the ground. Sparks kicked off from the cartwheeling lump of steel, which turned over several times in the letterbox before leaping into the air and out of sight. William ducked, waiting for the heavy vehicle part to land on top of them, but it slammed against the road behind them. He straightened just as the tank vanished over the brow of the hill in his small window. "I'd say they're out of missiles."

"No shit? How many do we have?"

"One."

"Make it count. Because right now I don't see us catching them." Still flat-out, Karl crested the hill. William's stomach lurched from the sudden drop. "In fact, it looks like now they've lost their turret, they might be even faster than us."

"I'm going to shoot the road."

"What?"

"It doesn't move."

"Which means?"

"I've got a chance of hitting it."

"And what good is that?"

They followed the tank into a valley. It hadn't yet reached the next climb. William aimed ahead. Directly in their enemy's path.

Fwomp!

The missile shot over the fleeing tank and slammed into the road. Higher than he'd aimed. Good job he hadn't tried to shoot them. It blew a ten-foot-wide crater with an eruption of mud and concrete.

They hit the bottom of the valley and chased the tank up the other side, their blocks up ahead on the left. Four clips held the turret in place. William undid three before the wind dragged it loose. He ducked just before it ripped his head off.

His heart beating like it might burst, he joined Karl in the cockpit.

The tank ahead reached the crater. It cut from the road into the meadow. The bumpy ground and long grass slowed them, but not enough. They navigated the crater and pulled back onto the road on the other side before vanishing over the brow of the next hill.

"Fuck it!" Karl slammed the heel of his hand against the steering wheel. He remained on the road, the crater in their path.

"Uh ... what are you doing?"

"This is the only way."

"This is suicide."

"Hang on."

William looked around the cab. "To what?"

"Your bollocks."

The tank's front dropped into the crater. The nose hit the ground with the screech of twisting steel.

The tank's back lifted, and William pressed against the ceiling. About as useful as the rookies clinging to the falling tower. "Oh, fuck!" The back kept going, turning their world upside down as they flipped.

Bouncing out of the crater, they slammed against the road again and turned sideways, barrel-rolling over the hill.

CHAPTER 29

William bounced around the cockpit like a pea in a cup. A buckle hit the side of his face. A boot cracked against his chin. A spent bullet case nearly took out his eye. He and Karl cracked heads as the tank screeched and banged. It turned over so many times the world no longer made sense. Gravity accelerated their crash from where they'd crested the hill's brow. He caught flashing glimpses of their blocks. The road. The meadow. The two tanks. Two?

They stopped with a final jolt. Every part of William ached as he lay across Karl, crushing him against the driver's side window.

His ears ringing, his legs weak, William dragged himself into the tank's rear, drawn to the daylight coming in through the hole left by the missing turret. Karl followed.

As if birthed from the wreckage, William poked his head out of the tank. The fresh early evening air cooled the red-hot bruising on his face. There were two tanks nearby. One on its roof, the other the right way up.

Dragging himself from the hole, William's leg caught on

the way out. He tripped and hit the road like a sack of shit. Before he could stand, Karl fell out and landed on top of him.

"Fucking hell, Karl." William kicked him away and got to his feet. He swayed like the surrounding meadow.

Karl ducked to get a better view into the upturned tank. "Is that ..."

William leaned over to peer in. The blood rushed to his head, making him dizzy. "Rayne, Matthew, and Katrina. What the hell are they doing here?"

The two men they'd chased lay slumped in the other tank's cockpit. They were dazed from colliding into their friends.

A horde screamed. Twenty strong. Maybe more. Downhill from the crash site. They sprinted through the meadow towards the road. Towards surer ground. William shoved Karl towards Rayne's tank. "Let's get them out before the diseased get here."

One of the men they'd chased stirred inside their tank. William changed course.

"What are you doing?"

The horde reached the road about one hundred feet away.

"Make sure Rayne and the others are okay."

"But what are you doing?"

"What Rayne would want me to do." And what Rayne would kick his arse for if he didn't. The man in the tank reached for a weapon. William opened the door with a *whoosh* and jumped aside.

Scaling the tank's side, William dived in through the turret hole as the man ran beneath him. He landed on his left shoulder. The impact lit up his already stinging body. With clumsy hands, he dragged his gun around and shot the man before he could shoot William. A quick burst. Six or seven bullets. They chewed into his chest. Tore his clothes. His arms flew away from his body, and he fell like a rag doll.

William clambered to his feet as the driver accelerated away. He turned a hard right, the tank jumping from where he ran over his dead mate.

William fired and missed. His laser target danced on the windscreen's inside.

The driver steered left and right, throwing William around in the back like a puck. He hit the wall beside the open door, and the top half of his body slipped outside.

Dragging himself back in, William shot the driver through the back of the head. He painted the inside of the windscreen with his brains. The driver slumped forwards over the wheel. The tank veered into the meadow and slowed.

William slumped on one of the back benches. His entire body throbbed. Until a diseased leaned in, its face torn to shreds. It fixed him with its bloody glare. Yellowed teeth, infected wounds, locked with pure hatred. It shrieked like an owl.

Yelling back, William fired.

The thing's head jolted, and it fell into the meadow.

Two more dived in.

William shot them both, dropping them in the open doorway.

Back on his feet, he kicked them clear and whacked the door's button.

Another diseased dived in through the closing door. It tackled William around the legs and landed on top of him.

It threw a flurry of wildly inaccurate swipes. It smacked the tank's floor around him with wet slaps. It bit at the air.

William grabbed it around the neck. It wore its loose skin like a scarf. He reached for his gun with his right hand, dragged it around, and wedged the barrel beneath the underside of its chin, forcing it to face the ceiling.

His gun kicked when he pulled the trigger. The diseased

fell limp. He shoved it aside and rolled away from the blood and mulch raining from the ceiling.

Tossing the cadaver aside, more diseased hammering against the tank's closed door, William grabbed the dead driver and dragged him clear of the cockpit. He took his place behind the wheel.

Stamping on the accelerator, William turned a hard right. The tank's wheels spun as he drove off, and the grass whipped against the vehicle's chassis.

At least fifteen of the twenty diseased had remained on the road. They headed for his friends. William hit the back of the pack. He mowed down at least half of them, the tank bouncing as it dragged their corpses beneath the wheels.

The decimated horde behind him, William raced to his friends. Karl had dragged them clear of the wreck. Katrina and Rayne were standing on either side of Matthew, supporting his weight from where one of his legs hung limp.

William halted. Karl whacked the tank's button to open the door. Rayne and Katrina dragged Matthew inside with them. William threw the driver's and the diseased's dead bodies out.

Karl fired down the hill at the remaining diseased, but more came at them from all sides.

Back at the wheel, William used his sleeve to rub the driver's brains from his line of sight. He called out through the open door, "We're ready to leave, Karl."

At the *whoosh* of the closing door, William stamped on the accelerator. They flew up the hill, back towards the hunting party.

"How's Matthew, Rayne?"

"Okay. I think."

"Good."

Karl patted William's shoulder. "Good work, man."

William smiled despite himself. Karl might be a prick, but they had worked well together.

"So," Rayne called from the back, "do either of you shits want to tell me what the shitting hell is going on?"

It only took for Karl's slight snort of laughter to set William off.

"You think this is funny?"

"No." William shook his head. "Sorry, Rayne, it's really not." He rocked where he sat, working some of the aches from his body.

"Then why are you laughing?"

All the while, Karl's eyes sparkled as he looked at William, daring him to giggle like a naughty schoolboy being reprimanded.

"Oh shit, Karl."

"Shitting shit?"

But William didn't smile this time. "The radio."

"Shit!"

"What?" Rayne said.

Karl grabbed the mic. "We shot the aerial when they drove away. We need to check it killed the radio."

"And if it didn't?"

"Then our cover's blown."

"*Eleanor's* cover."

"Maybe."

"Then what are you waiting for?"

"What if I get through to them?"

"If you do, then *they* already have. Just test it."

Karl winced, turned to Rayne in the back, and pressed the button.

"Nothing?" William swerved when he looked across at his passenger.

"No, it's dead."

"Yes!" He punched the air. "I don't know what we would have done had those shitting shitbags gotten away."

Once again, William and Karl broke into laughter.

CHAPTER 30

"And the radio's definitely dead?"

For the third time on their drive back, Karl held up the mic and pressed the button on the side. He twisted dials and flicked switches. "As a decapitated diseased."

Although William kept his eyes on the road so he had no visual reference, the tank's atmosphere eased from where Rayne must have relaxed. She spoke in a softer tone. "And you did all that to make sure they couldn't tell the blocks about Eleanor?"

Karl shrugged. "And our plan to attack."

"Which Hawk told them all about when he did his debrief before the hunt?"

"Go easy on Hawk. He didn't know." William rolled his shoulders, sending stabbing pains through his back.

"Hm."

"He didn't know they were there, Rayne."

"Isn't that something to be concerned about?"

"None of us knew until it was too late. Now hang on." William eased them off the road and back to the hunting party. Many stood on a nearby rock. He stopped and led the way in climbing from the turret hole. He hopped across from the tank's roof.

Pulling a tight-lipped smile, Matilda returned her attention to the vampire lookout tower in the meadow. She reached back and took his hand. The rookies and their mentor still clung to the rickety structure, which swayed more than ever. A hundred or more diseased gathered around them.

William turned back to his tank, but Karl thrust out an arm to stop him. "There's nothing you can do."

"But I have to try."

It only took another shake of his head for Karl to help William see reason. He didn't have to try. He wouldn't make it. And what could he do differently to the tank already heading over to the rookies? "Who's driving that?"

"Hawk," Matilda said.

"What took him so long?"

"He had to run to the closest tank."

He would have had one much closer had William and Karl not taken it. Not that Matilda would ever say that. She didn't need to.

The snap of splintering wood forced a gasp from those on the rock.

The tower swayed as if mimicking the meadow.

Hawk's tank bounced and hopped. Flat out.

The tower leaned with more splitting and splintering snaps. Several onlookers clapped their hands to their mouths. One of them cried out as the tower fell.

The diseased screamed. The rookies screamed louder. The tower crushed many of the wild cretins. Many more swarmed the small hunting party. One by one, in quick succession, the four hunters stopped screaming for their lives.

Fifty feet from the toppled tower, Hawk slowed his tank and turned around.

A woman close to William had tears in her eyes. "What's he doing?"

Nick reached out to her. "It's too late for them. There's no point in him endangering himself."

The ferocity of her narrowed glare forced William back a step. She jabbed a finger at him. "You went after that tank when you could have helped." She led the exodus, the hunters returning to their tanks to go back to the blocks.

William flinched at Rayne resting her hand on his back. "You did the right thing."

"Then why does it feel so wrong?"

"Because neither choice was good. But only one was right. This way, you've prevented the information from reaching the tower blocks. Not only have you kept Eleanor safe, but you've given the several hundred of us who are going to war a much better chance of winning. It might not feel like it, but this is a victory."

CHAPTER 31

"One, two, three, weeee!" Despite her heavy heart, Gracie laughed as the small boy swung between them, kicking his legs and giggling. Olga beamed while holding his other hand, so distracted by his antics she paid little mind to the cots beside them. Paid them little mind, but still stayed as far from them as she could.

They paused at Ash's bedside. Rowan sat in the small plastic chair beside her. The pair beamed at the boy. They'd have their own soon. Completion in an incomplete world. Ash winked at him. "Hi, Wilf."

The boy let go of Gracie's and Olga's hands, snapped his heels together, and saluted. They laughed again.

"You going for a walk?"

Wilf watched her with wide eyes, hanging on her every word at the attention from an adult he didn't know very well. He nodded. "I am. With Auntie Olga and Uncle Gracie."

Rowan raised his eyebrows, and Gracie shrugged.

"We're going to play tootball." His own joke tickled him so much, he bent forward at the waist with his guffawing laugh.

"That should wear you out." Ash covered her mouth and whispered at Gracie, "I reckon he'll have a lot of energy. He's about the only kid sleeping in these cots who doesn't wake up a thousand times a night."

Olga winked. "You have all that to come."

"I know, right? And I'm sure Little Aggie will want to be awake as much as possible. Like their namesake, I'm certain they'll have wicked FOMO."

The silence threatened to hang between them until Wilf broke it. "We're going to leave Mummy and Daddy to have some time alone."

Ash smiled. "We all need a little rest, eh?"

A moment together before Gracie and Olga took Bear away from his family again. What if they didn't come back? But they couldn't do this without him.

While swinging from Olga's hand, Wilf nodded with his entire body.

Nudging Rowan, Ash gestured towards Olga. "At least we know we have a keen babysitter for when the time comes."

Making a cutting motion with her hand, Olga fake heaved. "As long as you don't ask me to change nappies."

"That's Rowan's job."

Rowan's face fell slack.

Ash flicked her head towards Bear and Tammy. "I saw you tying Bear's plait."

Gracie shrugged. "He needed it."

"He certainly did. You'll have to do mine soon."

"Sure thing."

"Before you leave?"

"Uh … We're going soo …" Gracie trailed off and raised her eyebrows. Wilf listened in. Did he know they were taking his daddy from him again? That they were risking all of their safety by bringing an injured Kira along too? What if they were making a terrible choice?

Ash kept a hold of her hand. "Maybe after."

"Yeah."

"Good luck."

Wilf, aided by Olga, turned pirouettes. Gracie swallowed past the lump in her throat. Would they bring this boy's dad back to him? She coughed to keep the warble from her voice. "Thanks. We'll take all the luck we can get."

~

The boy giggled as he and Olga chased a flat football around the sports hall. Olga made monster noises and ran a step too slow to catch him.

She'd never seen her this carefree. Gracie waited as long as she could, the night creeping in. Nature's ticking clock. She clapped her hands, the crack of the contact whipping through the room. The lump had remained in her throat from earlier. It took the power from her raised voice. "Come on, you two. Let's get going."

~

Kira sat up in bed when they entered, Wilf coming in with the force of a natural disaster. She giggled at his chaos.

With a fake tut, Gracie rolled her eyes and smiled at the boy. "How are you doing?"

"A little sore still, but much better." Kira, dressed in a nightie, got out of bed. Yellow bruises smeared her leg like dirty grease, but she stood strong. She even jumped around with Wilf, holding her hands up like monster's claws and growling at him. She paused. "And how are you, little man?"

Wilf stood to attention and saluted her.

"How are your sit-ups coming along?"

The boy dropped and lay on his back. He grabbed his

hands behind his head and rolled around on the floor like a grub.

Holding her chin in a pinch, Kira nodded along with his effort. "*Very* impressive. It won't be long before you're as big and strong as Daddy."

The boy halted and glared at her from beneath his furrowed brow. "No one's as strong as Daddy."

Gracie's eyes itched. She turned her back on them. She blinked repeatedly like it might help.

"*Nearly* as strong as Daddy. How's that?"

He beamed at her. "*Nearly* as strong as Daddy."

∾

They returned to the maternity ward. To the screaming babies. To the stinking nappies. To the resting new mothers and to the anxious ones close to giving birth. Gracie walked through the room like her feet were too heavy. "We could do it without him?"

Wilf saluted Ash and Rowan on their way past.

Olga smiled at the pair before returning her attention to Gracie. "Can we?"

"Probably not."

"Daddy!" Wilf let go of Olga's hand and ran to his dad. He jumped into his arms, Bear wrapping him in a tight hug.

Her eyes itching again, Gracie sidled up to Tammy. "I'm sorry."

"It's not your fault." She smiled as Wilf got into bed with her.

"We could do it without him."

"Even if you could, and let's face it, you can't, we wouldn't want you to."

Bear sat straighter. Possessed with a zeal she'd not seen in him before. A noble acceptance of what lay ahead. An acceptance everyone in these blocks shared. In less than twenty-four hours, the blocks were going to war. Nothing would change that fact, and if they were to raise another Icarus tower, they needed to leave soon to get ahead of it.

"We'll bring him back to you. I prom—"

"Ah!" Tammy halted Gracie with her raised palm.

"We will."

She smiled through her tears. "I know you'll do all you can."

And what more could she promise? "Bear, we'll see you in the plaza in an hour, yeah?"

"Yep."

Gracie leaned over Tammy and hugged her. "We'll do our best."

"I know. And that's all I ask. Break a leg, yeah?"

"I'll tell Kira you said that." Gracie smiled despite herself. She and Olga left, Olga still walking as far from the cots as possible.

CHAPTER 32

Other than to make herself visible to Rayne on the walkways, Eleanor had remained in her room. She'd not eaten in days and made her solitary jug of water last the entire time. She took her final sip. If her throat got any drier, it'd crack like baked mud. She'd vomited, had an upset stomach, and had now fasted. Would it be enough to rid her system of what she'd eaten? And what would it take to remove the stain on her conscience?

But she'd not turned, and neither had anyone else. They'd all eaten from the same buffet. They'd all eaten diseased meat. She'd gotten this far without turning, so everything would be okay. "Right, Dad?"

His silence spoke volumes. How would he know? They were learning about the disease as they went.

On her feet, she paced the small room, gesticulating with her hands as she spoke. "The meat was awful. Vile. But it must have been sterilised when they boiled it." Bile crawled up her throat, and she swallowed it back. It burned with the meat's greasy and sickly-sweet flavour. "I've given it long enough to take effect. I have to assume I'll be okay, or take the risk at least. We're running out of time, Dad."

Entering her en-suite bathroom, she rested on her steel sink and leaned close to the mirror. Thick black bags hung like hammocks beneath her eyes. She turned on the tap and swallowed a dry gulp. "It might be drinkable, but should I trust them? Should I trust it?" She splashed some on her face, but kept her lips tight. Kept her dry tongue in her dry mouth. She'd drink later.

"You're right, Dad." The small frosted window made it hard to deny. "I have to get out of these blocks. And now is my best bet. While it's dark. I can't be here tomorrow."

Whoosh!

Eleanor spun towards her opening door. "What are *you* doing here?"

The ridiculous man with the ridiculous hair flashed his ridiculous grin at her as he wobbled in with his ridiculous gait. His rifle hung from its strap and rested against his ridiculously high waistline. People came in all shapes and sizes, but he wore his decadence with pride. A greedy and wasteful man, positively glowing with his own self-importance as he lorded it over a starving world. "You know, at first, I thought it was the meat making you talk. That you were just babbling some incoherent, fevered nonsense."

"What?"

Noris tapped his right ear. "I've been listening, sweetheart. For someone who seems to like solitude, you spend a lot of time talking. Daddy's dead, right? So your only friend's a ghost."

Eleanor stepped closer to the ridiculous man. He held his ground. At twice her size, what did he have to fear from this raving little lunatic?

"*Attack? Tomorrow?*" He gripped his chins in a contemplative pinch. "What on earth could that mean?" He hooked his thumb over his shoulder at the closed door. "I wonder if I should take it to the others to see if they can work out what you're talking about. What do you reckon? I wonder if they'll see what I've seen all along."

"And what have you seen?"

"That you're a snake." His smile stretched into a wide grin. "And your time's up!"

"And what if I told you to go fuck yourself?" She stepped closer.

The vile man beamed. He'd had her number from the very beginning.

She stepped closer still.

His right hand went to his gun.

Another step.

Just a few feet separated them.

He tightened his grip around the handle. Stretched his finger so it lay over the top of the trigger. He lifted the end a little. Come any closer and—

Eleanor dropped, snatched the canteen knife from her bedside table, and jumped up, leading with the blade. She wedged it into the bottom of his chin. She drove it so deep her hand slapped against his flesh, and she forced his face towards the ceiling, his tongue from his mouth, and his strength from his legs.

Gasping, his jaw flapping, Noris staggered left and spat blood.

She withdrew the knife and stabbed him again. In the stomach this time. Once, twice, three times, like she might burst him.

He gasped and gargled with every attack. Sent blood spraying away in a fine mist. But he somehow remained standing. Stumbling one way and the other, his gun swung from its strap while he clung to his neck wound with one hand and his stomach with the other. His blood soaked his clothes, and his wide eyes shone with a sudden clarity. He'd turned up to a knife fight with a gun.

Eleanor spun her knife around and gripped the handle so the blade poked from the side of her fist. She buried it into his temple. The diseased had taught her about the force it took to break through a skull. His cracked on her first try. She jumped aside as his legs went from beneath him.

Noris fell forwards. A dead weight. He slammed face-first into her wardrobe, rolled to the side, and whacked his head on her bedside table.

Eleanor stood panting over the corpse. Her pulse throbbed in her ears, and her head spun. Thirsty, hungry, and now covered in Noris' blood. "What shall I do with him, Dad? I can't leave him here."

She wiped her knife clean on the man. Dragged her sheet from her bed. She laid it over him and grunted with the effort of trying to lift him. But he was twice her size and three times her weight. "What the hell shall I do with him, Dad?"

CHAPTER 33

The best ideas always came in the shower. At least, that was what her dad used to say. She'd often find him dripping wet, a towel around his waist and a pen in his hand as he wrote some idea that would never go farther than the sparkle in his eyes and the ink marks on the sheet of paper. But he had a point. And while it might not be the best idea, it might just solve her problem. As long as she could get out of the blocks.

Showered, clean, and in a black, long-sleeved cocktail dress, Eleanor slipped on some flat shoes and hopped over Noris' corpse without looking at him. She landed on her toes, just on the other side of the ever-increasing pool of blood spreading out beneath the once white, now predominantly red, bedsheet. Her knife hidden up one sleeve, her tattoos hidden by the other, she filled her lungs and whacked the door's button.

Whoosh!

The hallway was as empty as ever. She'd always hated the carpets. They were a constant reminder of the red dye fed to the vampires to shame and oppress them. But at least it would cover up Noris' blood as it leaked beneath the door. Hide it should anyone throw a cursory glance down the corridor.

Whoosh!

The closing door rang through the block and up the stairwell, searching for any listening ears.

Eleanor stood statue still and held her breath. Waited for descending steps. Maybe someone knew Noris had come down here. Stan? He followed him everywhere, right? Did he already know Noris' hunch, or had the crude man kept it to himself?

"You're right, Dad. Too many what-ifs. How can I act based on assumptions? Just stick to the plan." She slipped her knife into the groove of one of the four screws holding the door button in place. She turned it several times, pinching the screw when it protruded far enough from the wall. She twisted it free with her fingers.

After removing the other three, Eleanor clung to them in her sweating grip. She pulled the door button away from the wall to reveal a mess of multicoloured wires. "Any ideas which one, Dad?"

"You're right. What does it matter?"

She ripped out several cables with a sharp tug. Her shoulders to her neck, she paused again. What if she'd triggered something else somewhere? Left evidence of her tampering by putting the power out somewhere she couldn't see? Or what if she'd opened all the doors on an abandoned floor?

Silence answered her anxiety.

She slipped the button back into place with shaking hands and slowly reattached it, one fiddly screw at a time.

The button secured, she looked up at the ceiling. "Please let this work." She closed her eyes and pressed the button.

She opened her eyes and tried again.

And again.

Other than the slight *clack* of the action, the button did nothing. The door wouldn't budge. After letting out a long sigh, Eleanor nodded to herself. At least something had gone well. Now she needed to get on a walkway so Rayne knew she'd survived another day. Then she had to find a way out of these hellish blocks where they ate diseased meat and turned navel-gazing into a full-time occupation.

~

She'd visited this spot more than any over the past few days. The top walkway in her block. As high as she could climb, and by being in the same place, it meant Rayne would easily find her.

The strong, cleansing wind had little impact. Where it could lighten many moods, and often did, nothing would change her mindset today. The dead man's essence clung to Eleanor like the fatty grease from a cooked corpse. It would take a bit more than fresh air to rid her of Noris. But he'd had it coming.

Eleanor blinked back her tears and wiped her eyes. It cleared her vision. A group of people were engaged in a meeting in the room at the walkway's other end. Many fixed on something or someone hidden from Eleanor's sight, but enough of them threw glances her way. Enough to have seen her. To have remembered her being there. To question why she'd come so close to a block meeting and not joined in. Did she have something to hide? Maybe they should check. See what's happening in her room. Find the dead body.

"Shit!"

Stan noticed her.

Walk away now and someone would follow. Most probably him.

"Fuck it." She marched towards the meeting like she

belonged. Shoulders back. Head held high. Fake it till you make it. Show these fuckers there's nothing to see here. Show them she belongs.

A man addressed the crowd. "So, we need a volunteer who will take a tank to the shining city and collect more supplies. They know we're coming, and they're waiting for us. It'll take a couple of days. Any volunteers?"

"I'll do it." Eleanor strode into the room with her hand raised.

The man addressing the crowd stood no taller than her. Rotund, he had scruffy hair clogged with grease. His mouth opened a little while he scanned the crowd for any other takers. He returned to her. "Uh …"

"Eleanor."

He laughed, as did several others. "I know your name, silly." The mirth left him. "Very good. I was just checking to see if we had any other volunteers. Someone more *capable*."

"Someone else who's survived in the wastelands on their own *without* a tank, you mean?"

His left eyebrow lifted. "Point taken." Yet he glanced over the crowd again. "Well, considering your experience, and in the absence of anyone else willing to go, we'll take you up on your offer."

"How gracious of you. Although, you should know that even if everyone volunteered, you wouldn't find anyone better to do the job."

"Well, they didn't. So it looks like there's no one to challenge your arrogance."

"Arrogance is when you don't understand your own capabilities. And while I accept it must be hard for you to see it in a young woman, what you're attacking right now is my confidence."

"We'll see."

Eleanor held her tongue. She'd pushed it far enough. Got

what she'd wanted. Goaded them into ejecting her from the blocks and hoping she'd fail. And she would. She'd never reach the shining city.

∼

THEY BRIDGED the gap in the walkway with the same strip of steel Eleanor had used to enter the blocks. About three feet wide and twenty feet long. It had supported her once. It would do so again. Diseased faces stared up from the meadow, waiting for her to fall. Others sprinted up the entrance ramp. Flat out, they charged with all they had. Even just a few weeks ago, this hellish image of determination would have stirred something in her. Bleeding eyes, clumsy gaits, slashing arms. But she'd met worse before they'd been a permanent fixture in her world, and if they were to take the shining city in the future, she had far worse to come. These poor creatures were victims. Sure, possessed with a hellish desire to inflict pain and suffering, but they didn't choose this life. People like Noris did.

Stretching a ladder from the pair of tanks parked across the ramp to the third solitary vehicle, Eleanor thrust her arms out to the sides for balance and stepped across a rung at a time. The diseased never gave up. Some jumped and swiped at the ladder. Some bit at the air, what remained of their teeth snapping together with a castanet *click!*

They'd removed the third tank's turret, giving Eleanor access via the hole in the top. She kneeled on the roof and peered in. You never knew with the fuckers in the blocks. At least forty of them watched from the safety of the plaza. But there were no diseased inside. Spinning around, she hung her legs into the tank and dropped into the steel vehicle.

Eleanor dropped into the cushioned seat and gripped the tank's steering wheel. She rested her finger's tip against the starter button and flinched. What if they'd rigged it to open the doors? If the power didn't work and they'd retracted the bridge? If the thing blew up for shits and giggles? If they knew about Noris? But the tank started, the headlights cutting through the night.

Exiting the ramp, Eleanor turned towards the shining city. She left the blocks behind, a super convoy parked in the elevated plaza's shadow. Had it always been there, or was it something they'd recently acquired? At least they hadn't asked her to drive that to pick up supplies.

Leaning back in her seat, she stared ahead into the night and cried again. Despite a lengthy shower, the warmth of Noris' spilled blood remained against her skin. His mutilated corpse flashed through her memory every time she blinked. She rubbed her sore eyes and stared into the darkness. The tyres hummed against the road with their usual monotonous tone. But it could have been much worse. She only had to drive far enough from the blocks to be out of sight. Then she'd turn around again. She'd return to William and the others with enough information to take the blocks. She'd be helping the vampires claim the life they deserved. In just a few weeks, she'd become a part of a community. Something she'd never had. And were her mum and dad still with her, they would have surely joined too. She wiped away her tears and smiled. "We're getting closer, Mum. Nearly there, Dad."

CHAPTER 34

William entered the meeting room last and held his hand up at those already sitting around the table. "Sorry to keep you waiting." He'd stopped to use the toilet. The same toilet Duncan had filled with the diseased who took Aggie. Same toilet, different block. But since that day, he'd stepped back after opening every door. Every time, it showed him what an idiot he'd been to not have adopted that process sooner.

Queen Bee and her mob were already around the top table. Matilda, Artan, and his lot back from the hunt. Even Hawk had joined them. He might have been the lead hunter and normally had little need or desire to be present at these meetings, but tomorrow night, whatever happened, they were going to war.

The only spare seat was beside Matilda. Matilda on one side and Karl with a K on the other. Of course he'd chosen to sit beside her. He smiled at his love and nodded at Karl. They'd been through too much together. So what if he liked Matilda? Could he blame him for that?

William rested his elbows on the cold table, linked his

fingers, and slowly scanned every face. They'd all watched him the entire time. "So, where are we at?"

Queen Bee cocked an eyebrow. "Waiting for you."

The prospect of war had hung over these blocks for days, but losing the rookies and their mentor had added a greater weight to the community's shoulders. It reminded everyone of their precarious existence. Many of the residents understood what had happened and the choice William and Karl had made. But some didn't. They reminded him of those they'd lost every chance they got. Jean, Bethan, and Craig. He'd had the three kids' names hollered at him so many times, they rang through his skull, filling the silence. And their mentor, a man named Salomon, had posthumously become everyone's best friend. But who was William to deny them their grief? Damn, he felt it as much as the next person. Had almost convinced himself he and Salomon went way back. He'd made the choice that had condemned them. But the consequences of letting the tank get back to the blocks would have been too great. Little consolation for those who grieved. "I have nothing."

Always beside Queen Bee, always ready to add her opinion, Katrina leaned on the table, mirroring William's posture. "Nothing?"

"What do you want from me? Since Eleanor's gone to the blocks, we've had to stay away. How can we get any information if we can't get close?"

Matilda scoffed. "It's not like we had much, anyway."

"Exactly. And until she returns—"

"*If* she returns." Artan wouldn't have been so forthcoming were Rayne in the room with them.

William shrugged. "I have nothing."

"But we have to attack tomorrow night."

"You think I don't know that? The best I can offer is we

find a way in through the food tube and take the blocks from the inside. Get in and improvise."

Queen Bee this time. "Improvise?"

"It's a shit plan when hundreds of people's lives depend on me. But it's all I have. If anyone else can do better, please don't be shy."

Dropping her focus to the large steel table, Queen Bee tapped it several times with the end of her nail before she looked up again. "So, what do I say in my broadcast?"

"The truth."

Slowly deflating with a sigh, Queen Bee scanned those around the table. Did anyone have anything better than their current plan?

Whoosh!

Flushed and out of breath, Rayne strode in. She looked at every person in turn before she stood aside to let Eleanor enter behind her.

Queen Bee nudged Katrina, who jumped up and offered Eleanor her seat.

"Are you okay?" Queen Bee said.

Eleanor took the seat with a nod and a polite smile. "I'm fine."

"They didn't suspect you?"

"Maybe a little, but I gave them no reason to suspect me further."

"And it wasn't hard getting out?"

"They asked for a volunteer to leave the blocks and go on an errand to the shining city. They're not expecting me back for a few days."

"So what did you find out?" The rest of the room turned to William. "Sorry. Eleanor, it's good to see you. Of course. And well done on getting out. But we have to make a plan and fast. Tell us everything you know."

CHAPTER 35

The gentle knock roused Eleanor from sleep. She groaned and stretched. The best night's rest she'd had in days.

They knocked again.

Closing her eyes, Eleanor let out a long sigh. She'd spent hours talking to William and the others. The best night's rest, but she could have done with a lot longer.

"Eleanor?" Rayne knocked and called again, "Eleanor?"

If she didn't reply, would Rayne leave her be?

Rayne knocked again. "I'm coming in, okay."

Whoosh!

"Didn't you hear me knock?"

"I did."

"Then why didn't you answer?"

"I've had a long night."

"*You've* had a long night? I've not slept all week because I've been worrying about you in those blocks." Rayne's lips tightened. "Why did you go without telling me?"

Eleanor sat up and held her throbbing head. She'd not had enough to eat or drink in days.

"That was not fucking cool, Eleanor."

"It must have been *so* hard for you."

Rayne stepped back a pace. "What?"

"Sitting here, eating Hawk's deer meat. Resting every night."

"I told you I didn't sleep."

"This isn't about you, Rayne."

"It never is, is it?"

"Do you know what I've been through? Were you even listening last night, or were you more focused on how it affected *you*?" Eleanor got out of bed. Dressed in just a nightshirt and underwear, she stepped up to Rayne. "You've not even asked me how I am. I did this for those poor bastards going to war tonight. Those people putting their lives on the line to help get control of the south so we don't have to live in fear."

"Like you know what that's like."

Eleanor jabbed her finger at Rayne and held it an inch from her face. "Don't you *fucking* dare! I can't help what I was born into, but I'm as committed to the cause as anyone. How dare you use that against me? I thought we were close. I trusted you."

Her face slackened, and Rayne lifted an apologetic hand. "I'm sorry. I've been so worried."

"And so you should have been. I was trapped in those blocks for days. Stalked by a buffoon of a man and his teenage sidekick, both of whom wanted me dead. I ate diseased meat thinking I was eating pork—"

Rayne clapped a hand to her mouth. "You didn't mention that."

"And my final act was to kill a man just so I could get out. I stabbed him so many times it took a ten-minute shower to get his blood off me. So I'm sorry you've had a few restless nights, but it's not been fun for me either."

"You ate diseased meat?"

"Just leave me alone, Rayne."

"But—"

Eleanor shoved her out into the hallway. "Leave me alone!" She whacked the button, shutting Rayne out with a *whoosh!*

CHAPTER 36

Knock, knock.

Eleanor rolled her eyes. Like a persistent parent, Rayne wouldn't let it go. When would she get the hint?

Knock, knock.

While biting her bottom lip hard, Eleanor thrust her middle finger at the closed door. She mouthed *fuck off!*

Whoosh!

She pulled her hand down and tucked it behind her back.

About three hours had passed since Rayne had last been in her room. Her face hung as slack now as it had then. The skinny, raven-haired woman entered carrying a tray holding a steaming bowl of broth and a glass of water.

Placing it on her bedside table, Rayne flashed her a weak smile. "It's vegetable soup. I figured you might be hungry."

Rubbing her flat stomach as she sat up, Eleanor snorted a mirthless laugh. "And I'm well off meat right now."

Now she'd penetrated enemy lines, Rayne sat on the corner of Eleanor's bed.

They stared at one another for a few seconds. Were it not

for the broth's spicy fragrance making her stomach rumble, Eleanor would have maintained it for longer. She spun from her bed, rested her feet on the cold steel floor, took a sip of water, and pulled the tray onto her lap. Rayne beamed as she watched her raise a spoonful to her lips.

"I'm sorry."

Eleanor slurped from the spoon. Even the very fist sip loosened her knot of hunger.

"I was worried." Rayne shifted, rocking the bed and sending some of Eleanor's broth slopping over the bowl's side. She stood up, sending more broth spilling onto the tray. Her hands behind her back, she paced the room like a caged dog. "I'm here to listen."

"For someone who's here to listen, you do a lot of talking."

"I want to shut up and hear you speak."

"You might want to, but does that mean you will?"

Rayne drew a breath in through her nose and nodded. "I will. How I reacted—"

"When you lost your shit?" Eleanor drank another salty spoonful.

"Yeah. That wasn't on. And you're right. I made it about me, and it's not. I was worried. I care about you."

"Funny way of showing it."

"But is it?"

An annoying parent. Exactly what her mum would have done. Eleanor slurped the next spoonful too soon. The hot liquid burned her throat on the way down.

"I'm here to listen *if* you want to talk?"

"You know what I'd really like?" Eleanor blew on the broth to cool it down. "I'd like to finish this and then go for a walk. This room's making me feel claustrophobic."

"Sure. I'll wait outside. You don't need me watching you eat."

They crossed walkway after walkway while Eleanor talked and Rayne listened. Properly listened. She winced when Eleanor talked about killing Noris. He had been onto her. Had she not acted, the blocks would have found out about their plans for war. She looked like she tried to hold on to her heave when Eleanor spoke about the infected meat. And that boiling it must have removed the infection, even if it did little for the taste. None of the residents looked ill. Iller. They all looked ill. Like they were lacking something. The way they dressed. The way they behaved. The dead glaze in their stares.

"You've earned a rest. The others think so too. They said they don't want you going back to the blocks with them tonight. And I'm going to stay here as well."

"The thought of going back so soon …" Eleanor knocked on the side of her head. "It's been running laps in my mind. I'll go back if they want me to."

Rayne held her hand. "They don't. You've done so much already."

"Okay. If I'm honest, I'm glad. I don't want to face those people again. That boiling vat of diseased. Stan. But I feel like I should do more."

"You've done enough. You're not going back."

Nodding as she walked, Eleanor straightened a little.

They descended a stairwell and reached the maternity ward. "How did we get here?"

"I brought us to see Ash and Rowan."

"They won't want to see me."

"Of course they will. I've been visiting them while you were away. Ranting about how you shouldn't have gone."

"And you want me to face a telling-off from them too?"

"They were on your side. Told me to trust that you knew

what you were doing. How you were helping more than most. Come on."

Beds lined either side of the large room. An old sports hall. They must have chosen it because of its wooden floor. It made it easier to keep warm than some of the other spaces. They'd blocked the doors leading to the walkways, leaving just a small space for ventilation. Eleanor loved babies, but twenty or more in a single room, no matter how large, stank almost as bad as a pile of rotting diseased.

"Ash still has a way to go." Rayne waved at the woman in the bed, Rowan beside her. "But she's one of the next mothers due to give birth, so she came up here early. She wanted to get a feel for the place. Get to know the other families." They approached the pair. "Maybe prepare a little for what's coming."

Ash laughed. "There ain't no preparing for this." She lay holding Rowan's hand. "But the time up here has shown me to expect utter carnage."

Rayne leaned on the bed and kissed Ash's cheek.

Rowan's smile forced Eleanor back a step. So natural and full. An alien gesture from this uptight man. "Thank you." His smile broadened. "You've sacrificed a lot. We appreciate it more than you know."

Eleanor pressed her lips tight and nodded. As much as Rayne had told her she could cry in public, it didn't mean she always should.

∼

Rayne, Ash, and Rowan talked while Eleanor listened. They talked about plans for the baby. If they'd remain in these blocks and for how long? What they'd call it. Aggie if it was a girl. And while they'd considered the same name were it a boy, they'd since changed their mind and would call him Ethan. They cried and laughed in equal measure, bouncing between hope and regret.

"Rayne! Eleanor!" Queen Bee marched in with Katrina beside her. Her loud call had startled several babies, their screams filling the room while scowling and exhausted parents fished them from their cribs.

The light shone off Queen Bee's bald head, and beamed a skeletal grin like she had no awareness of the impact of her entrance. She turned to Eleanor and Rayne. "I've been looking for you two."

"What's happened?" Rayne let go of Ash's hand.

"Will you come to the control room with us?"

"Is everything okay?"

"Yeah."

"You sure?"

Queen Bee shrugged. Pulled a face. "Yeah."

Kissing Ash, Rayne left, Eleanor nodding at the expecting pair as she followed. Her stomach churned, and her legs shook. What now?

∼

"Please, someone help me. I have no way out, and I don't know how long I'll last." The man's voice repeated on a loop. "Please, someone help me. I have—"

"You get the idea?" Queen Bee stood over the radio console and turned the volume down.

Rayne held her chin in a pinch. "That's a recording?"

"Obviously."

"From when?"

"An hour ago. Maybe two. And it wasn't the first message. They've put out a few calls."

Katrina pointed at Eleanor. "It's coming from her old blocks. Do you recognise the voice?"

Eleanor shook her head. "But we have to help them, right?"

"What if he's one of the block's residents?"

"*I'm* one of those blocks residents, Katrina."

"But you're different."

"How so?"

"You're a kid."

"A kid who'd kick your arse in the blink of an eye."

"I don't mean it like that." She winked at Eleanor. "And you wouldn't, by the way. But what I mean is you're a product of your environment. Raised by the regime. If this is a man rather than a boy, then he *is* the regime."

"My dad wasn't."

Rayne cut in, killing the argument before it gathered momentum. "It sounds like you've made a lot of assumptions. Have you done anything useful?"

"Like what, Rayne?"

"Like replied?"

Queen Bee threw her broad shoulders up with a shrug. "Radio silence, remember?"

Rayne took Eleanor's hand. "Want to check it out?"

"Yeah." Eleanor scowled at Katrina before nodding at Rayne. "Where's Matthew? He'll come with us."

Queen Bee scratched her bald head. "When will you go?"

"Tonight? When the others leave." Rayne glanced at Eleanor while she spoke, inviting her to interject should she disagree. "And don't tell them. They already have enough on their plate. We can drive up the ramp leading to the plaza and check it out. When we're close enough, we can use the local radio frequencies to make contact and maintain radio silence with the blocks farther south. And if we don't like what we see, we'll leave him there."

"Okay." Queen Bee shrugged at Katrina, who nodded along.

"Good." Rayne took Eleanor's hand and led her from the control room. "We'll find Matthew to see if he wants to come. Then we can get some more rest before we leave tonight."

CHAPTER 37

William gripped the handle above him and stood in the tank's gangway. Even if there had been space to sit, he would have remained on his feet. His stomach churned, alive with butterflies with razor-sharp wings. Rayne drove. She'd drop them off and head back to the blocks. Back to Eleanor, who'd already done more than enough to help the war effort.

Bending his legs at the knees, William dipped his head to peer through the front window, but the tank's interior lights polluted his view of the road ahead. Rayne had this. He blew out, his cheeks bulging. "After the time we spent in the meadow watching these blocks, it felt like this moment would never come."

The others all sat in silence. Hawk, as pallid as the rest of them, pulled a tight-lipped grimace that came close to a smile. A polite acknowledgement of his words. Nothing more. They had what they needed in Eleanor's plan. That didn't mean they had to like it.

"So we're all clear on the plan?"

Many of them nodded. Artan stared into the middle distance, lost in his own thoughts.

William told them anyway. Anything had to be better than the monotonous hum of the tank's tyres and the silent screaming of his own anxiety. "We get into the blocks, and we go straight for the control room—"

"Via the weapons storage."

He nodded at Artan. "Via the weapons storage. Then we need to open up the blocks. We'll stay in the control room so they can't go into lockdown again. When the super convoy brings our army in, we need to make sure they have total access. They'll be little use to us if they're locked outside in the plaza. I'd much rather it didn't end up with the seven of us against two hundred of them."

Hawk punched his palm with a *crack!* "Even if it does, we'll fuck them up. We'll show Duncan's mates who they've crossed. I can't wait to look them in the eye while they're begging for their lives."

After a quick glance at Matilda, William rested his hand on Hawk's shoulder. "You sure you're ready for this?"

"Just you try to fucking stop me."

"Hold on tight!" Rayne veered from the road and eased off the accelerator. The tank cut through the long grass as it bounced over the bumpy ground.

William stumbled with the slight jolt of her stopping, and the wind flooded the stuffy tank when she opened the side door.

William held back while the others exited. Hawk first. Then Karl, Knives, Matilda, Artan, and Nick. On his way out, Rayne grabbed his arm.

"What you did with chasing the tank to make sure it kept Eleanor safe …"

"I know."

"But I just wanted to say—"

"I know, Rayne. It's fine."

"I've been stressed. My behaviour wasn't on."

"Honestly, it's fine."

But she still clung on. Her eyes glistened. "Just make sure you come back, you prick."

"I love you too."

Rayne let go.

William landed on the damp ground with a squelch. The brow of the hill was twenty feet away. The eight locked-down tower blocks on the other side. The blocks had always looked quite empty when they'd visited to gather intel, but Eleanor had reported at least two hundred people inside. Were they mad? Seven of them against two hundred. But what choice did they have? They had to attack tonight, which meant they had to go with whatever plan seemed best. And as long as it worked, they'd have more than enough people to win this war. As long as it worked.

Just five feet before the brow of the hill, William and the others huddled around. He rubbed his cold head, Knives' tight shave leaving him exposed to the elements. "So we're all clear on the plan?"

Karl with a K rolled his eyes. "*Still* clear on it, William."

He pointed at the hill. "Once we go over, it's every man—"

"And woman!" Knives' blade glinted in the night.

"And woman for themselves. If we all focus on getting to the food tube and getting inside, then we'll be fine." The discontented diseased mob called to them. For some reason they favoured the other side of the blocks. It didn't matter why as long as they stayed there.

"Eleanor confirmed that if there's no spotlight, there won't be anyone on the plaza. We just need to make sure we stay quiet enough to not call them out."

"And you don't think the diseased will do that when they see us?" Karl said.

"They always make a lot of noise. Hopefully it won't be any different to that. Besides, I'm hopeful the diseased won't see us."

"Hopeful?"

"It'll work if we all make sure we're not seen and keep the noise down. So no guns, just knives. Gunfire will blow our cover. And you all have your saws?"

Nods passed around the group.

"We have to do the first part on our own, but if we're quiet and keep a low profile, we'll get inside and reach the control room. Our army will outnumber theirs, and the first they'll know of it is when we're storming their blocks." William reached into the middle, and the others covered his hand with theirs. "We can do this."

Patting Knives on the back, William stepped forwards with her. The best with a blade, it made sense to get her to the food tube first. If anyone had the skills to cut their way in … "You ready?"

"As I'll ever be."

William gave her a gentle shove, and she took off, vanishing from sight. Not only had they agreed Knives should go first, but she should also take the most direct route to the tube. The rest of them would take different paths down the hill. If any attracted diseased attention, they didn't want to blow it for the others.

Gripping a knife in one hand and his saw in the other, Artan went next, cutting left over the brow of the hill. Nick cut right. Hawk followed. Then Matilda. William let Karl go, and then he followed. The last one over, he cut right.

The food tube beneath the plaza was about two hundred feet away downhill. William's arms windmilled as he fought for balance across the soft and uneven ground.

The swish of the others' progress called out to him. The tall grass blocked his sight, and the dark night made sure. The diseased would be as blind, but not completely oblivious. They growled and howled. They snarled and grunted.

A silhouette broke from the meadow and sprinted across the flattened land beneath the plaza. The remains of the vampire camp popped and creaked with her progress, but the vast horde of diseased were on the other side of the blocks. Too far away to hear. For now.

As Artan broke from the meadow, Knives had already found a platform on which to stand and had buried her knife into the food tube's side. She plunged her saw in a second later.

The wet grass whipped William's face and dampened his clothes. Hawk, Matilda, and Nick ran beneath the plaza and joined the others. Knives stepped away, and Artan took over. A beast of a boy, he gripped the saw with both hands. With the force of a giant piston, he cut a wide slit in its side.

Diseased screeched over to William's left. He stumbled, but he remained on his feet. He continued to go with gravity down the hill. Just him and Karl remained in the tall grass.

Free of the meadow and into the shadowy space beneath the plaza, William ran over the collapsed vampire camp. Steel popped beneath his steps, and he jumped over the larger chunks of old debris. Hawk had taken Artan's place at the food tube. They'd nearly opened the slit wide enough.

Another screech behind. The diseased had something. Karl hadn't yet broken free from the meadow.

William tripped over a rock and fell onto a corrugated tin roof. It clattered like thunder, the acoustics beneath the plaza sending a jittering crash into the night.

Jumping up quicker than he'd gone down, William's mouth fell open. "Shit!"

They'd done a good job of not alerting the horde until that moment.

He stamped. "Shit!"

"We're in." Hawk stood back as Knives pulled the food tube's slit wide and climbed inside. Nick followed her. Artan, Hawk, and then Matilda. William smiled as his love vanished to safety.

The diseased came at them from the plaza's other side. Many fell crossing the treacherous ruins. But they didn't stay down long.

Back in the meadow, the grass swayed. The diseased behind them had found something. And Karl hadn't yet emerged.

Standing on the rock they'd all used, William gripped the thick plastic tube, pulled it wide, and poked his head in. It wobbled and swayed as the others climbed. Dirt and debris rained down on him. The noise swelled beneath the plaza. A hundred diseased. Two? Such a tightly packed crowd, they became a single entity. A wall of black.

"William!" Karl broke from the meadow and waved.

"Shit!" William paused. He wouldn't reach the food tube before the diseased. And there were too many in the meadow for him to turn back.

William poked his head into the food tube again. Each man and woman for themselves. They knew the rules. They'd all agreed. "Tilly!"

"William? What's up?"

"I love you."

"What are you doing?"

"I love you."

"I love you too. But …"

William pulled out of the food tube. He jumped from the rock as Karl sprinted towards him. Picking up a heavy lump of wood, he threw it to the left. It crashed against a sheet of corrugated tin. He ran after it, waving his hands, meeting the diseased's snarls with a cry of his own.

The fierce diseased had one major weakness: they were predictable. They ran after the most obvious target. They changed course and followed William, opening up a path for Karl to get to the food tube.

CHAPTER 38

Nearly a day had passed since they'd left the blocks. Gracie wanted to be out of the way before the others went to war, so they found somewhere safe and rested for the evening, one of them always on guard. They hunted for deer when they woke, ate well, and reached the next farm as evening closed in. The day grew darker as they descended the farm's deep staircase. By the time they'd reached the bottom stair, night peered down on them. The ominous drop had led them to another dimension. A dimension where the dead talked, and where her brother treated her with compassion.

In the previous tunnel, Bear had followed like a reluctant child, but he now kept pace, just a step or two behind Gracie and Kira. He and Olga walked side by side without the need for intervention.

The tedious march along the canted hallway sent a dull ache through Gracie's left hip and knee. Her gun swung with her progress, cultivating a sore spot from where it repeatedly slapped against her lower abdomen. Kira walked beside her, scanning their surroundings. She took in the weird images like they made sense. And to her, at least some of them did. But she must have seen nothing worth sharing.

They'd walked in silence for the past hour. The scuff of their weary steps called ahead of them as if searching for a response. A clue as to what they might encounter. Someone occasionally disturbed the quiet with a cough or sneeze, and Gracie added more than enough of her own sighs to the muted chorus. She frequently glanced back. Had they really done the right thing in separating Bear from his family? But would he have stayed in the blocks if they'd insisted?

"How do you think they're getting on?" Kira continued taking in their surroundings. "They should have reached the blocks by now, right?"

"Yeah." Gracie sighed. Again. "I can't help but feel like we're taking the easy option here. I feel so guilty."

Olga shook her head. "We have our job, and they have theirs."

Silence fell over them like a blanket until Bear cleared his throat, his words trembling. "I feel like I need to explain myself. With how I was in the last farm. I was reluctant at first, not because I disagreed with raising the Icarus tower—"

"We get it, Bear." Olga reached out to him. "You have a lot to lose."

"I have a lot to protect, too. We all need to do our bit to make sure we give the next generation something better than we have. Staying in the blocks won't do that. I was a lonely child." His humourless laugh chased their scuffing steps. Their sighs and sneezes. "I am going somewhere with this, trust me. My dad killed himself soon after they shut down my mum…"

Gracie frowned at him. "Shut down?"

Kira made a gesture of someone pressing a button.

"Damn."

"Dad couldn't cope. So he didn't."

"How old were you?"

"Six."

"Jeez. I'm so sorry." Gracie went to reach out to him, but pulled her hand back to her side and continued walking. "What did you do?"

"A family took me in and looked after me. They made their meals stretch a little farther. Made space for me in their small cluster of huts. They treated me like I belonged. Welcomed me with open arms."

"But?"

Gracie frowned at Olga.

Olga shrugged. "What? This feels like it's about to turn bad. Is it going to turn bad, Bear?"

His smile never made it to his eyes. "Turns out the dad had other reasons for getting me close. Turns out the shining city isn't the only place filled with beasts."

Even Kira's sunny demeanour faltered. She clapped a hand to her mouth. "What happened?"

"I saw what he had in mind, and I moved on before he could act."

Kira still held her mouth, muffling her words. "What about the rest of the family?"

"They all knew. It was their dark little secret. The truth behind their haunted glares. With me there, it gave him someone on which to focus his attention who wasn't them."

Olga's tut snapped through the tunnel. "How awful."

"It was all they knew. He had total control. Bringing me in was the only way they could think of to prevent it."

"You don't blame them?" Olga punched her open left hand with her balled right. "I would have killed them in their sleep."

"Blame doesn't get me anywhere. And by then, I'd lived with them for two years. I saw how much control he had over them all."

"So what did you do?"

"I was eight by that point. Old enough to survive. Although, barely sometimes. I remained in the camp. Safety in numbers and all that. But I kept to myself. I couldn't afford to be let down again. I pushed away anyone who got too close. Found people harder and harder to be around. Until I met Tammy. She accepted me for who I was. For the first time, I felt seen. Loved without condition."

"She seems like a good woman. And thanks for telling us this, but …" Olga turned her hand over the air.

"Where's this going?"

If Olga hadn't said it … Of course, Gracie was interested in what he told them. She wanted to get to know him better, but he'd said he wanted to explain himself …

"It's hard to have a sense of duty when you don't feel you're part of a community. My reluctance in the previous tunnel came from doing what I've always done in times of need. I was compelled to withdraw and look after me and mine. I couldn't see the bigger picture. Tammy showed me how things are different. How I'm not that vulnerable little boy anymore. That we're part of a supportive and caring community. So that's why I'm here. That's why I choose to be here. And that's why you shouldn't feel bad about separating me from my family. It's my choice. Okay?"

Gracie nodded along with the other two. But they'd gotten to know Wilf. To hear his laugh and see his funny little salute. Whatever their reasons, they'd separated Bear from his little boy. Nothing would change the fact.

"Wait!"

Kira's call froze Gracie mid-step. The other two halted.

Holding her chin in a pinch, Kira took in their surroundings, her eyes flitting from one symbol to the next.

Olga and Bear frowned.

Gracie stepped closer to Kira, but halted when the

woman showed her her palm. "Okay, fine. I'll stay here. But why have we stopped?"

"Fire!" Kira pointed to a crude carving. One amongst many on the busy walls.

"You're sure?" Olga said. "That *might* be a flame. It might be a flower. A drop of molten wax. A teardrop. A—"

"Give me your boot, Olga."

"What?"

Gracie nodded towards Kira. "Go on, Olga. Do it."

Tutting, Olga removed her left boot and threw it so it landed at Kira's feet. "There'd best be a good reason for this."

Kira tossed Olga's boot ahead of them. It spun through the air before landing the right way up with a *clop!*

Olga laughed. "Bet you couldn't do that agai—"

Whomp!

Highly concentrated flames burst from their surroundings like jet streams. The heat shoved Gracie back as they roasted the boot, disintegrating the laces and curling the leather.

Olga's mouth fell open. "That's my …"

Gracie wiped sweat from her brow and smiled at her.

"But that's my …"

Either choosing to ignore her or lost in reading the symbols, Kira approached the left wall. One carving depicted a pig unlike any Gracie had ever seen. Another image looked like an elephant with a giraffe's neck. A person with hands that hung to their feet. She pressed the symbol that looked like a small sun.

Thunk!

She smiled.

After a few seconds, and once again with Olga and Bear clearly as in the dark as her, Gracie raised an eyebrow. "You've turned it off?"

"Yep." Kira grinned and nodded.

"How do you know?"

"Olga, give me your boot."

"Fuck you."

"Olga." Gracie gestured towards Kira again. "Give her your boot. You look ridiculous wearing one, anyway."

Tutting and mumbling to herself, Olga removed her second boot and launched it at Kira, who jumped aside. The aggressive act did little to dampen her ever-hopeful disposition. She winked and saluted Olga. "Much obliged." She picked it up and launched it after the first. Like the first, it spun through the air and landed the right way up. *Clop.*

"Fuck me. It's like a hidden talent."

Gracie's shoulders lifted, but the fire blast never came.

"And that's it?" Olga threw her hands away from her body. They slapped back against her thighs. "We're ready?"

Kira nodded and showed Olga the way with her sweeping arm.

"And now you want me to go first? Look, I was happy to donate my boots ..."

Bear scoffed. "That's what happy looks like?"

Giggling, Gracie covered her mouth when Olga glared at her.

"You!" Olga, red-faced and tight-lipped, pointed at Kira. "You go if you're so confident."

"Fine."

Gracie fought the urge to grab Kira as she strode towards Olga's boots. One cremated, the other not. The girl half-turned away as she drew close to the spot that had triggered the trap. Like she could shield herself from being turned to ash. She remained tense even after she'd passed the spot and marched on down the tunnel. Bear shrugged and followed.

Gracie raised her eyebrows at Olga.

"Fuck you."

She nodded at her feet, her big toe pointing through a hole in her left sock.

"Fuck you!" Olga marched past Gracie and followed the others.

∼

Kira led them the rest of the way, triggering no traps. They followed the wonky tunnel as it bent around to the left and leaned to the right. They reached another circular control room with another computer console. This time, Bear typed in the password, loosing the deep *thunk* of another activating Icarus tower.

Gracie put her arm around Olga's shoulders. "Thanks for the boots." She couldn't contain her laugh this time, and from the way Bear and Kira joined in, they'd been holding onto their mirth too.

After a few seconds, where Olga stood like she might fight them all, she shrugged. "I suppose losing my boots is better than being cremated." She laughed with the rest of them.

CHAPTER 39

The weak moon did little for their visibility, and the tall grass kept the meadow's secrets. It strained Eleanor's eyes to pick out what lay ahead, but Rayne drove headlong into the night like she saw everything.

Thud!

And what Rayne couldn't see, she'd happily drive into. She sent the next canted diseased spinning away into the long grass.

Like those before it, the diseased proved to be little more than a punctuation to the friction hum of the tyres against the road. The monotonous tone was so jarringly dull, it quickly pulled Eleanor's heart rate down after the momentary spike from hitting another body.

Rayne clung to the wheel and stared through the windscreen with unblinking eyes. "Thanks for coming with us, Matthew. I know you wanted to go with the others."

He leaned forward from the back, poking his head between them. "I just feel bad about not helping."

"You are helping." The tank twitched from where Rayne

turned his way. "We needed someone to come with us, and you're one of the few people we'd choose."

"And seeing as your first five to ten choices had to go to the blocks or the farms ... Thanks, guys." Matthew clasped his hands in front of his chest. "You make me feel so special."

Eleanor smirked.

"But seriously," Matthew said, "the blocks were eerie when we left them. With over half the people gone, the place felt abandoned."

Eleanor's seat squeaked with her squirming. They closed in on the spot where her dad had crashed. She jumped at Matthew's hand on her shoulder. Rayne then reached across and laid her hand over her knee.

Eleanor let her tears flow.

A few hundred feet past the crash site, Eleanor wiped her face. "We're doing the right thing."

The tank twisted again with Rayne's movement. "In coming to help this man?"

"Yeah. It's what Dad would have done. He always helped where he could. Everyone deserves a chance. Some need more than one. He believed people were inherently good." Another wave of tears ran down her cheeks. "I used to think that was naïve, but Dad wasn't a fool. He was just a man with a big heart. He expected the very best from people and always allowed them the opportunity to deliver."

Still clinging to her shoulder, Matthew squeezed harder. "How are you feeling about returning to your old blocks?"

"Meh." Eleanor rose with her deep inhale and sank as she let it go again.

The prison wall loomed large up to their left. It ran along the hilltop like a spine. A silent and stoic protector. A demarcation of a rapidly fading world's boundaries. Now just an ugly scar to remind them of the segregation they were hoping to banish. Maybe one day, they'd celebrate it for the protection it provided.

Eleanor jumped at the radio's static hiss. She snatched up the microphone and twisted the dial.

"Please, someone help me. I have no way out, and I don't know how long I'll last." A dead tone. Someone who'd said it too many times. "It's not a recording." Eleanor lifted the mic so Rayne could see it.

The tank twitched again from where Rayne turned to her and nodded.

Eleanor pressed the talk button. "Hello?"

"Hello?" The man's tone lifted. "Who's that?"

"A friend." Eleanor shrugged at the others. Her dad might have believed in people's inherent goodness, but he'd still do his due diligence. "I hope."

"Who are you? Are you playing games?"

"No games." Eleanor shook her head and kept her voice soft. This man, whether they trusted him, was clearly distressed. "This isn't a nice world, friend. We heard your SOS, and we want to help. But we've waited until we're close enough to talk to you over a local signal. Can you switch too? A bit of privacy would be nice."

The line disconnected and reconnected. "Done. Who are you?"

"We want to help. And we really want to believe you are who you say you are. That we can trust you. But things are quite tense."

"No shit? There's a toppled tower here and diseased everywhere."

"Whose side are you on?"

The man paused. "No one's."

"Why the pause?"

"Why the question about sides?"

"It sounded to me like you didn't want to answer. Are you

hedging your bets to work out who you're talking to before you reveal your allegiances?"

"I'm just trying to stay alive. Can you blame me for that?"

"Trust is a hard thing to give in this new world."

"Have you come here to talk in riddles or to help? I genuinely don't know what you mean about sides. I used to live in the blocks. But I've been in the prison for a long time."

"As a prisoner?"

"A guard."

"Oh."

"That a problem?"

"I'm not sure, is it?"

"I'm not a zealot, if that's what you mean? What side should I be on?"

"I can't tell you that, friend."

The tank's front lifted when Rayne hit the ramp leading to the plaza. She aimed them at the seven blocks, the eighth lying in the meadow. She paused before the gap and turned them around, shunting diseased over the side with the slow manoeuvre.

"Is that you?"

Eleanor looked at Rayne, who shrugged.

"I'm coming down. Give me two minutes."

"Wait..."

Static responded.

Eleanor pressed the talk button a little harder, like it would help. "Hello?"

Matthew leaned between them again. "So what do we do now?"

Rayne stared down the ramp into the dark meadow. "We've come all this way..."

Eleanor nodded along. "And we could always drive off if we don't like the look of him."

"But what if he's one of them?" Matthew chewed on his

little finger's nail. "What if it's a mistake to give him a chance?"

Slotting the microphone back in its holder, Eleanor turned to him. "Like it was a mistake giving you a chance because of your affiliation with the coup? Like they gave me and my dad a chance despite us wearing the face of their oppressors? Do you think this man doesn't deserve that same grace?"

"Well…"

"I make that about a minute already." Rayne scanned the meadow ahead.

Eleanor fidgeted her way to two minutes. "Surely he was being ambitious saying he'd be here by now?"

"There's no radio equipment anywhere else?"

"Only in the control rooms." Eleanor turned around like she'd be able to see through the tank's steel chassis.

Rayne continued scowling out through the front window. "Then we give him longer."

Matthew clung to his rifle and paced in the back.

They'd been waiting for three minutes at least.

Four.

Rayne's chair squeaked as she leaned forwards. The light from the dials lit up her tired features. "Oh, fuck!"

Silhouettes crept from the meadow as if birthed from the long grass. Soldiers who'd been hiding in the darkness. Matthew shook his rifle. "They've been waiting for us. Baited us. I bet some of them have rocket launchers. There's no chance they're letting us leave. He's screwed us over."

Thud!

Something heavy hit the tank's roof.

It scrambled over the top.

It poked its head in through the turret hole.

Hairy.

Huge.

"Argh!" Matthew opened fire.

CHAPTER 40

Whatever happened, William needed a route back to the food tube. If he dragged them any farther away for Karl's sake, he wouldn't make it back himself. So he sprinted towards the diseased. The pack, a hundred or more strong, followed.

They charged as a massive, shadowy, wild-limbed entity. The wood cracked beneath their steps, and the tin roofs creaked and popped. Many fell and got trampled. Most got back up again.

Tens of diseased followed Karl from the meadow beneath the plaza. He weaved and hopped. His dexterity gave him an advantage over the murderous mob.

Six or seven front runners broke from the pack chasing William. He instinctively grabbed his gun, but let go a second later. Those above would hear. Diseased roars were nothing out of the ordinary. A fired gun, however … And what would he achieve? He'd run out of bullets well before they ran out of diseased.

William scooped up a rough brick from the ground and

launched it. He scored a direct hit, straight into the lead diseased's face. It fell. It tripped the beast directly behind.

Throwing another brick, William missed. He threw a third and slowed the next diseased. Five more took its place.

Karl tripped. The diseased on his tail closed in. He scrambled to his feet again, but they were close.

If William bought Karl any more time, he wouldn't make it back himself. He'd done what he could. He sprinted towards the food tube. He'd reach it first.

His cry echoing up the tube, William yelled as he pulled the rigid plastic wide and entered. Like being shit out in reverse, he braced against the rubbery colon's insides and climbed. The tight space threw his own quickened breaths back at him. The stench of rotten food was damn near intoxicating. But at least it had dried out from not being used.

The tube had a ribbed inside. They'd come here with a half-baked plan, and if they found the entire tube to be as smooth as the top section like in the block they'd left, it would have taken every inch of their strength to complete the climb. They'd be knackered before they attacked. But the raised rings on the inside worked as steps. Ledges that supported William's weight. Dragging himself higher, he climbed about ten feet up the tube.

Grunting and thrashing, Karl wriggled in through the slit. The light from outside made him easier to see as he pulled himself higher.

William stepped up to another ring. Several pairs of arms reached in after Karl, thrashing about like fighting snakes. They struck and swiped. Swayed and twisted. But Karl dragged his legs from their reach.

Karl rested. Panting, he looked down at the diseased arms.

"You good?"

Sweat beaded Karl's face. His mouth hung open as he

fought to get his breath back. He swallowed several times. William gulped, his own throat bone dry. He looked down again, more arms stretching through, the food tube swaying from the disturbance. One more gulp, his voice barely more than a croak, Karl nodded. "Thanks, man."

William resumed his climb.

"William?"

"Tilly?" She was at least twenty feet above them.

"Karl?"

"Yeah."

She laughed, but it quickly died. "Wait ... have either of you been ..."

"No." But William couldn't speak for Karl.

"No."

Matilda laughed again. "Thank the heavens. See you at the top."

CHAPTER 41

Like when they'd raised the other two towers, they exited the control room to find a recess in the left and right wall. Gracie rubbed Kira's back when she momentarily froze. "Come on, it'll be okay." She led them to the cart on the right and jumped into the driver's seat.

"Who made you the driver?"

Gracie tutted at Olga. "For a start, I'm wearing appropriate footwear."

Biting down on her bottom lip as if to add force to her gesture, Olga flipped Gracie the bird.

"And last time … you kind of … uh … well, cras—"

"That wasn't my fault."

"Uh …" Kira stopped their argument before it began. Something about the tone of her voice sent Gracie's stomach plummeting. She'd clearly gotten distracted on her way to the cart and now stood over to the left, studying the markings on the sandstone wall. Vehicles and buildings, animals and humanoids. Amongst the indecipherable scrawl sat a three-pronged handprint. A hoof-print. Like it belonged to something crossed between a human and a goat.

Gracie held her breath while Kira placed her hand into the shape. Her thumb slotted into the left of the three prongs, which jutted away from the other two at a forty-five-degree angle. The other two slots were in the shape of a V. She slipped her index and middle finger into one side, and her ring and small finger into the other.

Thunk!

Gracie thrust her arms out like she might fall. Her pulse raced. Olga's mouth hung open, and Bear shifted from one foot to the other as if the ground had grown hotter.

"We've had water, sand, and fire," Gracie said. "What now? A plague of fucking locusts?"

A landslide rumble rolled through the ground like the raising of an Icarus tower, but much closer.

A wall beside Kira pulled away to reveal a dark and tight tunnel.

Olga shook her head and stepped back. "Fuck no!"

The tunnel, too dark for Gracie's eyes to penetrate, stretched only a little wider than her shoulders and stood no more than five feet tall. Like everything else in this subterranean funhouse world, it leaned at an angle that stood in direct competition with every surrounding plane. Should Gracie enter it, she'd have to walk with a lean and a stoop. "I'm inclined to agree with Olga on this one."

"There's a first!"

"Now wait a minute." Kira raised her right index finger.

"No!" Olga pointed into the darkness. "I'm not waiting for anything. I'm not going in there. Fact!"

"You're not even curious where it leads?"

"Where does it lead?"

Kira paused. "I'm not sure."

"If you don't know, and you're the one who talks to the walls, then I'm even more reluctant to enter. What if it floods? Or fills with fire? Or there's more sand? A landslide?

An ice storm?" Betrayed by the warble in her voice, Olga lost focus.

Gracie stepped towards her, but Olga shuffled away.

"But it's here for a reason," Kira said.

"To kill curious idiots? Like every other trap in these fucking tunnels."

Folding her arms, Gracie nodded at Kira. "You have an idea where it leads, don't you?"

"It's a guess."

"From what you've shown us so far, I'd say an educated guess."

Olga tutted. "The operative word still being *guess*."

"Don't be shy, Kira. Tell us what you think."

"I think it leads to another control room." Her big brown eyes shifted from Gracie to Olga and then to Bear. Her curly black hair bounced with her moving head.

"That'll lift another Icarus tower?"

"I think so." Kira nodded. "I'm pretty sure it's a shortcut to the end of another tunnel."

Olga's breathing sped up. "But what if it's not? You've been right a couple of times—"

"*Every* time, Olga."

"It looks like a fucking tomb, *Gracie*. Besides"—she stepped closer to Bear—"we shouldn't take him away from his family for any longer than is necessary. We need to get back."

"Now that, I agree with."

"You were seriously considering going in there, Gracie?"

"If Kira's right, it could save us a lot of hassle."

"If she's wrong, we'll be marching to our deaths down a tunnel that's darker than the devil's arsehole."

"As opposed to the leisurely stroll we've been on whenever we've come down here? You're talking like our other choices for raising the next tower are ideal."

"Better the devil you know."

"Like yet another trap we've never encountered before? It was fire this time. Water the first time. San—"

"I *was* there, you know. Besides, Bear d—"

"I don't need anyone making choices for me, Olga." Until that moment, Bear had stood to the side, watching it all play out. The edges of his mouth turned down. "Kira's been correct so far. Even when it came to rescuing you from your sandy tomb."

Her chest rising with her deep inhale, Olga rubbed her face with both hands.

"Now, I get it must have been claustrophobic in there, and I can imagine this tunnel is a bit triggering."

"Don't patronise me, Bear."

"I don't mean to."

"Then what *do* you mean?"

"My point is, as Gracie said, if we're down here already, and if this cuts through to another tunnel, then why don't we take it? Save time in the long run. You're right, I don't want to be away from my family for any longer than is necessary. So if you're showing me a shortcut …"

Olga's cheeks bulged with her exhale. She fixed on Gracie. The one person who should have backed her up.

"It makes sense, Olga."

"It sounds like you three have decided." Olga turned from one to the other.

"We do this all together or not at all." Gracie waited for Kira and Bear to nod along with her. "If you're not okay with that tunnel, we'll find another way."

Olga's furrowed brow pressed down over her eyes. She rocked from side to side as if trying to spend the murderous energy pumping through her.

"I mean it, Olga."

"Fuck off, Gracie." Olga marched towards the tunnel and vanished into the darkness.

Kira followed her in, and Gracie remained outside with Bear. "You sure this is the right choice?"

"No. And I won't be until we see it to its conclusion. But, while I appreciate you looking out for my family, this is my choice. I'd ask to go back if that's what I wanted." Bear followed and paused just before the entrance. He saluted and looked exactly like Wilf.

Gracie scooped up her gun, which hung from the strap around her neck. She clung to it with both hands like it would help. She entered last. Into the dark and musty embrace of the gloomy tunnel. Towards an end they couldn't see, in the hope they'd find another Icarus tower. But if these tunnels had proven anything, they'd proven the wrong choice could be fatal.

CHAPTER 42

A combination of the beast's quick movement and Matthew's poor aim meant the monster got away. It pulled its head from the hatch as Matthew's ricocheting bullets sparked off the inside of the tank.

Still screaming, Matthew charged after the monster, but Eleanor reached back from her seat and caught him, gripping a handful of shirt. "Wait!" She spun him around and pointed out the front window. "Look!"

Breathing heavily, Matthew ducked to get a better view down the ramp. "It's not an ambush?"

"They're diseased." Eleanor slipped from her seat, putting herself between Matthew and the hatch. "Now wait there, and put that gun down." She stepped closer to the hole leading outside. "Hello? Are you still up there?"

The monster of a man banged his fist against the tank's roof with a *boom!*

"I'm sorry. My friend got spooked. Thought this was an ambush. Are you okay?"

The man banged again.

"Am I safe to poke my head from the hatch?"

Once more, the man turned the tank into a drum with another heavy whack.

The diseased's yells grew louder when she poked her head out into the night. A monster of a man, he hunched close to the hole like a bear waiting to catch a fish. Broad shouldered and stocky. Farmer strong. He had a thick black beard and messy hair. But for all his rough edges, his brown eyes were soft. Kind. Fearful. Eleanor reached out to him, and he shuffled back. "I'm Eleanor."

His enormous paw enveloped hers. In that moment, if he'd wanted to, he could have ripped her arm from its socket, but he had a gentle touch.

The first of the diseased attacked the tank's chassis. Some slapped it. Some ran into it. Others kicked out. Eleanor's stomach churned, and she swallowed like she might vomit again. The fatty essence of mealtimes in the blocks flooded her senses. Clogged her nose. But she shook her head like she could discard the experience. "Do you want to come in?"

The man glanced down as if he knew exactly where Matthew stood.

"He won't shoot again." Eleanor pointed at the diseased breaking from the meadow. Spawned from the long grass. "Like I said, when we saw them, we thought we'd been ambushed. Like I said to you on the radio, there are sides, and we're at war. Everyone's a little jittery right now." Eleanor pulled back inside and put her arm across Matthew, easing him back a step.

"Jeez!" Rayne's mouth fell open as the monstrous man slid into the tank. Not only did he fill the space, but he wore the uniform of a prison guard. "You're a big one, aren't ya?"

The man dropped his gaze.

"I suppose you've heard that a lot?"

The man rolled his eyes. "And it's like those who tell me think I don't know."

"Point taken. Sorry."

The man dipped a half-nod.

"Now, hold onto something!" Rayne stamped on the accelerator, sending the tank lurching forwards into the diseased mob. They yielded and made for a bumpy ride. Yet the ones from the meadow still ran straight at them. Like they backed themselves to win this fight.

The tank's tyres hummed against the concrete. The man and Matthew stood as far away from one another as they could.

"Put your rifle down."

Matthew leaned closer to Eleanor. "Huh?"

"Your rifle. Put it down."

Lifting the strap over his head, Matthew went to put his rifle on the tank's passenger seat, but Eleanor took it from him and laid it on the bench, closer to the man than Matthew.

Lingering on the weapon for a few seconds, the man coughed to clear his throat. His baritone boom went off like a fired cannon. "Thank you for coming for me. And for explaining about the war. It makes sense why you're so …" He glanced at Matthew again. "Jumpy."

The mood between the two had stabilised, so Eleanor stepped between them to keep it that way. "We're at war with those who used to run the tower blocks."

The large man scratched his head as he looked her up and down. "Forgive me, but aren't you one of th—"

"Yeah. I was never on board with their oppressive regime. With how they treated the v …"

"Just say it." Rayne slammed into another diseased.

"Vampires."

The man's brown hair shook with his shaking head. "Me either."

"They're being overthrown tonight. A large chunk of

them, at least. If we're successful, it'll take us one step closer to winning this war. But we still have to take the shining city."

"Something similar's happened with the prison. The old regime has gone."

"Louis?"

"You saw the footage?"

Eleanor rolled her eyes. "Who didn't? So you understand why I asked about sides?"

The man nodded.

"And …"

"Didn't I just make it clear? I hate any form of oppression. Control." His words caught in his throat, and he coughed to clear them. "Intolerance. A lot's happened to me in my life. I know it's never as simple as good guys and bad guys. Black and white. But I also understand we have to pick what we stand for in times of war. Seeing how they ran the prison has made me realise I was born into the wrong side. And seeing as you're offering me a choice. And if you'll allow it, I choose to be on the side of the revolution."

Again, Eleanor offered him her hand. "In that case, I'm pleased to meet you. I'm Eleanor."

For the first time since they'd met him, he smiled. He took her hand and dipped his massive head. "Pleased to meet you too, Eleanor. I'm Ralph."

CHAPTER 43

Every part of William's body trembled, and his clothes clung to his sweating body. He reached out with one hand and caught the food tube's entrance, or exit in their case. He grabbed it with his other hand and pulled himself out. The reverse shit completed, he flopped onto the steel floor, falling on top of his rifle. Matilda helped him stand on shaking legs and pulled him close. They both carried a tang of sweat and rotting food. But they'd made it. All of them.

Karl smiled as he exited the tube. The climb had been nothing to him. The diseased screeched and screamed below. They were furious, but many had lost their zeal. Had forgotten the cause of their irritation.

Although the others gathered around smiling, Karl winked at Matilda. "Were you worried about me?"

"Of course."

"Fucking hell."

William's response stopped them all dead. He lowered his voice. "Give it a rest, will ya?"

"What?" Karl laid a hand against his chest.

"Stop being a creep."

"I … I'm not sure what you're talking about, William."

"You clearly fancy her."

"Who?"

"Just stop it, Karl. Don't make me regret helping you out down there."

Karl's mouth fell open, and he threw his arms out in an exaggerated shrug. William left him where he stood, and the rest of the room followed. If he'd been out of line in how he just spoke to Karl, someone would have pulled him up on it. Their silence spoke volumes. But would Karl hear it? He pressed the door's button, the *whoosh* of automation calling along the quiet corridor.

The blood-red carpet softened their steps, but the dim lighting created shadows in every corner and crevice, made worse by the shutter blocking the only window at the end. "We still going with the plan?" William pointed up. "Three floors above us, right? Third room on the left?"

Knives nodded. She turned back to the others in case any disagreed. None did. And if they felt anything like William, the sooner they got through this place, the better.

"And don't eat the meat." Artan screwed up his face.

Nick covered his mouth, his words muffled. "You think Eleanor really ate diseased?"

"I think she thinks she did."

"And boiling it removes the infection?"

Artan shrugged. "To be honest, I'll die happy if I never find out the answer to that question."

When no one stepped up, William took the lead. The carpet muted their progress, but he still walked on tiptoes. They needed to be ready to fight. Plan for the worst and hope for the best. And with two hundred residents or more, the worst could get pretty fucking bad pretty fucking fast.

They entered the stairwell, passing beneath a camera

pointing back down the hallway. Deactivated, according to Eleanor.

Even darker on the stairs, William strained his ears to the point where he could hear the whine of electricity running through the place.

They climbed the stairs with little more than the scuff of an occasional step and the slap of a slightly heavy foot.

William relaxed a little to be leading them down another carpeted hallway.

He passed the first room on the left and then the second.

Whoosh!

William spun around, his gun raised.

Nick stood before the open door. The second room on the left. They'd packed it with furniture. It looked like they'd had a clear-out in another part of the block and didn't know where to put it. Nick winced. "This isn't the right room, is it?"

"Does it look like the right room?"

The door automatically closed. Nick dropped his head. "Sorry."

William tutted. "Third floor up, *third* room on the left."

His head still lowered, Nick muttered to the floor, "Sorry."

They waited. They listened. With their eyes and their ears. Many of them looking up at the ceiling as if it would somehow help them hear better.

William waited for them all to look at him and nod. One after the other. Clear of guards. As far as they could tell. At the next door along, the third on the left, like Eleanor had said, he pressed the button, and the door opened.

Whoosh!

The room contained about twenty metal crates. William smiled as he entered, the others following him in.

The crates were about four feet wide and two feet deep.

William lifted one from the top of the stack and placed it on the floor. He waited for Karl, who still wouldn't look at him, to come in last before he undid the catches around the lid and lifted it clear.

"What the …?" Hawk leaned over the box like a different angle would change what he saw. "Didn't Eleanor say this is where they kept the weapons?"

"That's what she said." William grabbed another steel box, but froze.

Whoosh!

Artan kicked the empty crate towards the door. It spun and slid, the closing door pinning it against the frame. It bent from the door's force.

Artan shoved Nick. "Get out. Now!"

He grabbed his sister and sent her out next. The crate buckled further as she stepped over it.

Before anyone else could break from the room, Artan slipped into the gap. He pressed his back to the doorframe and pushed with the sole of his boot against the closing door. He bared his teeth, and his leg shook. "I can't hold it much longer."

Knives kicked the crate out into the hall and ducked beneath his leg. Hawk and Karl followed. William left last. On the other side, he reached out to Artan.

The boy ignored his gesture and yelled. His leg bent and shook.

William squirmed where he stood. Waited for the pop of Artan's kneecap.

Artan shrieked. The door slammed shut across his lower stomach and hip, shattering bones and pinning him in place. His gun hung from his leaning form like a trinket from a tree branch.

"Artan!" Matilda grabbed his face with both hands. "Artan, are you okay?"

William slipped his fingers into the inch-wide gap between the frame and the door and pulled. Nick joined him lower down, but the door wouldn't budge.

Artan sprayed blood as he spoke. "It's a trap."

"What?"

"They've fucked us, Matilda. They've set this up. They've …" His eyes rolled, and his face turned beetroot. "They've …"

"Just hang on, Artan. Please." Matilda squeezed his face, puckering his lips with the force of her desperation.

He regained consciousness. "Stand back."

"What?"

"Stand back, Matilda." Blood cascaded down his chin. "I have a plan."

But Matilda remained still.

Despite Karl, Knives, and Hawk joining them on the door, they'd not opened it any wider. They'd only managed to delay the door cutting Artan in two like a guillotine. It would win, the force of the door's mechanism more than a match for William and the others. And when it closed, it would take every one of their fingers. "Let go on three."

The others nodded at William.

"No!" Matilda stamped her foot. "Hold on."

"We can't overpower the door, Tilly."

"You have to try."

"We have!" Knives said. "William's right."

"No!"

"On three?"

The others nodded at William.

"One. Two. Three."

William, Hawk, Knives, and Karl let go of the door.

Nick clung on. He fixed on Artan and cried out before he also let go, the door cutting into Artan as it closed further. They'd lost him the second he'd wedged himself in the door frame. Their efforts had only delayed the inevitable.

Piss stained Artan's trousers, and blood bubbled on his lips. "I love you."

Nick mouthed it back, his words abandoning him.

Artan turned to Matilda. "I'm sorry. I was …" His head rolled like he'd lost the strength to support it. "I was looking forward to meeting my niece or nephew."

She loosed a sound like something inside her broke. In a world filled with grief, she let go of something so profound she might have lost it forever.

With clumsy hands, Artan dragged his gun around and placed the barrel beneath his chin while looking at his sister.

"This was your plan?" Matilda turned away and leaned into William.

Artan pulled the trigger, spraying the ceiling with blood and brain matter.

As he stood there, hugging his love, Artan's sister, William stared at the now sagging form of the boy he'd known since birth. The fierce boy who'd survived so much. Who'd murdered a man who deserved it and was prepared to face eternal punishment for the sake of his family. Resilient, and now just a limp and broken body leaking blood and piss in a deserted hallway. His resting place a loveless steel block because they had no time for anything else. William clung onto Matilda as hard as she clung onto him, and with every other person along that hallway, he wept for the loss of their humble hero.

CHAPTER 44

The new tunnel forced Gracie to walk with both a stoop and a lean. At the back of the line, she fought to match Olga's pace while striding into complete darkness. Her friends' steps were her only guide. Those and Olga's occasional swear as she whacked another part of herself on the walls.

Gracie's shoulders scraped the sandstone. She adjusted her position as best she could. When both shoulders scraped simultaneously, she momentarily paused. But her friends kept moving, determined to wedge themselves into this tunnel like corks into bottles.

The ceiling dropped lower, forcing Gracie's head down like an abuser. The back of her neck ached, and her heart beat harder in her tight chest. "You all right up there, Olga?"

The tunnel's twists and turns deadened Olga's reply. "Just you worry about you."

She was. Gracie sped up. What if the path forked ahead? What if they went one way and she another? If she fell too far behind, she could end up wandering these tunnels in solitude for days. Maybe she should have backed Olga. It must have been awful to lie in that small space while the sand fell outside. To accept the only way out would be suffocation or your own gun wedged beneath your chin. She tilted her gun upwards, the barrel scraping the left wall.

Jump!

"Ah!" Gracie whacked her head on the tunnel's roof.

"Gracie?"

"I'm fine."

"You don't sound it."

"Sorry. Got a fright, is all."

"That I can understand."

"Are *you* okay, Olga?" She kept moving. Closing the distance between them.

"You've already asked me that."

"But are you?"

"I'll be better when we're out of here."

"Me too."

Jump!

This time, Aus' face appeared in her mind's eye. The old Aus. The cruelty of a brother who kicked her when she was down. Who dared her to jump when he knew she'd whack her head. Jump hard enough and she'd crack open her skull. Do the world a favour.

Jump!

She clenched her jaw to bite back her response. Aus could go fuck himself. He'd haunted her while he was alive. No way would she give him that same power in death.

A deep rumbling shook the ground. Gracie thrust out her arms, grazing the backs of her hands on the rough walls. "Have you just activated something, Kira?"

"No."

"Anyone else know what's going on?"

Splitting and cracking like shattering ice called from the tunnel they'd left behind. The dry scrape of shifting rock.

Whomp!

Gracie spun around. A wave of dust crashed into her. It burned her eyes and instantly clogged her airways. She coughed and spluttered.

"Gracie?"

Gracie fell to her knees. The narrow tunnel forced her to hold her arms at her sides. She leaned forward at the waist and loosed a series of hacking barks. Each one burned her throat like she'd inhaled glass. Her nose and eyes ran.

"Gracie?" Olga came closer.

Wheezing and coughing, Gracie reached towards her friend. She swallowed several dry gulps and gagged on the grit.

White light flashed through Gracie's vision as Olga kneed her in the side of the head and toppled over her. "Gracie, where are you?" She scrambled back around and grabbed her arm. "Gracie, are you okay?"

Gracie wheezed. "I'm fine."

"Thank the heavens. I thought the worst."

"I'm all right." Her tight throat strangled her words. "What about you? Are you okay?"

"Yea—no, not really." She laughed. "This is a bit triggering."

Fumbling in the darkness, Gracie found Olga's shoulders and pulled her in for a hug. Her short friend trembled in her arms.

Olga's laugh lacked humour. "But what's the point of being worried? It's not like we have an exit. We're all in now, eh?"

"It certainly looks that way."

"*Looks?*"

Gracie snorted. "Seems. Sounds. Smells." She coughed, turned away from Olga, and spat dust onto the floor. "Bear? Kira?" She coughed again.

"Yeah?"

"Yep?"

"You both all right?"

"Yeah."

"Yep."

Bracing against the close walls, Gracie took Olga's hand and stood up again. Even when they were back on their feet, Olga still clung on.

Kira called back, "Are you two ready to keep going?"

Olga said, "Define ready?"

"We're fine, Kira." Gracie pulled Olga along with her, reaching out ahead to find where the tunnel bent as she followed their friends' shuffling steps.

"Ew!"

Olga froze, pulling Gracie to a halt like a stubborn horse. "You okay, Kira?"

"Yeah. It's squelchy down here."

Gracie's neck ached more than ever. Her temples throbbed, and her thighs burned from maintaining the stoop. "*Squelchy?*"

"Squelchy."

"But passable?"

"So far."

Leading Olga on again, Gracie winced as the sandstone walls changed from dry to moist and slick. She kept going, even when her steps sank like she was walking on a damp sponge. Even when cold drops fell on her head and ran down the back of her neck.

Olga panted behind her. Her panic was dragging her under. Gracie squeezed her hand harder. "Everything's okay. We're going to be okay."

"How do you know?"

Jump!

Gracie flinched.

"What?" Olga's single syllable ran away from her. "What is it?"

"Nothing. Just a particularly slimy part." The slimiest. If she could bring her brother back from the dead, she'd kill him all over again.

Olga's words wavered. "I don't like it down here, Gracie."

"Kira, how ar—" Gracie heaved and pressed her free hand to the back of her nose. Rotting meat and soured milk all in one. "What the fuck is that smell?"

Olga retched behind her, and Gracie pulled her on. They could only go forwards. She ducked lower with every squelching step. The lubricated walls eased their tight passage. Even if it did coat them in the rancid slime. If it got them out of there ...

An exercise in managing panic. They'd only get out by going forwards. Even then, there were no guarantees. A tightening dread crawled up through Gracie. It gripped her dust-filled lungs tighter than Olga clung to her hand. But they had to keep going.

Jump!

Clang! Clang! Clang!

The sound rang through the tunnel like a gargantuan hammer clattering into steel.

Clang! Clang! Clang!

Thunk!

Kira and Bear screamed.

"What's happening?" Olga's shrill cry hurt Gracie's ears. "What's happening, Gracie?"

Clang! Clang! Clang!

It drew closer. Fighting to keep her own breaths even, Gracie spoke slow and deliberate words. "I don't know. Kira?"

Her voice echoed through the tunnel, searching for a reply.

"Bear?"

Olga said, "Where have they gone?"

Clang! Clang! Clang!

Jump!

"What do we do, Gracie?"

Clang! Clang! Clang!

The drops from the ceiling turned into a thick ooze. A snotty grease. It landed on Gracie's head and coated her hair.

Clang! Clang! Clang!

Small stones rained down on them like the hammering blows were working them loose.

Jump!

"Go away!"

"Me?"

"No, Olga. Not you."

"Then who?"

Gracie took another step, and were it not for Olga holding onto her like an anchor, she would have fallen down the hole. She jumped back. "There's no floor."

"No floor?"

"A hole, Olga."

Jump!

"That's where Bear and Kira have gone?"

"That's my guess."

"Then we follow?"

"Unless you have a better option?"

Olga whimpered.

Jump!

Gracie stepped forwards again and fell several feet. She landed hard, the rocky ground jarring her hip. The ground slick with slime and angled like a slide, she shot into the darkness. Olga screamed behind her.

Clattering through a hatch, Gracie fell again, this time about ten feet. She landed on rough sandstone. "Oomph!"

She rolled aside, the hatch swinging open and shut again as it birthed Olga, who landed where she'd been.

The weak light stung her burning eyes. She blinked, and her vision cleared. Kira and Bear stood over her, their faces streaked with red. "What happened?"

"It's not blood." Kira wiped her face. "We think it's some kind of iron ore."

Olga stood up first and wiped herself down. She turned on the spot. "There's no way out?"

They were in a small, circular, windowless dungeon. Images similar to those in the tunnels above scored the sandstone walls. The cell stretched ten feet from wall to wall. Their only light came from a round glass semi-sphere embedded in the ceiling. It gave off a dull yellow glow, like it didn't have long left.

Taking Olga's hand, Gracie stood up next and hugged her friend. "I'm sorry. You were right. Entering the tunnel was the wrong choice."

"I wasn't right. I was scared. And that's no fit state in which to decide. We followed what we believed to be the best path."

Gracie sighed. "And we were wrong."

CHAPTER 45

William took Matilda's hand to drag her away, but she held firm and stared through unblinking eyes at her brother's mangled corpse.

He pulled again, but Matilda snapped away from him. She went to Artan. The bullets had blown a jagged hole in the top of his head, exposing his mulched brain. She lifted one of his limp arms and tugged.

"Matilda." William rubbed her back.

She spun around. "Fuck off!" Wild like a diseased, her face as hateful.

"But he's gone."

"We don't give up on anyone!"

"He's dead, Matilda."

She charged and hammered her fists against William's chest. Turning his face away from her attack, he pulled her in tight and clung on.

Tense, she shivered and twisted, but her voice turned febrile. "We don't leave anyone behind."

"We have no choice, Tilly. What else can we do?"

Her face buckled. She threw a weak arm towards her dead brother. "But look at him, William."

Choked by the lump in his throat, William's eyes burned. He gulped, but he still only managed a croak. "I know." The once strong boy. Someone who'd had his back time and again. Now weak and broken by the force of the closing door. Immobilised. Invalidated. Defunct. "Believe me, I wish I could say something else, but there's nothing we can do."

The others waited with them. Knives comforted Nick while Karl and Hawk had walked a few feet closer to the stairwell.

"You hear that?" Karl pointed at the ceiling. Something on a floor above.

The diseased scream lifted the hairs on the back of William's neck.

Knives drew a pair of blades. The weak light glinted off their polished and sharpened steel. "You think they're recordings?"

The diseased drew closer. William rubbed his eyes and wiped his nose with the back of his sleeve. He lifted his gun. "Maybe? Hopefully. It sounds like we're about to find out."

Clack!

William turned towards the sound. It came from behind. Somewhere down the hall near the shuttered window at the end.

"The sprinklers!" Hawk pointed at the nozzles now protruding from the ceiling. They turned on, clogging the air with a fine mist. He sniffed. "And that's—"

"Gasoline." Knives stepped back towards the stairwell. William, Matilda, and the others followed. "They're going to torch the place."

Thunk!

The hallway went dark before being bathed in the blood-red glow of emergency lighting.

They continued towards the stairwell.

A spark flared at the other end of the hallway beneath the shuttered window. A wink. A flash. A failed attempt. For now. It burst from the gloom again. Once. Twice. William flinched with each one, ready for the *whomp* of ignition.

Karl ran into the stairwell.

Matilda walked like she didn't care. Let the fire take her.

Another spark.

"Up or down?" Hawk pointed both ways.

"I'm leaving." Matilda pointed down. "I'm done. I'm done with everything. With this war. With this fight for survival. With this shitty life. Nothing matters anymore."

William winced, but she had every right to feel that way. She needed to say whatever came to mind. She'd just lost her brother. This wasn't about his feelings. He turned his gun around, gripped it by the barrel, and whacked the security camera above the door as he ran into the stairwell. He shrugged. "Eleanor said they were off. I wouldn't mind betting they're back on now. I think it's safe to assume they're listening to *everything*."

The spark flashed again at the end of the hallway.

Her blades still drawn, Knives used them to point up. The diseased above drew closer. Or the recordings grew louder. Whichever it was, they'd find out soon enough. She stepped closer to Matilda. "We have an army waiting to come in and help us. What if we leave and they try to get in anyway?"

"What if they don't?"

"Can we risk that, Matilda? That's hundreds of lives."

"Don't talk to me about lost lives." Her mouth twitched, and her eyes shimmered. "We told them to wait until we'd opened up the blocks. If they can't follow orders, that's not on us."

Whomp!

The far end of the hallway went up in a ball of flames.

William turned his back, the heat slamming into him. Only half of the hallway burned for now. The flames chewed through the carpet, and the rooms' doors opened. All save for the one they'd trapped Artan in.

"That must have been what the furniture was about," Nick said. "They stacked that room with some highly combustible shit. I'm guessing the others are the same to make this floor burn. They must have hoped we'd still be in that weapons room. They'd planned to slowly roast us."

"Fuckers." Karl spat on the floor as if disrespecting the block would somehow be a slight on those who'd just set fire to their own home. But what other power did they have right now?

Hawk ran down a flight of stairs to the plateau between floors and ran back. "There's also a fire down there."

All the while, the diseased above grew louder. One thumped from where it must have tripped and fallen. A clang rang out. Like a skull slamming into a steel wall. Knives said, "That's no recording."

Swaying from side to side, Karl gripped his gun. "They've well and truly screwed us."

William jumped aside as Nick fired up the stairs at a diseased. A quick burst, his muzzle flare cutting through the gloom, his laser target predicting his bullet's path. The diseased stumbled and clattered into the wall before slumping to the ground on the plateau above. Limp and lifeless. Like Artan.

The same glaze as before, Matilda watched her brother's body burn.

Grief shredded Nick's words. Like losing Artan had lacerated his vocal cords. He clung to his gun, and his tears flowed freely. "Whatever happens from this moment on, I can tell you one thing that's for sure. Artan's life won't count for naught. Even if I could retreat now, I wouldn't." He pointed up and cleared his throat. "I can't speak for anyone else, but those fuckers up there have taken the most precious thing from my life."

Still dazed, Matilda nodded along.

Karl glanced at William.

"And I, for one, am going to make sure I do everything in my power to make them pay." He shot another diseased with another flash of muzzle flare. He raised a balled fist. "I'm going to take what they've inflicted on me, and I'm going to use it as fuel to make them feel a pain they couldn't even imagine. It might only be a shred of what I feel, but even if it kills me before I pass, I'm going to make sure these fuckers suffer."

Firing for a third time, Nick charged up the stairs. He'd not asked anyone to follow, but of course they did. All of them. Even the dazed Matilda.

CHAPTER 46

They'd passed her dad's crash site and the spot where they'd ended the coup. Their blocks, their destination, loomed large. Even from this distance, they looked abandoned by an army heading out to war. Rayne kept a steady humming pace, Matthew riding shotgun. Eleanor sat on the bench opposite Ralph. "So, you knew that man in the broadcast?"

Ralph's features darkened.

Eleanor squirmed in her seat. "I'm sorry. Did I say something wrong?"

"He was the worst kind of human being. Worse than the diseased. And he's the reason they're all loose now. The prison was secure until he set those creatures free. He's the reason the south's overrun. And what if I told you that's not the worst of it? He ran the prison like a sadist."

"Now that I can believe. I lived in these blocks, remember?"

Ralph rolled his eyes.

"And even from the short piece of footage, you could see his pleasure at turning the prisoners into diseased."

"I had a friend." The fire left Ralph, his broad shoulders sagging. "A lover. I won't hide that anymore. But we had to hide it from him. Except Warren didn't."

"He told him?"

Ralph nodded.

Eleanor took the man's large hand, holding on with both of hers. "What happened?"

"Louis killed him. Like so many other people who lived a life different from his. We thought people left from time to time, but it turned out they didn't. Those who left were made to disappear."

"I'm so sorry. Is that why you left the prison?"

Ralph's deep brown eyes shimmered with his tears. "I left some good friends behind. But I couldn't stay there. Not after I found out the truth. Not with that memory hanging over my head."

"I understand."

"I left with several other people." Ralph looked back towards Eleanor's old blocks. "The blocks were so close to the prison's exit. I thought we'd all make it."

"You were the only one?"

Ralph bit his trembling lip.

"I'm sorry."

"Me too. But who hasn't lost people?"

Eleanor sighed. "Maybe you'll get a chance to go back and see your friends from the prison again?"

"Maybe. And I think the prison will be much more improved for this. Eventually. The prisoners and the guards are working together."

"If only we could say the same of the south. Unfortunately, those who ran the blocks are not for turning."

"Sounds like the kind of toxic drivel they'd spout. I bet those morons in the blocks ate it up too. Like not changing your mind—even when presented with compelling evidence to the contrary—is some kind of virtue." He sneered. "Fucking idiots."

Rayne leaned back in her seat. "Which is why we have to crush them all."

A static hiss burst from the radio. "Help us."

Matthew snatched the radio's mic. "Hello?"

"Help us!"

The tyres' hum grew higher in pitch as Rayne sped up, closing in on the blocks. "Is it coming from us?"

Matthew leaned forward and looked up into the sky at the blocks. "It's local, and we're close enough. It must be them."

"What's happening?"

Matthew pressed the button. "What's going on?"

"The maternity ward. Help!"

"Ash!" Rayne gripped the wheel tighter.

Another static burst.

Rayne snatched the mic from Matthew. Her fingers turned white with her grip. "What's happened?"

Static.

"Hello?"

Static.

"Shit!" She threw the mic across the cab. She turned left up the entrance ramp leading to the tower blocks just as another tank fled, the driver avoiding them at the last minute.

Rayne slammed on the brakes. "Whoever's in that tank did it! We can't let them get away."

"You get into the blocks." Ralph stood up from the back. "I'll go after that tank."

Rayne snatched up her rifle, slipped past Matthew, and opened the tank's door. She jumped out firing, holding back the diseased running up the ramp. Eleanor leaped out beside her and shot the diseased. Matthew joined them and closed the tank's door.

Reversing off the ramp, Ralph knocked over many of the approaching diseased. He yanked the tank around, knocking more flying as he set off after the fleeing vehicle.

Chasing after Rayne, Eleanor climbed the tank already parked there and followed her across the ladder stretching over the gap. It bowed and bounced with their progress. Her gun swung from its strap. The diseased below reached up, ever-hopeful someone would fall.

Climbing clear on the other side, Matthew behind her, Eleanor sprinted after Rayne towards the block. Towards those in the maternity ward. Hopefully it wasn't already too late.

CHAPTER 47

Gracie crouched opposite Bear in their sandstone prison. They linked arms, and Olga sat on the bridge they'd made between them. He nodded at her, and she nodded back.

"On three?"

She nodded again, bracing against the sandstone wall in front of them with her free hand.

"One ... two ... three."

They stood up together, lifting their short friend towards the ceiling. She reached up and scraped her fingers against the sandstone.

"How's it looking?" Sand rained down on Gracie's face. She dropped her head again, and she blinked repeatedly to ease the sting in her watering eyes.

Olga ran her fingers along the rough stone. "There's no join."

Gracie stumbled beneath her weight. "Huh?"

"It's like the hatch was never there."

"But I saw it."

"We all *saw* it, Gracie. We shot through it when we slid in here. That doesn't change the fact …"

Bear shrugged, lifting one side of Olga and shoving Gracie a step to the left. "So it's vanished?"

Olga tutted. "Yes."

"And we're in the right spot?"

"Yes."

"And you're sure—"

"Yes, Bear, I'm *sure*. There's no hatch."

"There must be a hatch."

"Obviously. And if you have anything useful to add, I'm all ears." Olga slid forwards and landed between them with the slap of her feet against the hard floor. She cocked an eyebrow at Gracie, who rubbed her shoulder. "I'm not *that* heavy, am I?"

"No." She shouldn't have replied so quickly.

"So what now?" Olga continued studying the ceiling.

"Here!" All the while, Kira had stood over to Gracie's left, examining the symbols carved into the wall. The slimy ore had turned her as red as the rest of them. She pointed at a small square and waved Gracie over. "I need you to press this when I say."

Gracie lifted her hand, but Kira caught her wrist. She gripped a little too hard. "*Only* when I say. Okay?"

Gracie snarled at Kira until she let go. "Why?"

"Just trust me. Bear …" She took Bear's hand and led him to a spot on the wall directly opposite. To another square identical to the one she'd shown Gracie. The uniformity of the two stood out in the abstract chaos. Every symbol different. At least at first glance. Or unless you were Kira.

Olga next, she stood her close to another square and walked over to a fourth directly opposite.

"On the count of three, I want you all to press your square

at the same time." She held up three fingers like they needed a visual count. "One … two … three."

Gracie pressed her square in time with the others.

Thunk!

A tunnel, lit by the same weak glow as their dungeon, opened up in the wall between Gracie and Olga. But three brushed-steel doors closed it off. They slammed down in front of them, each one closer than the previous. Each one shortened the tunnel further with their hammering closure.

Clang! Clang! Clang!

They shook the ground. Gracie folded her arms. "I'm not convinced this is much better, Kira. There's no other way?"

"There was—"

"*Was*? But not anymore?"

Kira gestured at the other shapes in the walls. "We had one choice." She glanced at the gates as they slowly lifted. "We could have pressed a circle. A pair of lines. Or a triangle. But the more sides or lines the shape had, the more people it required to press them. I believe this is easier than if I'd only pressed the circle." She pressed it now and looked up like she expected a response from a higher power. She pressed it again. "And I was right. We had only one chance to decide."

"You."

"Huh?"

Gracie said, "*You* only had one chance to decide."

"If you put it like that."

"Unless I missed the consultation?"

Olga opened her mouth to speak, but paused as the three steel gates, which had lifted several feet from the ground, slammed shut again.

Clang! Clang! Clang!

"So we could have made a different, better choice?"

"Different, Olga. Yes. For sure. Better? Who knows?"

Olga stared at the slowly lifting gates as if hypnotised by them. "But we might have made the worst choice?"

"The worst choice is to choose to believe it's the worst choice."

"Huh?"

"We'll never know if it was the worst or not, seeing as we could only make one. But that train of thought will certainly make you feel like it was the worst, which amounts to the same thing."

"Which is?"

"A useless waste of time. We're here now, so let's find a way out."

Gracie raised her eyebrows. Kira had a point.

Clang! Clang! Clang!

Being trapped in the wall on their previous trip had really shaken Olga. It had stolen some of her fire. She shifted her stance again. Uncomfortable in her own skin. "And if we stay here?"

"If we stay here, we die. Most likely of dehydration. That is"—Kira looked up at the ceiling—"if this dungeon doesn't cave in on us."

Clang! Clang! Clang!

Each steel door hit the ground like a gargantuan hammer.

Just go!

Real or imagined, Aus' words gave Gracie the spark she needed. She strode into the tunnel, avoiding Olga's reaching hand as she tried to drag her back. If she didn't go now, she never would.

Clang! Clang! Clang!

The farthest of the three gates dropped first, the other two following suit. Faced with her blurred reflection in the closest wall of brushed steel, Gracie rocked from side to side as it slowly lifted again. The gap beneath it stretched to about three feet.

Now.

She rocked forwards, but held her ground.

Now.

She remained in front of the slamming doors.

Go!

Gracie darted through the first three. She ducked as the final door closed with a *whoosh* of brushed steel in a sandstone sleeve.

Clang! Clang! Clang!

She blew out hard. Her friends remained on the other side of the three closed gates. The path ahead bent around to the right. It revealed another pair of slamming doors.

Now.

Gracie hopped through, the pair closing behind her and sending a shot of wind after her with the clap of their connection.

Kira on her tail, Bear and Olga behind, Gracie pushed on through another two sets of doors without breaking stride.

Clang! Clang! Clang!

Stop!

She halted. The next set of doors only opened halfway before they slammed shut again.

Clang! Clang! Clang!

Now!

Gracie jumped through, the doors having opened fully for the first time. "Wait!" She showed Kira her halting hand and counted several cycles.

Clang! Clang! Clang!

"Every third open."

"What?"

Clang! Clang! Clang!

"The gates open wider on every third cycle."

Now.

She might have trusted Aus, but Kira needed to make her

own choice. She jumped through, and the other two copied the pattern.

With all of them together and the tunnel now open ahead of them, Gracie pointed forwards. "You ready to move on?"

Clang! Clang! Clang!

The sandstone on Gracie's right creaked and groaned. A crack had formed in the rock. She shared a glance with Kira. She'd seen it too. The others seemed oblivious. Olga stood immobilised, with the wide eyes of someone in distress. Telling them would only make it worse. Especially when the fact remained … they needed to get out of there and fast. And if they didn't keep moving forwards, where would they go?

Gracie took off, and Kira followed closely behind. The tunnel ran in a straight line for about twenty feet before taking another sharp turn. She followed the twisting path, left and right. They passed more symbols on the walls.

"Down!"

She turned to Kira. "What?"

Kira tackled Gracie to the ground and landed on top of her, driving the air from her lungs.

"What are you—"

Clang!

A steel sheet slammed above them, instantly halving the tunnel's height.

Still on top of her, Kira pointed at a symbol up to their left. It showed a horizontal line beside a vertical one.

"I'm glad that means something to you." Gracie's heart galloped. "Even if I'd have seen it, I would have still run into the trap."

Bear and Olga caught up and dropped to all fours. Gracie let Kira lead, the symbols a better guide than a dead vindictive brother. If she put too much trust in him, she'd surely die.

The hard ground hurt Gracie's knees as she crawled after Kira, panting from trying to keep up. But they needed to keep moving. More cracks formed around them. The tunnel creaked like an old wooden tower in the wind.

Kira crawled into a recess on their left. She stood up. Gracie and the others copied her.

On her feet last, Olga scanned the ceiling. She must have heard the creaking too. "What are we waiting for?"

"Now, don't panic. Just stand still, okay?"

Olga sneered. "I'm *not* panicking."

"I'm just saying."

"Well, stop saying. It's a waste of time."

Kira rolled her eyes.

"So what are you doing, Kira?"

"You want me to hurry, but you also want a running commentary?"

Olga shrugged.

Kira pressed a symbol beside them. A bright light shone in the recess. Water rained down on them. It was so cold Gracie gasped.

Clang! Clang! Clang!

Kira wiped the red ore from her face and hair. "I didn't expect the shower."

"Yet you want us to trust your judgement?"

She turned her back on Olga. "But look at this." Kira pointed at a steel panel on the wall. It had a single button with two similar symbols. One sat above the button, and the other beside it.

The downpour halted, and Gracie let her shoulders relax. She wrung the last of the ore from her clothes while the gates continued slamming.

Clang! Clang! Clang!

Olga shoved Kira aside. "What are we looking at?"

Kira smiled as she traced the first symbol with her finger.

A circle with six lines coming off it. It looked like a basic depiction of a sun. "See it?"

Leaning closer, Olga then turned to Gracie and raised her eyebrows.

Gracie said, "I don't think we do, Kira."

"What does this look like?"

"A circle?" Bear said. "A sun?"

Clang! Clang! Clang!

"You've seen maps of the south, right? What would you think if you saw this symbol on a map?"

Bear shrugged. "I'd think it was a sun on a map."

Gracie sniggered. "Bear has a point. But I also see what you mean, Kira."

Kira nodded and smiled. "You see it?"

"See what?" Olga glowered at Gracie. At this stage, she'd fight anyone for an answer.

"The shining city. Right, Kira?"

Kira grinned. She traced the symbol beneath it. The same circle and the same lines, but this time, the lines were much farther away from the circle. Like the sun had burst.

"You think this button will open up the shining city?" Olga pointed at it, and Kira caught her wrist.

Olga dragged her hand away. "I wasn't going to press it. Obviously."

"Kira's right."

"I wasn't going to press it, Gracie."

"It looked like you were."

"Well, I wasn't."

"Anyway, Kira's right. We can't press it yet. We need to tell the others. If this button opens the shining city—and Kira's not been wrong yet—then we need to decide on when we press it. This is a one-time-only kind of action."

Clang! Clang! Clang!

Bear peered down the tunnel they were yet to walk. "*If* we get out of here."

You will.

"We will." Gracie dropped to her knees and crawled off, the sand from the sandstone sticking to her damp clothes, her trousers chafing against her thighs.

Clang! Clang! Clang!

Gracie rounded the next bend and stood up again. They'd reached a flight of stairs carved into the sandstone. They led up. The others joined her. "You all ready?"

They each nodded.

The stairs emerged into another wide tunnel close to another Icarus tower control room. Gracie hugged Kira and Olga as they followed her out. Bear last, she saluted the man, and he saluted back before they threw their arms around one another. "Not only do we have a way to open up the shining city"—she gestured at the door just a few feet away—"but it would seem we've found the control room for another Icarus tower."

Olga's smile banished her stress lines. "And a better way to approach the shining city's button."

Gracie squeezed Kira's shoulder. "Am I glad we have you with us. Now let's raise this tower and get the hell out of here."

CHAPTER 48

Had William not been so close behind Nick, he would have missed it in the chaos. The moaning. The clattering of falling diseased bodies. The squeals of discomfort. The *clack* of Nick's firing gun. But he caught the glow in the darkness. Two red zeros on the ammo counter.

Had William not been so close behind Nick, he would have missed him when he reached out.

But as Nick spun his gun around, turning it into a bludgeon by waving the stock in the air, William caught his backpack bulging with ammo and dragged him back. "Reload, you lunatic."

Nick came forwards like he might fight William, but Karl stepped between them.

Nick's cheeks bulged from his hard exhale. He had to let it out somehow. He locked eyes on William as he reached into his backpack and pulled out another magazine.

William led them away. He turned up the stairs, his gun raised. The red dot of his laser target danced on the wall close to the bend. A landslide of clumsy steps called down to him. He widened his stance, closed one eye, and shot the first diseased. It fell and tripped those behind it.

The diseased might have outnumbered William and his friends, but the stairs, combined with their clumsy gaits, shattered any advantage they might have had. William shot them as they stumbled into view.

The emergency lighting bathed everything in a deep red glow. It showed the fallen diseased. They were down, but how could they be sure they were out? William shot another one in the head before stepping over its prone form. Better to be safe than infected.

They made progress. A flight of stairs at a time, the stairwell filling with noxious smoke from the fire below. Cloying and plastic, it wound William's lungs tight and burned his already stinging eyes.

Clack! Out of bullets, William stepped aside to let Nick lead again. Artan's lover scowled as he passed.

At the final flight of stairs, Nick screamed and took off. He vanished into the first communal room, his cries a match for the diseased horde beyond.

In the abandoned classroom, William went right where Nick had gone left. Fifty or more wild diseased sprinted at them, knocking over tables and chairs. Many tripped over the furniture before they got close. While the others came in and fanned out, all of them fixed on the diseased, William held his trigger down and dragged his target from one diseased to the next. Their heads snapped back, their legs buckled, and while they kept reaching with their hands, they fell well short of grabbing a hold of anything.

Knives and Matilda came in last. Knives threw blades, but Matilda's gun hung from her strap as she stared into space.

Having taken down the diseased on his side of the room, William fired across to the other side. He nailed a beast as it jumped up from a fall.

With all the diseased down, everyone stopped shooting. William's ears rang. While everyone else either reloaded or lowered their weapons, Matilda remained at the top of the stairs, frozen. She flinched when he took her hand. "Are you …" Of course she wasn't all right. His stomach tightened. What a moron. "Are …" For the first time since he'd known her, he didn't know what to say.

A bright light cut through the gloom. Birthed from a small ceiling projector, which painted the far wall with Louis' face. The man's dead stare made William shiver.

"Argh!" Matilda opened fire on the ceiling. Bullets sparked off the steel surrounding the projector. She finally caught the small box, obliterating it and sending it raining down in tiny pieces.

William touched the back of her arm.

She jumped and turned her weapon on him.

Backing away, he raised his hands in the air. "Tilly, it's me!"

She blinked. Once. Twice. Something pierced her numbness. The slightest twitch. A flash of who she was, and who he was to her. A connection that dropped almost as soon as it had registered. But it had registered. She lowered her weapon. Her features once more misted over. She turned away from him and followed Nick and Hawk, who picked their way through the destroyed classroom, resting their laser targets on the diseased corpses as they stepped over them.

Knives patted William's back before she followed the others.

Karl, on the walkway, pointed out across the meadow. "Who do you think it is?"

William jogged to catch up with them. Away from the smoking stairwell. From the vinegar rot of diseased. He rubbed his shaven head to counter the night's cold nip, and like the others, tracked the tank driving away from the blocks. Flat out, it raced along the road heading for the shining city.

Hawk said, "Should we go after it?"

Smoke billowed out of the blocks' bases. It squeezed through the gaps in the shutters. They were all ablaze, the air thick with the noxious clouds.

"It's a rabbit."

They all turned to Matilda, who'd fallen back into her daze.

Karl raised an eyebrow at William. "A rabbit?"

"Something designed to chase, right, Tilly?"

But they'd lost her again.

William said, "To distract us. Lure us away from something."

"And probably into a trap." Hawk scratched his scarred neck.

"Exactly."

The super convoy containing their army would still be waiting on the other side of the hill. Hidden from the block's line of sight, but there, ready for the call to action.

"Look." Knives pointed into the distance at the newly raised Icarus towers. "That's two more."

"They're doing their job."

The others turned to William.

"What I mean is, we came here with a job to do. Like they went into the farms with a job to do. I say we focus on that rather than getting distracted by that tank, whoever it is and wherever it's going. Let's open up the blocks first, and hopefully, those waiting to come in will deal with the fires."

Nick led them on.

The communal room at the other end of the walkway was an abandoned dining room. Like the classroom, they'd laid out a maze of tables. A great way to slow the diseased charge.

If there were any diseased to charge. The empty room threw the scuff and knock of their movements back at them. The steel walls turned the open space into an echo chamber.

Nick pointed up, and William nodded. They were in the right block. Now they just needed to get to the top floor.

William entered the stairwell last, Matilda a foot or two ahead of him, but light years away. And who could blame her? He'd grieve for Artan, but he had the luxury of being slightly further removed than her. He could compartmentalise for now.

Clinging to his gun, William followed the others' gentle steps as they slowly ascended to the top floor. They weaved through the theatre's chairs, Nick and Hawk reaching the stage first and climbing up. They bent down to help the others, all of them taking a hand save for Matilda. She climbed up as if she'd made the journey alone.

The theatre was as quiet as the rest of this block. It reported them crossing the stage with their steps against the wooden platform.

His eyes still swollen and red, but a little calmer than before, Nick paused by the control room's door. He waited for William to get close, and he looked at every one of them in turn. Were they ready? They all nodded back.

Nick pressed the button, and the door opened with a *whoosh!*

CHAPTER 49

This time, Gracie and Olga sat in the back of the buggy while Bear drove. Her gun in her lap, the wind in her face, she took in their surroundings like she might make sense of the strange carvings in the poor light. Even though they had Kira riding shotgun for a reason.

Like Gracie, Olga clung to the truck as if she feared she might blow away. Like Gracie, she took in their surroundings. She raised her voice to be heard over the hum of the cart's small tyres and the whine of its little engine. "We've had water, fire, and collapsing ceilings." Kira threw a glance back at Olga. "So what now?"

"Hopefully nothing." Gracie squeezed Kira's shoulder. "Right, Kira?"

She remained focused ahead this time. "Right." She pointed. "There it is!"

The cart lifted with the lump in the road. Gracie turned to look back at the embossed sun as they left it behind. "So what does that mean?"

Clinging to the cart's dashboard, Kira leaned forwards. "Dunno."

Olga tutted. "Helpful."

Her stomach in knots, her leg bouncing, Gracie barely blinked, even with the headwind blowing all the moisture from her sore eyes. The stair's zigzagging structure slowly came into definition in the shadowy distance. The Icarus tower's struts in front of them, an elevator on the ground. Just fifty feet away. So close. Surely—

"We've made it?" Olga sat up straighter. "But what about the trap?"

Kira remained fixed ahead, and Gracie shrugged.

The cart's suspension squeaked as Bear brought them to a halt by the elevator. Gracie and Olga jumped out.

Kira, still looking around, reading the symbols like a book, paused as if waiting for something. Did she have an insight she needed to share?

Yanking up the handbrake with a grating creak, Bear got out last, the lightweight buggy rocking as he stepped clear.

Gracie dragged open the elevator door and entered. She waited inside, holding her breath. They weren't out of there yet. But as the others got in and Olga closed the door behind them, she relaxed ever so slightly.

Raising her eyebrows at Gracie, Olga hovered over the button to activate the elevator. Gracie held onto the handrail and nodded.

The elevator took off, shooting into the sky as they whipped past field after field, leaving each one behind with a clap of wind. *Thwip! Thwip! Thwip!*

They broke the surface and shot up the side of the Icarus tower, accelerating like they wouldn't stop. Until they did. Right at the top. Despite their momentum threatening to turn them to mush against the elevator's ceiling, they came to an inexplicably gentle halt.

Exposed to the night and the wind's chilly nip, Gracie rested her forehead against the elevator's caged sides. Uninterrupted wastelands all around. "That was easier than I was expecting."

"Tell me about it." Kira laughed.

"Did you get a sense of the trap in that tunnel?"

Kira shook her head. "That's what worried me. We were moving too fast."

Still hovering by the button, Olga waited, ready to press it. "Does anyone know where we are?"

Gracie shrugged.

Kira shook her head.

Bear stared down at the vehicles in the quarantine zone surrounding the farm.

The road away from the farm led downhill. A horde of a hundred or more diseased gathered at the bottom like gravity had guided their path. They squabbled and squalled. Shrieked and wailed. Their usual discontent rippled through the dormant mob.

Olga said, "And any idea how we might get out of here?" She looked at them all in turn. "Bear?"

"That tractor." He pointed at a vehicle with small front wheels compared to the massive chunky tyres on the back. "Hopefully, I can get that started. It'll plow through those diseased. And it's high enough to keep us out of reach."

"Hopefully?" Olga still kept her hand close to the button.

"I'll have to look at it to be sure."

∼

WITH HER HACKING device in her left hand, Olga crouched by the gates' control button. It took her about five seconds to open them, giving them access to the quarantine zone.

The barrel of her gun resting in her shoulder, Gracie closed an eye and shot the first diseased. Her laser target on its face, she blew its brains out the back of its head.

Olga took down the next one.

Gracie the third.

Side by side, the pair of them led Kira and Bear out into the quarantine zone. Their guns raised, they took slow steps towards the tractor and scanned for more.

Kira joined them on guard by the tractor while Bear climbed into the driver's seat. He flicked switches and pressed buttons.

Gracie scanned their surroundings. "I think we're clear?"

Olga nodded.

"Bear, what are you saying? What's happening?"

More switches and more button presses. He blew out hard, his cheeks bulging. "It won't start."

"Of course it won't." Gracie's head dropped. "That would be *too* easy."

Bear climbed from the tractor's cab and opened the bonnet. He reached in and tugged a few things. Tapped some others. Back in the driver's seat, he pressed the start button again.

Gracie said, "Still nothing?"

Olga sneered. "What do *you* think?"

"All right. How about you try to be helpful for once in your life?"

"How about you fuck off?" A slight glint in her eye. At a different time, Gracie might have seen the humour in it. "But seriously, come on, Bear. There must be a way?"

"Maybe."

Olga took over now. "Go on?"

"A jump start."

Olga glanced at Kira and Gracie. "A what now?"

Bear turned his hands over one another, gesturing motion. "Get it moving. Rolling. And then use the momentum to start it."

"And if it doesn't start?"

"How much ammo have you got?"

Olga sagged, and Gracie cut in. "There are no other ways?"

"Maybe." Bear threw up his shoulders. "But I've not thought of them yet."

Olga raised her hand. "I'll be the contingency plan. I'll wait behind. When it works, when you start the tractor, you can sweep by and pick me up."

"And if it doesn't?" Kira this time.

"That's what a contingency plan is."

"A contingency plan is an actual plan, Olga."

Olga rolled her eyes. "If it doesn't work, I'll think of something. I'll get help."

~

THEY WERE DOWNHILL ALL the way, so the second Olga got the external gates open, it took little more than a gentle shove to get the tractor moving. Gracie pushed with Kira and Olga.

The diseased wails lit up the night. The horde at the bottom of the hill waited to receive them.

The tractor gained momentum with their push. The large and chunky tyres turned. Even though they'd be out of arm's reach when they scaled the tractor, the sharper squeals and cries from the bottom of the hill lifted gooseflesh on Gracie's skin. Only a few had been alerted to their presence. Soon, they'd all be baying for their blood.

Kira climbed up the tractor's back first. Gracie, jogging to keep up with the quickening vehicle, followed her up, leaving Olga to push. She gripped on with one hand and, with her other, pressed her palm to her face and blew Olga a kiss. "Be safe!"

Olga continued pushing and smiled. "I'll be fi—"

Diseased screams cut her off. A horde appeared behind her. They ran around the side of the farm.

Olga's smile fell.

Holding onto the tractor's frame with one hand, Gracie reached down and grabbed Olga's wrist with the other.

Olga continued pushing the tractor. "What are you doing?"

"Diseased."

"I can see that. Let go of me."

"Get on the tractor."

The massive vehicle gained momentum, and Olga shook her head. Her face reddened with the effort of her run. "We need a backup."

"We need you alive."

"Let go, Gracie." She ripped her hand free.

Gracie reached out again and grabbed air. Fifty diseased or more streamed around the side of the farm. Olga didn't stand a chance. Gracie jumped from the tractor, and her legs buckled beneath her. She crashed down on the road.

"Gracie!" Olga stopped pushing to drag her to her feet. "What are you doing?"

"I won't leave you on your own."

The tractor rolled away.

"But we'll die here."

"That's what I've been trying to tell you, Olga."

Fifty diseased behind turned into seventy. Soon there'd be a hundred and as many ahead. Olga covered her face with her hands, muting her cry. "Damn it, Gracie. You should have left me!"

CHAPTER 50

"Now will you run?" Gracie shoved Olga after the rolling tractor. Over twenty feet away, it gathered momentum. She jogged behind her friend and shoved her again, hard enough to make her stumble, but not so hard she fell. "Quicker!"

Olga dropped her head and pumped her arms.

Gracie had more to give. She could overtake her short friend and reach the tractor before her, but they were in this together. She held back and remained focused on the vehicle's massive tyres and Kira halfway up the tractor's back between them.

They closed the distance, but had to run faster to match the tractor's increasing speed.

Diseased wailed around them, but one stood out amongst the collective. Alone in its charge, it raced up the hill towards them, passing the tractor on its right. Gracie shoved Olga towards the tractor again, raised her gun, and fired. The diseased fell and rolled, Olga jumping it in her pursuit of the farm vehicle.

Kira climbed higher up the tractor and fired down the

hill. Its massive tyres crushed the fallen diseased and slowed its roll by a beat.

Kira fired again. The diseased horde wailed back like white-hot bullets meant nothing to them. The tractor's left side lifted as it rolled over another dropped diseased.

Olga grabbed the tractor's frame. She clung on, hopping and skipping behind it with wide strides where it dragged her forwards. On her fourth or fifth bound, she kicked hard, landed on the back, and climbed up.

Gassed from the run, Gracie dug deep and found a burst of speed. She grabbed a cold steel bar running along the tractor's rear. A diseased came around the tractor's right side. Still hanging on, she jumped and kicked out, catching the creature in the face with both feet, sending it spinning into the meadow.

Two more bouncing steps on the hard road, each with the potential to break ankles, she dragged herself clear and climbed up the tractor's back.

Panting, she dragged herself up beside Olga and put her arm around her.

Olga sneered. "You idiot."

Gracie kissed her friend's forehead. "I couldn't leave you."

"Let's hope we don't need rescuing now."

"Even if we do, had you stayed back, you would have been too dead to help."

"I'd have found a way."

"This was the only way."

Some of the colour drained from Olga's flushed face when she glanced back at the mob that had cut off her retreat. Well over a hundred diseased ran down the hill after them. She said it so only Gracie heard. "Thank you."

Gracie kissed her forehead again.

The tractor gathered momentum, mowing down the

diseased like they weren't there. The wind cooled Gracie's sweating skin. They'd done all they could.

Bear clung to the steering wheel and leaned back to shout over the mounting chaos, "Hang on!"

Gripping the frame tighter, Gracie leaned over Bear as he ripped his foot clear of one pedal.

The tractor lurched and slowed a little. They rolled closer to the pack at the bottom of the hill, now only about forty feet away.

Gracie raised her eyebrows at Olga and Kira. They both shrugged back. "Everything okay, Bear?"

"No."

"No?"

"Hang on!" Bear did something with his foot again.

The tractor lurched again.

Gracie gripped on again.

The hope in her chest died again.

They slowed and rolled into the diseased horde at the bottom of the hill, coming to a complete halt.

Surrounded by the funk of vinegar rot and the slapping of clumsy hands against the tank's chassis, Gracie gripped on tighter and climbed a little higher. Away from hateful faces. From bleeding eyes and snapping jaws. Away from the reaching hands and wriggling fingers. Their skin slashed with deep lacerations. Infected bite marks. Ripped-open throats. Rotting flesh, alive with maggots. A writhing and highly volatile mess. They were trapped with no way out.

Olga sighed and looked back. "I should have stayed behind."

"If you had, you'd already be dead."

"I know. At least it would have been quick."

"Damn." Gracie dropped her head. Living in a world like this, she'd always had her *when the time comes* plan. Everyone in Dout had talked about it. In hers, she'd always given up.

Why fight the inevitable? She loosened her grip a little and leaned back, ready to let go. Bear broke her out of it when he climbed from the driver's seat. She pulled closer to the tank and avoided Olga's confused stare. "What are you doing, Bear?"

Having left the bonnet open after inspecting it in the farm, the lithe Bear crawled over the front of the tractor like a lizard. He reached into the engine, burying his arm deep inside the vehicle. He turned his head sideways so he could get even deeper. He pulled something out and cleaned it on his shirt before plunging his arm back in again. His tongue poked from his mouth like it helped him explore the unseen parts of the engine.

Kira shouted over the furore, "What's he doing?"

Olga shook her head. "Dunno." And then lowered her voice as she leaned close to Gracie. "But I saw what you were about to do." She pointed at her. "How dare you? After forcing me to get on the tractor!"

Bear climbed back into the driver's seat, closed his eyes, and stared up at the night sky. His lips moved, but the diseased drowned out his utterance.

Twisting in his seat as if to get comfortable, Bear pressed the tractor's start button.

The vehicle kicked. Kira gasped, and Gracie clung on tighter. But the tractor halted.

Bear pressed the start button again, sending another shimmy through the tractor.

On his final press, it came to life with a splutter. Leaning forwards, Bear rested his forehead against the steering wheel, his lips still moving. He turned back and flashed them a wonky grin. His eyes were bloodshot. He'd been stripped back to a father who might never again see his son. Who might never meet his unborn child. Who might leave a woman he loved to survive in this awful world alone. He saluted Gracie, and despite his smile, his grief dampened his words. "Hold tight, ladies. We're going home."

Nodding to herself, Gracie gripped on as they drove away. She had a plan for when the time came. Maybe she needed to plan how to better recognise that time. Powered by the massive back wheels, the tractor crushed the diseased in its path. It popped their bones and wrung wild screams from their rattling lungs.

CHAPTER 51

William stepped over Nick's discarded backpack as he followed him into the control room. He'd done an essential job in carrying the ammo. He now carried a much heavier burden, so who could blame him for handing it off to someone else? Anyone else. Artan's death had affected them all, but Nick had lost a lover, and Matilda a brother. What right did William have to dwell on his own grief?

The control room was quiet. As abandoned as the rest of the blocks. "Where is everyone?" William moved aside to let the others pass, and waited for Matilda. She entered and stepped over the bag, walking as if on autopilot.

Turning his gun around so he held the barrel, William swung for the camera above the door. He dislodged it with a hard blow, sending the small box flying across the room and crashing into a wall.

Having learned a bit from Gracie, Nick tapped on the control console's keyboard. The screen remained black. Not only off, but cut off. Powerless. He hit the keys harder with each press, like he might resuscitate them with force. He gripped his chin in a pinch. "Eleanor said this is the right roo—"

Three of the four walls glowed white. Each one a massive monitor. A man laughed. A speaker hung in each of the room's corners, broadcasting his smug mirth from all angles.

Black lines crisscrossed the monitors, breaking the screens into grids. Each box played a unique piece of footage. Each showed a view through one of the blocks' many security cameras. Hundreds of rooms, many lit red and a few blacked out from where the cameras had clearly stopped working. Or been knocked clean off.

"What?" The man laughed again. "Did you really think we knew nothing about what that little bitch was up to?"

"Shit!" Hawk pointed at one of the many small screens. It showed a hallway with its doors opening and tens of diseased spilling out.

"Do you think we'd be so stupid as to trust a kid who appeared from nowhere and was far too nosy for her own good? We're not fools, you know?"

More and more rooms opened on other tiny screens. More diseased stumbled out into the blocks. The ground shook with a bass-line thud. The diseased on the screens responded to the call and ran towards the communal rooms.

"But the fact you've gone straight to the defunct control room would suggest you fell for it. Maybe you need to be a bit more discerning about whom you trust. At least question everything. It's naïve to take things at face value, wouldn't you say? Especially in this world."

"We didn't come here for a lecture, you fucking prick." Nick thrust his middle finger in the air.

The diseased cleared the residential floors, all of them drawn to the bassy call.

"As for these blocks?" The man laughed again. "Have them. They're useless. We're on our way to the shining city, and good luck trying to get in there. You'll need much more than a silly little tart with doe eyes and a sob story to penetrate that fortress."

"He's right." Nick cried while he spoke. "We should have been more discerning. If we'd stopped to question what Eleanor told us, Artan would still be alive."

"Now wait." William reached out to him. "Thinking like that will get us nowhere."

"It might help us learn from our mistakes. Make sure Artan's life counted for something."

"As you can probably see, there are hundreds of diseased throughout these blocks." The monotonous man continued, the rumbling bass throb shaking the floor from where it drew the diseased to the theatre outside. "We've spent the past day, since the child left, putting them in every room we could secure. Didn't dumb little Eleanor ever wonder why we kept the basements locked? Or did she really believe we had bountiful supplies of food down there?"

William's cheeks flushed, and he dropped his focus to the floor. He should have known better than to send her.

"You'd have thought she'd smell them. But she was right about there being a control room that operates these blocks. You've just chosen the wrong one. And good luck with reaching the other. There are a shitload of diseased between you and it. And if the diseased don't get you, I'm sure you'll choke on the smoke or burn alive. You could always take the easy option by getting to a walkway and seeing if you can learn how to fly. Spoiler"—he giggled—"you can't."

The grids fell away to be replaced by a single large image on each of the three walls. They showed different hallways. The sprinklers activated, and William's stomach lurched. He flinched in time with the firing spark at the hallway's end. The flash. The flare of ignition. The birthed flames galloping down the corridor's length like wild horses. "We've rigged every residential floor to burn. Good luck!"

The man laughed again. "Oh, and before I forget, you're probably wondering how we knew?"

Nick shook his head. "You've already said it was Eleanor. We get it. We fucked up."

The recording continued, "I mean, Eleanor's performance was far from convincing, but that wasn't it. We used her naïveté against her. Had a buffoon called Noris distract her while she was here. And he did such a good job. It's a shame she killed him in the end."

"Damn." William sagged where he stood. "Poor kid."

"She even believed she'd stumbled into a meeting about someone leaving the blocks to go to the shining city. Of course we knew she'd head back to you and tell you everything. But we knew of your plans well before she arrived. Of the hundreds of people in these blocks, you were foolish to think we didn't have someone who could speak high vamp. Didn't you even consider it? In those little back-and-forths in the VR rooms, you told us everything. You're lucky we've maintained radio silence. We couldn't tell the other fifteen communities they were about to be attacked. But don't worry, I'd be surprised if they didn't know too. However, you might get lucky. There might be a few blocks who are completely oblivious to your plans."

Sneering, Karl, like the others, stared up at the ceiling. "Motherfucker."

"Oh, there's one thing I will give you. We tried to convince Eleanor we ate diseased meat. We set up a boiling vat and chucked in some severed heads just to mess with her little mind. To make her think she'd eaten it too. Maybe you'll be able to appease her worries if you ever make it out of here. But were I a betting man, I'd guess you'll neve—"

Nick screamed and shot the speakers. Four cubes, one in

each corner of the room. They dropped to the floor. Silenced and dented. "He was getting on my tits."

Knives cut the air with her blades as if it helped her spend her frustration. "We need to get to the other control room." The gridded screens returned, playing footage from all the burning blocks. Of the diseased ambling through the thick smoke on their way to the communal floors.

"Matilda?" Karl pointed at the monitor.

William checked behind. He spun back to the gridded screen, and his voice broke. "Matilda!" She ran over a walkway, firing her gun, Nick's ammo bag on her back.

Hawks' jaw hung slack. The screen's glow reflected in his blue eyes. "What's she doing?"

Nick said, "She's not even heading for the control room. What does she hope to achieve?"

"I'm not sure she hopes to achieve anything." Her vacant gaze dominated William's mind's eye. "I think she's beyond caring."

CHAPTER 52

Blowing hard, Eleanor matched Rayne's pace up the stairs, the pair of them leaving Matthew behind on the elevated plaza. Desperation to get to Ash and Rowan drove Rayne, while Eleanor relied on conditioning. She'd spent her entire life running up and down the towers.

Guards blocked the stairwell, denying them access to the top residential floor—the one directly beneath the maternity ward, where the families stayed before and after giving birth. Where Ash and Rowan had come when they'd first arrived. "What's going on?" Rayne shoved a guard, but he stood strong, preventing her from going any higher. She shoved him again, her breathing ragged and her scream wild. "What's happening?"

The wall of a man showed Rayne his halting hand. "Wait here."

Diseased screams called from above. Rayne yelled as she swung for the guard. She caught him clean and caught him cold. He stumbled, and it gave her an opening. She slipped through the gap, and Eleanor followed, driving her elbow into the guard's ribs, forcing his reaching hands back as he bent over double and dropped to his knees. Her dad always told her if she got in trouble, it wasn't always about the force of your blow but, rather, where you hit them.

The diseased screamed.

Gunfire responded.

For the first time since they'd entered the blocks, Eleanor eased her pace as Rayne ran into the maternity ward. Several people moved through the room, guns raised as they shot diseased. Dead bodies everywhere, their blood stained the white sheets. Many lay on their backs, their stomachs riddled with leaking bullet holes. Some of those stomachs had almost reached full term.

The small army shot the remaining diseased. They mowed down new parents and parents to be.

Rayne loosed a primal roar and ran to a pair of corpses. She lifted Ash's head, her face covered in a glistening mask of blood. Beneath her crimson right eye, she had a bullet hole large enough to poke a finger through. She lay in bed on her back, holding Rowan's hand. Inseparable even when infected. Inseparable even when dead.

The bullet fire and diseased cries faded into the background. The guards had it covered, and more stood on the walkways to keep it contained. Too late for the families, but it clearly hadn't spread. Eleanor stumbled over to Rayne and rubbed her back. An utterly useless gesture, but she had nothing better.

The gunfire abated. A stillness settled across the room. Diseased corpses littered the space. Some were in beds, but many were sprawled across the floor. Unborn babies slain. Mothers. Fathers. Eleanor leaned on a nearby cot for support, and her legs shook. "Oh no."

Rayne stumbled over and peered in beside Eleanor. She pulled her hair back, scraping it away from her sweating face. Tears fell from her blinking eyes and landed beside the squirming baby. It wore a coating of blood like a slug wears slime. It looked upon the world through crimson eyes. Its small mouth searched, not for a teat, but for someone into which it could drive the disease.

"No!" Rayne shook the cot, the baby snarling at the disturbance. "No! No! No! No!"

Eleanor moved along the line, her tears blurring her vision. Baby after baby. All of them infected. Some of them were so little, the diseased's crimson veil had blinded them before they'd looked upon the world for the first time. She caught the arm of a passing guard. "What about the babies?"

The guard's pale face hung slack. Her bloodshot eyes glazed as if she'd succumbed to her own infection. She stared into the middle distance before twisting away from Eleanor's grip. She left the room with the others, chased by Eleanor's ragged cries. "What about the babies?"

"No!"

A man charged in, shoving Eleanor aside as he passed. Like Rayne, the man dropped beside a dead mother. He gripped her face with both hands, her head rolling from where her dead neck could no longer support its weight. He rested his forehead against hers. He shouted like his words would revive her. Like his scream would reach her in the afterlife. "No!" Like his wails would remove the bullets from her womb. He punched the bed, the corpse rocking with the blow.

Eleanor jumped as a hand stroked the back of her arm. Gracie stood with Olga beside her. Olga reached out to the man as he stumbled towards a crib. "Leave it, Bear."

But he raised his gun, the red laser target drawing a line from it to the baby's face. Gracie dragged Eleanor back as he pulled the trigger, killing the kid.

Olga marched from the room with her head down. She strode out onto one walkway.

Gracie pulled Eleanor in for a tight hug, and Eleanor cried on her shoulder as the man moved down the room, screaming while killing the diseased babies one after the other.

Gracie rocked her and made a shushing noise. "Someone has to do it."

"But why him? He's suffered enough already. What toll will it take?"

"Ask Olga."

The man paused at the final cot.

Eleanor dragged in a wet sniff.

The gun fell from the man's grip like he could no longer hold on.

"No!" Eleanor reached out too late. He'd already leaned into the crib and pulled out a toddler. The thing thrashed and twisted. It screamed and snarled. It snapped and bit at the air. The man held the once-boy at arm's length, his face an ever-shifting grieving grimace.

Eleanor twisted away from Gracie. She reached towards the man again.

But the man pulled the boy towards him. The little kid opened his mouth wide and sank his teeth into his dad's neck.

Her gun raised, Eleanor's laser target danced on the side of the man's face. Her finger locked momentarily. She yelled through her inaction and dragged bullets from father to son. Obliterating both their heads, she stumbled back when Gracie pulled her away.

The man and his boy fell.

Dead before he'd turned, the man lay on his back as the only corpse in the room without a crimson glare.

CHAPTER 53

Anger, grief, plans, and counter-plans. The others' fierce debate faded into the background as William chewed on his bottom lip and tracked Matilda from one small screen to the next. Tiny and alone. When she vanished from one camera, it took him a few frantic seconds to find her on another. Some screens were blank. Some blinded by smoke.

Out on a walkway, Matilda's gun flashed with muzzle flare. "What's she doing?"

Karl joined William.

He threw his hand up at the screen. "Doesn't she realise how many diseased are in these blocks? Does she even care?"

Even Karl knew when to keep his mouth shut.

Matilda fired one way and the other. Shooting the diseased coming from both blocks. The buildings spat them out like they were sentient. Generals sending soldiers into battle. The muzzle flare stopped. "What—"

"She's out of ammo."

"Shit!" William bounced on his toes as Matilda tossed the

empty magazine over the walkway. The night consumed the small metal object.

The diseased drew closer.

Matilda dropped her backpack—Nick's backpack—at her feet and pulled it open.

Leading with reaching hands, the diseased stumbled with their clumsy charge. They slashed at the air, battling invisible foes. They fought the white-hot poison running through their veins. They got close. Too fucking close. "Get them!"

Like she'd heard him, Matilda sprang up from the bag and kicked out. She caught the first diseased clean in the stomach. It bent over double. Clinging to her gun with both hands, she slammed the butt into the side of the cretin's face, knocking them flat. She stamped on the beast's head, pulled a magazine from her bag, and reloaded by slapping it into place.

The end of her gun flared as she opened up on the diseased, turning one way and then the other. The creatures carried their momentum for a few more steps before their legs failed them, and they dropped to the walkway, tripping those behind.

She ran out of bullets and reloaded again. The images made her look tiny, but they also showed her great will. Or her recklessness. She'd take on an army, and she didn't care if she lived or died.

Sweating like he'd been fighting with her, William relaxed as the final diseased fell. They littered her path. She reshouldered her backpack and ran, skipping over the tops of the corpses and vanishing into …

It took a few seconds to find her on the next screen. Into a sports hall. Another useless sports hall. Cast in the same red glow as many other parts of the blocks, her gun flared, diseased fell, and she darted into a stairwell.

William jumped at Hawk's touch.

"We have to get to the other control room."

"Are you mad?"

Hawk frowned at him.

"What about Matilda?"

A slight pause, like William had caught him off guard. Had Hawk really not considered it? "Do you expect me to give up on her? Would you have given up on Aggie?"

Hawk winced. He rubbed his temples. "What do you suggest we do?"

"We get her." William pointed at one wall. But after a few seconds of scanning, he turned to another and found her in a burning hallway. "There!"

Hawk sighed. "Where's *there*, William?"

"In block …" His cheeks grew hot. "I …" Matilda ran through another communal room. A dining room. Or a classroom. Hard to tell. She left it and appeared on another screen. Appearing and disappearing every few seconds. "If I need to, I'll find her on my own."

William's chest tightened with his every breath. More and more smoke entered the room. And if he struggled up here, what would it be like for Matilda? Would she run out of oxygen before they found her?

Knives took Hawk's place. "It's not that we're not with you, William."

"It feels like it."

"But how do we follow her if we don't know where she is? What's your plan?"

"Sometimes you just have to go with your gut." Matilda ran from one camera to the next. He turned left and right to find her. A shadow in the gloom. She shot past another camera and vanished.

William jumped as Matilda clattered into another

diseased. The collision sent them both stumbling, but she kicked it back before it grabbed her. She battered it with the butt of her gun. She beat it down and kept going, pulping the thing's head. She turned her weapon around and fired on the diseased rushing towards her.

"Someone could stay here." He raised his eyebrows at Knives. "If I go after her, they can guide me. Between us, we'll find her."

Still over the control console, Nick jabbed several keys on the keyboard. "Guide you how? Nothing works in this room. We can see where you both are, but we can't help you."

"There must be radios."

Nick shrugged.

"The tannoy? Like Queen Bee used. A broadcast?"

"We think that's all in the other control room."

"Think?"

"We know it's not here, William. We also need to be in there to open up the blocks. Maybe the others can help us not get burned alive." Nick pointed at the control room's door. "It's only three blocks away." He drew closer, and William backed away. "Trust me, I want nothing more than to go after her. Artan would want nothing more." He rubbed his watering eyes. "But she'll be impossible to find. The best thing we can do is get somewhere where we can communicate with her. We can let her know where we are. Then we can get these blocks open and hopefully extinguish these fires. We can fan out and kill the diseased. Those outside can come in and help. We might not find Matilda, but we can massively reduce the threat to her life. We can't stop you following her, but we can't go with you either. And trust me when I say I believe this is the best way. The *only* way for us to find her again."

None of the others spoke. They clearly all agreed with

Nick. And he made a compelling argument. "Okay, fine. Then we must go now."

Nick clapped his hand on William's shoulder and ran for the room's exit. "We'll get her back."

"I hope so."

CHAPTER 54

The cots' high sides hid the massacred babies, but it didn't remove what Eleanor had already seen. The bloody little eyes. The nasty little twist of hate distorting the features of a being who shouldn't have any concept of malice. The burning desire to spread the disease.

She followed Rayne and Gracie towards the walkways. Guards had prevented Matthew from entering the ward at first, but they'd since let him in, and he now helped clean up the mess.

The walkways had always helped Eleanor find solace. Somewhere she could still her mind. But this time, it'd take more than a strong breeze and a shitty view to clear her thoughts.

Eleanor slipped in beside Olga, who shivered from the cold and stared out into the night. "You okay?"

Although Olga turned her way, her features remained dull, like she didn't recognise the girl.

"Olga, are you …" How could she ask it again? "Of course you're not okay. None of us are. I'm sorry you've lost a friend. And you, Gracie."

Gracie acknowledged her with a tight-lipped and utterly humourless smile. This life had taken its pound of flesh from them all. Had left Eleanor as an orphan and a murderer. She'd taken two lives recently, and while the dad would have turned, she'd still shot him before the disease took hold. And Noris had had it coming, but his wide-eyed panic as his life slipped away had taken up residence inside her skull. It joined the infected babies and the crunching finality of her dad's crash.

"*Ralph?*" Olga leaned farther over the railing and rubbed her eyes like she didn't believe it. Like the man who'd just climbed from the tank on the block's ramp didn't exist. "Am I seeing things?"

Gracie shook her head. "No, Olga, you're not. What's he doing here?"

"You know him?" Rayne said. "He told us he's from the prison. That he was a guard."

Olga nodded. "He is. And he was."

"Do you trust him?"

"With my life."

Gracie pointed down at the hulking man dragging someone from his tank. "But who's that with him?"

Rayne's voice lowered. "That's the fucker who set the disease loose in the maternity ward." She took off at a sprint towards the neighbouring block.

~

Eleanor had chased Rayne all the way, still on her tail when they reached the elevated plaza and the ladder leading to the tank beside Ralph's. Ralph had dragged his prisoner onto its roof and had bound his wrists and ankles with electric cables. His prisoner's head hung like he no longer had the strength to hold it. Blood dribbled from his nose and mouth.

His shaggy black hair covered his forehead and eyes. A thick black beard hid the lower half of his face.

Olga threw herself at Ralph. The large man wrapped her in a hug and kissed the top of her head. They both winced when Rayne kicked the bound man in the face. He fell onto his back, and she pulled him upright again.

"You'd best talk now, fucker! Where did you come from?"

"Fishy fishy." The man smiled at her. Even now, with a waterfall of blood running over his lips and cascading down his chin, he wore the superiority of someone from the blocks. "Little fat worm catches the fishy fishy."

Rayne kicked him again. His head snapped to the side, and blood sprayed away from the attack. But he remained kneeling.

"Fishy worm, fishy worm. We know all. We see all. You think you're smarter than us? We speak the mother tongue. Knew about the maternity ward."

"What?" Rayne threw up her arms. She cried freely. "Who are you? Where have you come from?"

"Fishy fishy. Little fat worm."

Rayne yelled in his face, "*What?*"

Eleanor pulled her back.

"I put him on a hook and went fishing. Although, it could have been a she. Didn't want to check, and it's always hard to tell. Safer to not say anything, don't you think? It saves upsetting people."

"What's he saying?" Rayne turned to Gracie, who shrugged back at her.

"I put him, her, *it* on a hook. Hung it from the plaza."

Eleanor's entire being sank. "No."

Rayne looked at her. "What?"

The man on his knees laughed. "Swaddled it nice and tight. Fat little thing. Wrapped it so tight, it woke no one when I slipped back in and replaced it. But the swaddling would come loose. It thrashed so much it was bound to happen." The man grinned. "I tied it that way. And then it cried. And what happens when one cries?" Spit-bubbles of blood burst from his mouth. "A mother has to pick it up." His glee widened his grin.

"No!" Rayne twisted away from Eleanor.

"Has to pick it up. An instinct to protect. But she should have checked. It only takes one."

"Yeargh!" Rayne kicked him so hard in the chest, she launched him from the tank's roof through the gap in the ramp.

His laugh ended when he hit the ground with a *thump!* Not even the diseased bothered with him after that.

Rayne walked back across the bouncing ladder. It bowed with her steps, but she strode with the reckless abandon of someone who cared not if they fell.

While Ralph still clung to Olga, Eleanor rested a hand on the big man's arm. "Thank you for bringing him back."

He threw a shrug through his massive shoulders. "I can't believe he used a baby as bait."

Eleanor shrugged back. "Most from the blocks would have done the same thing." She followed Rayne. And like Rayne, who cared if she fell? They'd fought long and hard already, and things only seemed to be getting worse.

CHAPTER 55

The burning block turned the stairwell into a chimney. Smoke thickened the theatre's air, and since they'd been in the control room, diseased had filled the place, called up by the bass-note throb, which had since abated. The shambling silhouettes stumbled through the acrid fog tinged red from the emergency lighting. They wandered blind. They threw furious swings at the air like they could defeat the elements. William followed the others with his gun raised. They'd all reloaded in the control room. At the back of the line, he jumped from the stage last. He landed with a gentle pat of his feet against the hard floor. And they might have gone unnoticed had he managed to hold onto his cough.

Nick, Hawk, and Karl opened fire. They shot the charging diseased and pushed forwards, stepping closer to their exit, and closer to the stairwell.

Tears streamed from William's burning eyes. He fired with the others. The diseased fell with thuds, with the clattering of chairs, and with the *tonk* of running into walls.

The air thinned as they drew closer to the walkway. The wind sucked the smoke outside. Karl remained close to the exit, giving them cover while William, as the last of them, stumbled out into the night.

William blinked and rubbed his eyes. The dark night yielded ever so slightly to the grainy awakening of a new day. He wheezed, and his head spun. He and Karl stood shoulder to shoulder and fired as they walked backwards, dropping the diseased on their tail before they left the theatre. Knives, Nick, and Hawk shot the diseased ahead.

Even with William's improving vision, he cried harder than before. The lump in his throat had finally burst like the burning blocks' windows. Artan was gone. That little boy he'd known for all of Artan's life and most of his. Snuffed out in an instant. One mistake. All it took. And now Matilda had charged into the unknown with seemingly little purpose. How long before she went the way of her brother? And what then? What did he have left to fight for?

"Reloading!" Karl had a backpack, from which he fished a fresh magazine. He slipped the first one into William's pocket before reaching in and taking the second for himself.

William's gun rattled. The fallen diseased clogged the walkways, tripping those following them out. The pile grew larger and more impassable. They didn't need to kill them all, just slow them down enough to get to the next control room.

Clack!

"Reloading!" William ripped out his spent magazine and tossed it from the walkway. It spun through the darkness while he reloaded and slapped the replacement in with the palm of his hand.

Nick, Knives, and Hawk had killed as many diseased as them. Bodies littered their path. As Knives led, crossing over the corpses, William pointed to where they were heading. "These fuckers have more sports halls than they do morals."

Karl grimaced while firing into the theatre. "I'd imagine they have more pet unicorns than they do morals."

William smiled despite himself.

Remaining by the entrance, Hawk waited for William and Karl. He aimed back down the bridge while Knives and Nick crossed the smokey sports hall.

"Where are they?" William blinked like it would help, but he remained as blind in the sports hall as he'd been in the theatre. His grief throttled his words. "Knives and Nick. Where are they?"

Hawk had little more to offer than a hand thrown in their general direction and a shrug.

Thunk!

Spinning one way and then the other, Karl kept his gun raised. "What's that?"

Two silhouettes charged towards them.

William used the end of his own gun to knock the bottom of Karl's, sending his bullets into the ceiling. The smoke seared his throat. "It's Knives and Nick."

As the pair emerged, Karl raised an apologetic hand. At any other time, Knives would have put him on his arse.

Nick said, "The door to the next walkway. It just locked."

"Locked?"

Something screeched on William's right. Something in the sports hall with them. He turned to the wall of smoke.

Hawk fired. The screech died. A body hit the floor with a hard *slap!*

"So what now?" Karl shrugged. Diseased wailed around them, but the thick smoke hid them from view.

Pulling her shirt up over her mouth, Knives pointed away from them. "We have to go down a level." She ran off.

William copied her, dragging his top up over the bottom half of his face. Maybe the shirt made a difference, but he still wheezed and gasped as he tried to drag something breathable from the atmosphere.

Inside the stairwell, William found the handrail. He

followed Nick while Karl came down behind him. They descended in single file.

A wheezing, crying mess, and throttled by grief and smoke, William saw stars by the time they reached the plateau between floors. But they pushed on, the visibility so low he'd lose sight of Nick and Karl were they even a foot farther away.

Hawk and Nick followed Knives down to the floor below and out onto the walkway towards the next block. William and Karl took up the rear and covered their backs like before.

There were fewer active diseased on this level. Many already lay dead on the walkway. "This is the bridge Matilda was on when we were in the control room."

Karl shot back into the room they'd left. There were so few diseased, he had it covered. More diseased charged from the block they were heading for. Even Knives used a gun. She had no chance of retrieving any tossed blades in the smoke.

The door that had closed on them on the floor above was now open again. It let smoke out into the night. Karl jumped when William rested his hand on his shoulder. "Cover me."

"What are you doing?"

William pointed at the room they'd just left. "Can you hold them back?"

"Yes."

"Good. Then cover me."

The corpses shifted and slipped beneath William's steps as he ran to Knives and the others. They were laying down almost continuous fire, dropping diseased as they appeared.

"Stop shooting!" William slipped past them and shot the door's control button. He then laid the red dot of his laser target on the camera above the door. He paused for a moment. Those cameras had shown him Matilda's location. He fired, and the small box dropped to the walkway.

Her face streaked with soot, Knives let William past as he pulled back. She shot the emerging diseased. She pulled her shirt down from her mouth and shouted over her clattering gun, "What was that for?"

"We're being watched." He pointed up at the previously closed door. "They closed that door so we couldn't get out. Look, it's now open again."

"Damn. Then we need to blind them."

William's gulp tasted like charcoal. "And we need to destroy the doors' buttons so they can't control them."

"But what about Matilda?" Knives' cheeks shook with her gun's recoil. "If we kill the cameras, how will we know where she is?"

"We need to prioritise getting to the control room safely."

Knives stopped shooting and grabbed his hand. Her eyes streamed as much as his. Bloodshot like a diseased on the turn. "We'll find her."

"I hope so."

Knives pulled her shirt over her mouth again and sprinted into the next room.

Nick followed her in and shot the cameras over the other doors. He shot their control panels too. Hawk backed them up.

"Nick!" William screamed. Nick had been so focused on blinding those watching, he'd blinded himself. A diseased slammed into his side, taking them both down.

Knives shot the diseased before the pair hit the ground. Nick jumped straight back up again, and William let go of a small sigh. Side by side, the pair led the charge onto the next walkway, shooting the diseased in front of them.

The noxious smoke clung to William like a second skin. He followed Hawk, who ran close to Knives and Nick into the next block. He stumbled out onto the top floor, the door's control button fizzing and spitting electricity from where Nick had already shot it.

Out onto the walkway directly behind Hawk and Knives, William grabbed Knives' shoulder as she aimed for another camera. "Stop."

"What? Why?"

"I don't think anyone else is watching us." William pointed. A burning rope ladder ran from their walkway all the way down and over the plaza's edge. A tank drove off into the distance. "Whoever was screwing with us—"

"Has just left the building." Knives shot a diseased and ran for the ballroom with the mirrored floor. Towards the main control room. Towards a chance at survival for them and Matilda.

CHAPTER 56

Gracie rested her elbow on the meeting room table and her other hand on Olga's back. Of course the maternity ward had affected them all, but none of them had had to kill a baby in a bathtub before. Eight of them sat around the table in near silence.

"I know I shouldn't have killed him." Rayne looked up at the others. Eleanor sat beside her, holding her hand. "But I couldn't control myself."

"If it hadn't been you, one of us would have done it." Gracie cleared her throat. "I'm not sure there's a person in these blocks who would have acted any differently."

Olga's voice trembled. "I just wish we'd never separated Bear from his family. If he'd have been there with them ..."

"He would have also been turned." Queen Bee scratched her bald head. "The man who did this waited for the right moment to strike." She held eye contact with Olga.

Gracie rubbed Olga's back. "We told Bear we didn't want him to come. He made the choice, and he'd make it again. How could we possibly know that was going to happen? It's hard to even comprehend that level of evil."

Sniffing, Olga wiped her nose with the back of her sleeve and rocked as she nodded. "And without Bear, we wouldn't be here now. He was integral in getting us home and, before that, helping us find out how to open up the shining city."

Queen Bee leaned forwards. "What?" She checked around her. Glanced at Rayne. Katrina. Ralph. And back to Olga. "Have I missed something? Did you just say you have a way to open up the shining city?"

"We *think* we do." Gracie showed Queen Bee her palm like it would temper her expectations. "We *hope* it will work."

"That's huge!"

"If we're right."

Queen Bee turned her hand over in front of her. She needed more information. "Are you confident it'll work?"

"Kira's been on the money so far."

"Kira?"

"She went with us to raise the Icarus towers. There are lots of strange symbols down there."

"I remember you saying."

"Nonsensical."

Queen Bee raised her eyebrows. "Until Kira made sense of them?"

"Exactly. To her, many of the symbols are as easy to read as words on a page."

"And she thinks you have a way to open up the shining city?"

"Yep. But, for obvious reasons, we can't test it out. We'll only get to drop their defences once. And that needs to be—"

"When we're outside the city and ready for war?"

"Exactly. And we can't discuss it over the airwaves. We have to wait until we're face to face with the other communities."

Queen Bee's mouth turned down at the edges. "Okay. Well, at least we have a plan."

"Speaking of plans, what's happening with William and the others? What was their plan of attack?"

"A small group of them were to infiltrate the blocks and open them up from the inside to let in the waiting army."

Gracie said, "And we don't know how that's going?"

"No. We've agreed on radio silence."

They could do little else but wait. And having taken all the limelight, Gracie leaned back in her seat to let someone else speak.

"Margot."

Gracie sat up straighter. "Huh?"

Playing with her hands, Queen Bee directed it at Rayne. "Margot."

Rayne cocked an eyebrow. "What?"

"That's my name. Margot."

"Margot?"

"Margot Largo."

"You're shitting me."

"I shit you not."

"Your parents must have hated you."

Olga snorted a laugh that made Gracie jump.

Queen Bee smiled. "Cruel, isn't it?"

"No kidding."

Eleanor giggled.

Biting her lip like she could chew back her mirth, Rayne's voice wavered with her tethered chuckle. "I'm guessing you'd prefer me to stick with Queen Bee?"

Even Katrina giggled. "I didn't know that was your surname."

"It's not something I like to shout about."

Grinning along with them, Gracie said, "I wonder why."

"This is William. You need to hear us out before you go ahead with the plan. Over."

The radio cut through the room.

Gracie said, "What happened to radio silence?"

Ashen-faced, Queen Bee turned towards the radio console. "Something must have gone wrong."

"Shit!" Rayne's head dropped, but before Queen Bee could stand, she shoved a halting hand in her direction. "Don't tell them about the maternity ward. Whatever they're dealing with, knowing that will only make things worse."

"And obviously nothing about the shining city," Gracie said.

"Then what can I say?"

Ralph's chair screeched as he stood up from the table. The monster of a man cast a shadow over them all. "I don't mind talking to them. I'd like to help if I can? And if we're breaking radio silence, I'd like to see if I can contact the prison too?"

Throwing a sweeping hand in the radio's direction, Queen Bee then folded her arms and rocked back in her seat. "Have at it."

The small mic in his large grip, Ralph lifted it to his mouth. "William?"

"Who's that?"

CHAPTER 57

The smoke clearer in the mirrored ballroom, William breathed more easily as he walked beside Karl. "They must have engineered it this way."

Karl cocked his head to one side. "Huh?"

"The smoke." William cut through the thinner clouds with a wave of his arm. "This room's clearer than any of the other top floors we've been on."

"They must have been in this control room as late as possible before they fled." Karl lowered his voice to a raspy and smoke-damaged growl. "Rats from a sinking ship."

"Well, let's make sure we keep it afloat." William paused at the door leading to the stairwell. "Maybe this explains it." He still had his knife from when they'd entered the food tube. Removing it from its sheath, he cut the thick tape they'd used to seal the doorframe. He pulled the door open a crack, letting in a thick churn of inky smoke.

Karl's mouth hung open from watching William free the doors.

"If Matilda comes up those stairs, I want to make sure she can get in."

"Okay. That makes more sense."

They set off towards the control room at the end of the short corridor.

"You're really quite capable, you know?"

Halfway between the stairwell and the control room, William paused and looked Karl up and down. "What do you want?"

"Huh?"

"Why are you being nice to me? Well, sort of nice. *Quite capable?*"

"Fucking hell, William. You're formidable. Is that what you want to hear?"

"I mean ... that's better. But what do you want?"

"I'm not sure what you mean?"

"Since you've been with us, all you've done is try to steal my girlfriend."

"Tilly?"

"You've not earned the right to call her that."

"That's why you were calling me a creep?"

"So you don't deny it?"

"I mean ... sure—"

"Wow. You really don't deny it. Fucking hell, Karl. When this is all over, do me a favour and stay away from me, yeah?"

"Let me finish, William. I've been showing off, sure, but not to impress Matilda."

"Then who?"

William followed Karl's line of sight. "Really?"

Karl shrugged.

"Knives?"

"What?" She had her blades drawn as she kicked the button for the control room's door.

Karl frowned at William.

"Nothing."

Knives, Hawk, and Nick entered the control room, its white glow spilling out into the emergency red of the hallway. Even with everything else they had going on, William smiled.

"I don't see what's so funny. She's wonderful."

"Knives?"

"At least you said it quieter this time. And yes, Knives."

"Wonderful is a word, I suppose."

Karl grabbed William's forearm just before he entered the control room. He gripped on a little too tight. "Don't say anything. Please."

"It's not for me to say."

"Thank you."

Nick's sweaty face glistened, illuminated by the control console's light. He typed quickly and finished by jabbing one key harder than the others. The *click* came as a punctuation to his furious typing. An echoing *thunk* called through the blocks.

"Good work, Nick."

Haggard with grief, his eyes sallow and his cheeks slack, Nick gripped the microphone. "Tilly, we're in the other control room. I've just opened up the blocks. Come back to us. Please."

William said, "Can we contact the other blocks while we wait for her to get here?"

"Uh …"

"Aren't we past radio silence by now, Nick? If what they said about understanding high vamp is true, then our secret's out. And even if there are some blocks who weren't aware of tonight's assault, surely they know by now? I just think we need to communicate with them so they understand our situation. The blocks are on fire and filled with diseased. If we can tell that to the army waiting to come in, we could end up saving a lot of lives."

After twisting several dials, Nick turned the mic in William's direction and stepped away from the console.

Smoke damage and anxiety ran a tight twist through William's lungs. He tried to inhale deeply, but it was like breathing through a straw. He coughed several times, each one harder and more raking than the last. He coughed until he heaved. His throat still tight, he drew another desperate gasp. He pressed the radio's talk button. "This is William. You need to hear us out before you go ahead with the plan. Over."

"William?" A man's voice.

"Who's that?"

"Ralph."

"Ralph?"

Hawk said, "From the prison?"

"From the prison?"

"You know any other Ralphs?"

"Where's Joni?"

"Still there."

"But what … actually, hang on. Have you heard me outside the block? I'm talking to those waiting to come in. Can you hear me? Over."

A woman's voice he didn't recognise said, "Yes, William, we hear you. Over."

"What's the safe word? Over."

"Hugh. Over."

William gulped twice, but the lump in his throat endured. His voice was more strained than before. "Good." He pushed through the restriction. "Now, hold tight. The blocks are on fire—"

"We can see that. Over."

"And the place is filled with diseased. It's a death trap. We need a better plan than you lot storming in. Over."

"Can we action stage one of the plan? Over."

Knives mouthed *the plaza*.

"Yes, you can. I can't see many diseased coming down through the burning floors. But hold tight after that. Over."

"Ralph?"

"Yeah."

"And those outside. Over."

The woman's voice. "We're listening. Over."

"We're using the radio because the people in this block had someone who knew high vamp. We have to assume the other blocks might have seen their attacks coming too. And even if they didn't, they would have attacked by now, so it's not like we have anything left to hide. Who knows how many have walked straight into traps like we did? Artan's dead—"

"Dead?"

"Is that you, Eleanor?"

"Yeah. I'm so sorry, William."

"They understood high vamp, Eleanor. They knew what was coming even when you were here with them. I'm sorry for putting you in that position."

"I was going into those blocks whether you helped me or not."

"Well, we're grateful you're still okay. But Artan was caught in a trap in the ammo room. He's dead. And M ..."

He stared up at the ceiling's bright lights and blinked back his burning tears. "Matilda's missing."

Eleanor gasped.

The woman leading their backup team said, "So we action phase one, and what then? Over."

"Do you see a burning rope ladder? Over."

"Yeah. Over."

"We're in the block beside that. Over."

"Okay. We'll get you out of there. And once you're free, we're going to put an end to this regime once and for all. Over."

William nodded. "I'm glad we're on the same page."

Whoosh!

Stumbling back from the console, William clapped a hand to his heart. "Tilly?"

Her hair dishevelled, Matilda stumbled in panting and crying. Sweat and soot streaked her face.

William ran and wrapped her in a tight hug. He kissed her head, her cheek, her lips. "Am I glad to see you." He held the sides of her face and kissed her again. "I was so worried. So, so worried."

She leaned her forehead against his. "Sorry."

"It's okay. Are you all right?"

"No. But what did I miss?"

William remained leaning against his love, the pair of them watching the steel floor between them. "I'm sorry about Artan."

"I don't know what I'll do without him. But going off on a suicidal rampage won't fix anything, will it?"

"I'm here for you. Always."

Her tears fell from her dipped head. "I know. Thank you."

The others gathered around. All save for Nick. Had Matilda not just walked in, someone might have noticed he'd pulled into himself. Might have paid more attention to his rounded shoulders. His slumped frame. The cut on the back of his hand. He'd lost so much. They all had. His love. His best friend. But he'd also lost something else. And now, as his top lip spasmed with an involuntary twitch, and he shuffled close to the others, surely someone would notice before it was too late. Surely someone would see how the once kind Nick now snarled with hatred. How he scowled at the world. How he now viewed it through eyes glazed with blood.

END OF BOOK EIGHTEEN.

Thank you for reading *Revolution:* Book eighteen of Beyond These Walls.

The Shining City: Book nineteen of Beyond These Walls is available to order now. To find out where, go to www.michaelrobertson.co.uk

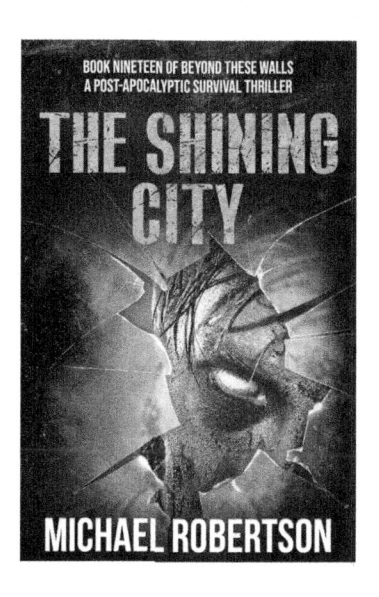

∽

Would you like a FREE exclusive standalone novel set in my Beyond These Walls universe?

Fury: Book one in Tales from Beyond These Walls is available to everyone who joins my spam-free reader group at www.michaelrobertson.co.uk

You can unsubscribe at any time.

Support The Author

Dear reader, as an independent author I don't have the resources of a huge publisher. If you like my work and would like to see more from me in the future, there are two things you can do to help: leaving a review, and a word-of-mouth referral.

Releasing a book takes many hours and hundreds of dollars. I love to write, and would love to continue to do so. All I ask is that you leave a review. It shows other readers that you've enjoyed the book and will encourage them to give it a try too. The review can be just one sentence, or as long as you like.

ABOUT THE AUTHOR

Like most children born in the seventies, Michael grew up with Star Wars in his life, along with other great stories like Labyrinth, The Neverending Story, and as he grew older, the Alien franchise. An obsessive watcher of movies and consumer of stories, he found his mind wandering to stories of his own.

Those stories had to come out.

He hopes you enjoy reading his work as much as he does creating it.

Contact
www.michaelrobertson.co.uk
subscribers@michaelrobertson.co.uk

ALSO BY MICHAEL ROBERTSON

THE SHADOW ORDER:

The Shadow Order

The First Mission - Book Two of The Shadow Order

The Crimson War - Book Three of The Shadow Order

Eradication - Book Four of The Shadow Order

Fugitive - Book Five of The Shadow Order

Enigma - Book Six of The Shadow Order

Prophecy - Book Seven of The Shadow Order

The Faradis - Book Eight of The Shadow Order

The Complete Shadow Order Box Set - Books 1 - 8

∽

GALACTIC TERROR:

Galactic Terror: A Space Opera

Galactic Retribution: Galactic Terror Book Two

Galactic Force: Galactic Terror Book Three

Galactic Liberation: Galactic Terror Book Four

Galactic Confrontation - Part One: Galactic Terror Book Five

∽

NEON HORIZON:

The Blind Spot - A Cyberpunk Thriller - Neon Horizon Book One.

Prime City - A Cyberpunk Thriller - Neon Horizon Book Two.

Bounty Hunter - A Cyberpunk Thriller - Neon Horizon Book

Three.

Connection - A Cyberpunk Thriller - Neon Horizon Book Four.

Reunion - A Cyberpunk Thriller - Neon Horizon Book Five.

Eight Ways to Kill a Rat - A Cyberpunk Thriller - Neon Horizon Book Six.

Neon Horizon - Books 1 - 3 Box Set - A Cyberpunk Thriller.

∽

THE ALPHA PLAGUE:

The Alpha Plague: A Post-Apocalyptic Action Thriller

The Alpha Plague 2

The Alpha Plague 3

The Alpha Plague 4

The Alpha Plague 5

The Alpha Plague 6

The Alpha Plague 7

The Alpha Plague 8

The Complete Alpha Plague Box Set - Books 1 - 8

∽

BEYOND THESE WALLS:

Protectors - Book one of Beyond These Walls

National Service - Book two of Beyond These Walls

Retribution - Book three of Beyond These Walls

Collapse - Book four of Beyond These Walls

After Edin - Book five of Beyond These Walls

Three Days - Book six of Beyond These Walls

The Asylum - Book seven of Beyond These Walls

Between Fury and Fear - Book eight of Beyond These Walls

Before the Dawn - Book nine of Beyond These Walls

The Wall - Book ten of Beyond These Walls

Divided - Book eleven of Beyond These Walls

Escape - Book twelve of Beyond These Walls

It Only Takes One - Book thirteen of Beyond These Walls

Trapped - Book fourteen of Beyond These Walls

This World of Corpses - Book fifteen of Beyond These Walls

Blackout - Book sixteen of Beyond These Walls

An Interesting Alliance - Book seventeen of Beyond These Walls

Revolution - Book eighteen of Beyond These Walls

The Shining City - Book nineteen of Beyond These Walls

Beyond These Walls - Books 1 - 6 Box Set

Beyond These Walls - Books 7 - 9 Box Set

Beyond These Walls - Books 10 - 12 Box Set

Beyond These Walls - Books 13 - 15 Box Set

∼

OFF-KILTER TALES:

The Girl in the Woods - A Ghost's Story - Off-Kilter Tales Book One

Rat Run - A Post-Apocalyptic Tale - Off-Kilter Tales Book Two

∼

Masked - A Psychological Horror

∼

CRASH:

Crash - A Dark Post-Apocalyptic Tale
Crash II: Highrise Hell
Crash III: There's No Place Like Home
Crash IV: Run Free
Crash V: The Final Showdown

∼

NEW REALITY:
New Reality: Truth
New Reality 2: Justice
New Reality 3: Fear

∼

Audiobooks:

CLICK HERE TO VIEW MY FULL AUDIOBOOK LIBRARY.

Printed in Great Britain
by Amazon